ROUGH JUSTICE

Jessica McEncroe

Contents

CHAPTER 1

I had been going to Tattoo Rogue for years to get tattooes drawn onto my skin. I had tattooes everywhere on my body, like a canvas now painted. I was mad on them, I relished the pain and I relished the look of my skin, I hoped it covered all of me so I didn't have to see it.

My mother was totally against the first tattoo I ever had, especially because I was so young too. She was always worrying that I had some never lasting tattoo addiction and worried I'd regret them all one day in my life.

She'd go, "what if your wife doesn't like tattooes?" She didn't know I wouldn't be marrying any girl who didn't like me for me, tattooes and all.

In fact, I didn't even think I wanted to marry at all. I liked women, hell, I loved women. I loved women in my apartment and on my bed for a few hours, and that was it. Never anything more, never anything less.

I had my own recommendation anyway in Tattoo Rogue, he was called Glenn and every single one of his designs were legit. He gave me discounts too.

I loved all of his work, he could draw pretty much anything given the chance. It was a talent and he was extremely talented. He was the owner of Tattoo Rogue and had tattooed every single design onto my skin since the first.

So you could imagine my surprise when Glenn came in one day to tell me he was training his daughter to take over the company when he was gone. He was training her to become one of the best tattoo artists in the country just like himself.

My brows rose to my hairline.

"Where are you going?" I had asked him. The man chuckled.

"No where, it's just in case I die."

And that was that. Glenn had a sense of humour. It was quite morbid really and you never could predict what would leave his mouth next. He was great company when I had to spend hours getting my sleeve done all in one go. It cost a bomb too so I didn't expect him to complain. Luckily, he didn't.

But right now, I was here to get my new tattoo done. I had wanted a tattoo on my knuckle for a while now and I had booked my appointment a few weeks back with Glenn. I guess the dick wasn't going to give me one today but instead dump his daughter on to me instead.

"I didn't pay you for this." I asked for Glenn specifically. He was the only person I trusted.

"You haven't paid me at all yet." Glenn shot back. I slouched further in my chair.

"Come on, Glenn. You've been tattooing me for years, don't let me down." I pleaded as I shot out of my chair and made my way over the counter he was standing behind. I couldn't trust any other fucker with my skin and a tattoo needle. What if it turned out looking like shit?

Glenn had even tattooed me when I was underage. Of course, he would never do that now, but he did it for me years ago when I was sixteen. It took a hell of a lot of persuading.

I was now 28 and I was starting to think there was no where else to tattoo on my skin. The thought made me scowl.

"Don't try and make me feel guilty." He took his thick framed glasses off his nose and his highly tattooed arm came over the counter to punch me in the bicep. "Let my daughter practice on you. She's really good, if I must say." Pride shot through his eyes and I wanted to gag at his stupid fatherly love for his daughter.

I was never going to win this.

"Fine." I grumbled. "But don't let her fuck up." I had OCD when it came to the pictures on my skin.

"God forbid." He stated. I rolled my eyes before sitting back down on the plastic chairs like a sulking child.

Glenn had a thin mop of hair on his head with splatters of grey and silver in his dark brown hair. He was lean, lanky and tattooed. His brown eyes were genuine and they twinkled with interest and entertainment.

I had trusted him the moment I met him.

I waited a few minutes, it wasn't busy here so I didn't understand why Glenn's daughter was taking so long to tattoo me. I didn't have all day.

I had known Glenn for 12 years and I was surprised I had never met his daughter until now. I had heard about his wife, his ex wife and I had heard stories about when his daughter was a child, but I had never seen her.

I couldn't even remember her name.

Glenn sat behind his counter and hummed along to the music as he traced a drawing a client had given him. I loved it here. Drawing was the only thing I knew how to do.

If I hadn't been getting so much money with the job I currently had I would have taken this job up quickly. Maybe I would one day.

"Glenn, how long is she gonna be?" I tapped my watch impatiently. Glenn rolled his eyes but lifted himself off his chair and made his way to the back room where his daughter must have been.

It didn't take long before Glenn came back into the room.

"She'll be here now." He stated, I nodded my head. "You impatient fuck." I chuckled at his reply. He held a twinkle in his eye and a smile on his face.

Just as I was about to go outside for a quick cigarette, Glenn's daughter came from out of the back room. My eyes widened at the look of her.

Fuck me.

"Fucking hell, dad, can't you tell him to be a little more patient." She came storming out of the room. As soon as she saw me she closed her mouth from saying anything else.

"I think you just told him yourself." Glenn muttered as he continued to draw.

She had long almost black hair that came just below her chest. Her body, just like mine was covered with tattooes. She wore a vest top and short denim shorts. Her legs were sky high and her black heels made me fidget in my chair.

Glenn didn't tell me his daughter was fucking smoking hot.

"Nick." I nodded my greetings. She leaned against the counter and raised her brow.

"Aren't you a sort huh?" She tutted and then her tongue came out to lick her plump bottom lip. I stared at her, I couldn't help it. Glenn would have my balls for this.

"You could say that." I stood up from my chair and stalked forward. "Are we ready then?" I asked, willing to get my tattoo done now. I had waited long enough.

Her scent wafted my way. She smelt sweet and floral. It was so feminine, I felt wild.

"Yes, come this way." She led me towards one of the tattoo benches. She changed all the covers before telling me to sit. I laid down just like instructed.

She got all of the equipment. She moved around the room with such ease and grace, she was so sexy and confident, I knew that much.

Even with my eyes on her, she didn't fault. Not like other women who fell to their feet for me. It was like she didn't even know I was there.

I told her what I wanted when she was back and she listened intently. I could smell her still, stronger now, it was all I could think about. My body felt weird being this close to her. But God, she smelt so good.

"You know." I swallowed. Christ, I was effected by her. "No colour, I don't do much colour." I was a boring fuck.

"I get it." She noted. She looked up to me with those big blue eyes and I could honestly say for once, Nicholas was speechless. "Any colour?" She asked. I hadn't recovered. "Cat got your tongue has it?" Her eyes were playful. I shook my head and tried to gain some concentration.

"No, thanks." I croaked. She nodded and got ready with her tattoo pen. "You didn't tell me your name?"

"It is what you want it to be." She looked to me and winked. Oh, playful and very mysterious. I kind of liked it.

"Okay then, babe." I smirked her way.

"Are you flirting with me?" She laughed as she laid the needle to my skin after disinfecting it. I sighed with relaxation at the contact.

"Do you want me to?"

"Maybe, maybe not." She shrugged but a smile played on her lips. She was just like her father, playful. She seemed a tease too.

Did she know how much I loved teases?

"Seriously, what's your name?" I asked for the second time. "And your number."

"Smooth." She giggled and it played in my mind for minutes. So sweet. "It's Cathy."

"Cathy." I rolled it on my tongue. I liked that too. It suited her.

I was a flirt. I flirted with every girl I came across, I loved doing it to see the reaction I received. I wasn't anything like my cousin, Xavier, who hated, well, used to hate any kind of contact with the female anatomy.

I was the polar opposite, I loved the female anatomy, maybe even a little too much.

And right now, I was loving Cathys anatomy. She had a smoking hot body. She was curvy and had large assets. Her boobs, they weren't the biggest, her arse, now that was something special. She had long legs that travelled for miles, even though she was at least half a foot smaller than me still.

I looked to one of Cathy's tattoos and concentrated on the one she had on the back of her hand and all the way up her arm. It was sick. It was bright and bold and full of colour. It was a sickening contrast to the tattooes on my skin which were void of any colour at all.

"I love this." I trailed my finger up her arm and relished in the electricity shooting through it. Goosebumps rose from her skin. I smirked.

Just before Cathy could reply, Glenn came barreling into the room. I straightened up in the chair and scowled his way.

"Get your filthy hands off my daughter." Glenn's voice came out as he went to one of the draws with all the files in. Cathy laughed.

"He can't keep away from me." She stated. The little minx. I looked to her and narrowed my eyes. She held a twinkle in her eye.

God, the things I wanted to do to her.

"Don't listen to her, Glenn, I wouldn't touch her with a barge pole." Glenn chuckled and what a fucking lie that was. I wanted to touch her in every way I knew how.

"I'll ram this tattoo needle up your arse." Cathy replied. I laughed. There was just something about her that I really liked. She was hot as fuck and I wanted her in my bed.

"I've been wanting to do that for years." Glenn sighed. "Resist the temptation, Cat, it's worth it in the end, we don't want a law suit."

"Cheeky fucker." I replied.

Minutes went by and Cathy had actually been doing an amazing job. I hated to admit it, she was as good as Glenn had stated. I was actually really happy with the outcome so far.

Glenn had left the room with a small warning before getting back to his work. As if I was going to listen to him.

I wanted this girl in my bed. I hope she knew it too.

And Christ it was fucking turning me on seeing her tattoo me and for fuck sake she kept touching my skin so softly, almost as if I couldn't feel it, but I could.

No woman had effected me like this before. I usually had better control. I was usually the one seducing the women, not the other way around.

Luckily, it didn't take long before Cathy had finished her work.

"Go and have a look in the mirror if you want." She stated. I shook my head, I could see it, it was perfect, it was everything I imagined.

"Nah, it's perfect." I exclaimed truthfully. She smiled my way, beaming, my skin tingled in awareness.

"I'm glad you like it." Her smile was breathtaking.

Fuck, I was becoming poetic.

She did all the other necessities before smiling my way as soon as we were fully done. I could finally breathe without the scent of her driving me wild.

"You've done a great job. Thanks."

"No problem, sweetie." She patted my shoulder before getting off her stool and chucking all of the supplies and replacing them with new ones.

I looked at her ass in those tight denim shorts. Jesus.

Without a thought, I got up from the tattoo bench and made my way around it until I was standing behind her body. I knew I shouldn't have, I knew I couldn't come on to her like this, right now, this soon, but I had to, I couldn't help it.

She stilled as soon as she knew I was there. I could feel the warmth radiating off of her small little frame. My body fitted behind hers like a puzzle. So many thoughts went through my mind, the things I could have done, I wanted them so badly.

Fuck.

"So about that number?"

CHAPTER 2

I came down stairs to the smell of bacon and sausages. My father, Glenn, was at the stove in a small apron, a white shirt and black jeans.

"Morning." I yawned. It was nearly ten in the morning, I hadn't even changed for breakfast, I was still in my dressing gown and slippers. It was hard getting used to the cold weather here.

"Morning. Sausage and bacon sandwiches okay for you?"

"Is that even a question?" I snickered. Anything greasy and tasty was definitely a yes from me. Food was a massive guilty pleasure of mine, my ass probably showed that.

"It's all I've got time for I'm afraid, birdie." His nickname still stuck. He had called me it ever since I was born, he never told me why. God, I missed my father so much. I was so happy to be back. He truly understood me and I was a massive daddy's girl. We both had tattoos, sleeves full. He loved me for who I was. "I've got to open the shop."

"No worries. What time do you usually open?" I questioned. I had worked yesterday but not until late in the afternoon. I was asleep before I even saw my father leave. I was pretty much jet lagged.

"Now, but I'll open half an hour later today, just for you." He turned around and gave me a wink. I smiled.

"Christ, I am flattered."

"I'm glad to hear that." He gave the pan a shake with his highly tattooed arm and I smiled.

Before I was born my father worked in an office somewhere in the city. He discovered I was a talented artist when I had started to grow up and I then discovered he was too. It wasn't until then he had decided to make something out of his talents, he was already tattooed then, not as much as now but he was definitely fascinated. The shop he owned now was the result. I was very proud of what he had accomplished.

I'm happy his genes were passed down to me.

"There you are." He laid a plate down on the counter. My belly grumbled in response. He kissed my forehead. "I'll go and get ready. Eat up."

"Cheers, dad." And I got tucked in.

I had practiced tattooing when I was living with my mum, many of my friends were interested in it and I had trained up for around a year. It came naturally to me just like it did my father.

My first shift with my dad was yesterday in Tattoo Rogue and I loved it there. Plus, I had met some of the most fascinating people. One person had stuck in my mind all day and night afterwards. Nick, I think his name was. I wasn't really listening, he was a fine specimen of a man and I couldn't help but stare.

I tried to play it cool, I really hoped it had worked because I really didn't want to make a fool out of myself, especially when he was so composed and cool.

"So about that number?" He had asked. I didn't give it to him, I couldn't even remember the number quick enough. Secondly,

I knew how men like him worked, he wanted fun not anything serious.

I was almost 23, young and looking for fun, of course, but I didn't want to be used. I had already had my fair share in foolish men thinking they could use me, my body, when I didn't want that, not now, not ever. I wasn't 18 anymore, I wasn't looking for that.

He effected me anyway, in more ways than I wanted to admit.

Dad said he came there often, I could see that, he was tattooed literally from chest to foot. He was so hot, it was hard trying to concentrate on tattooing him when he looked like he did. I had managed it by some unknown miracle. Glenn had also mentioned how close he was to Nick, they were almost the best of friends even with the considerable age gap.

I didn't like to admit it, but I think I'd be seeing him again and a part of me couldn't wait to feast my eyes upon him.

I could look, after all.

"I'm going now, you'll come up when you're ready to help though yeah?" He came into the room and I swallowed the remaining bit of food on my plate. I stood up and took it to the sink. I'd wash them later.

"Sure." And I couldn't wait to get started again.

Once he had left, I went upstairs to take a shower. Afterwards, I chucked on a white t shirt, skinny jeans and converse.

I wasn't ever self conscious of my apprearance. I was a little bit of a tom boy, there wasn't an ounce of glamorous in me. I wore what was comfortable rather than what was stylish. I had tried to be a little more glam, but I thought I just looked weird.

Once I had done my makeup and my hair, I grabbed the set of keys in the bowl which was left on a table in the hallway and left.

The shop was down the street from the house so it was easily accessible and dad could keep an eye on it from home. It was convenient.

The walk was nice, yet short. It was chilly out, that time of year. I had missed it.

Living with my mother meant hot weather constantly in Australia. I loved it, don't get me wrong, Australia was amazing but here was my home town and it meant more to me than any other place in the world. I missed it like mad when I was away and I missed my dad more than anything.

Once I opened the door to the shop I spotted him at his desk drawing and designing a new tattoo.

"Interesting." I mused once I had rounded the counter to look at it. The drawing was bold, colourful and floral. My dad could draw pretty much anything.

"This would suit you." I snickered.

"Flowers aren't really my thing." I stated. I had one flower tattoo and that was about it.

"Can I do you another tattoo soon?" He asked. He continued to draw.

"Definitely." I loved his work even when saying that was being biased. We bonded in the only way we knew how.

"I had missed you so much, Birdie, nobody entertains me as much as you." He swivelled around in his chair to face me. He was a vibrant colour even when the walls were full of colourful pictures and designs.

"I missed you too, dad, you soppy git." I squeezed his shoulder before turning around and making my way to the coffee machine.

"Can I have one too?"

"I knew you wanted something." He laughed in the background.

Everything was so relaxed and normal here. This was definitely where I wanted to be.

Suddenly, the phone rang. It was situated on Glenn's desk and he reached over to answer it. I turned around to watch him as the coffee brewed.

"Hello?" He continued to draw whilst the phone balanced on his shoulder and his cheek pressed to it. I didn't know how he did it, he was a better multi tasker than anyone I had ever met. "Nick, what do I owe this pleasure?"

My heart stuttered at his name. I was a pretty confident girl, but my belly couldn't help but flip.

"Again? Jesus, you don't hang about do you." He flipped the page over in his notebook. "You're a pain in the arse." I snickered. "Yes, I know you pay me but bloody hell, Nick."

I turned around to continue with the coffee and listened.

"I'll design one now. Come in around two." He put down the phone. Come in around two?

"What's up?" I asked.

"Nick wants another tattoo, that boy will have no room left on his skin soon."

"What part of his body?" I asked and brought the two mugs over to the counter. The shop was dead quiet at the moment, some tattoo artists already were at work.

"His other knuckle apparently."

"Sounds good." I loved a tattooed man.

The day flew by and my dad had been laying it on easy for me. I wanted to work, but he hadn't been giving me much to do. I sat there most of the day and stupidly thought about Nick.

I was nervous, I was. I wasn't used to being so close to someone so hot and intense. He had effected me so much on our first meeting.

I didn't know why I was so fascinated with him.

Just as I was about to get up to check on my father, the door opened and the air changed. I could feel him even before I saw him.

Nick.

I wasn't mentally prepared, especially when he came in to the shop in his uniform. He was a police officer? God, this was just getting better and better.

I rubbed at my jeans nervously and waited until he had sauntered his way to the counter.

"Hello there again, you." His voice was like rich melted chocolate. My skin buzzed at the sound. His uniform was so hot.

His muscles bulged out of his tight top and his legs looked lean in his tight trousers. Shit. He had the most intense green eyes I had ever seen.

"Hello, sweetcheeks." I batted my eyelashes his way even when my belly was flipping inside. Keep cool, keep cool.

"You look radiant this afternoon." His eyes twinkled.

"As do you, officer." I smirked his way as his eyes darkened.

"Less of that, Angel." His voice lowered. I shivered at the nickname and everything else about him. "Are you tattooing me today?"

"I'm not sure, I need to ask dad." I stated. Nick leaned against the counter as if it were the most natural thing to him. He looked damn fine.

"You're free aren't you?" He raked his eyes down my body. I wanted to blush under his gaze. Christ, I never blushed. "I want you to do it."

"I thought you preferred Glenn?" I questioned as I flipped through his notebook to try and find the drawing he drew for Nick earlier.

"Glenn isn't fucking sexy, though." I looked to him, he watched me as I bent over the counter. I straightened and pulled the book up to the top of the counter so I was standing. He smirked. Cocky ass.

"You have a beautiful way with words." I stated sarcastically.

"You want to hear more?" His smirk grew.

"Maybe, are you free after work?" I joked. He stood up straighter.

"Sure." And he looked dead serious. I couldn't help but laugh at his face.

"I was joking." I stated.

"Tease." He breathed before going into his back pocket and pulling out a pack of cigarettes. "I'll be back in five, call me in when you're ready." He pulled one cigarette out of its packet and put the packet back into his pocket. I couldn't help but stare. Tattoos and cigarettes.

"Do you have a motorbike too?"

"Huh?" He turned around to look at me, one perfectly arched brow risen.

"Tattoos, cigarettes, you're the ultimate bad boy, where's your motorbike?"

"Why? Do you want to ride it?"

Just as I was about to reply, my father came in from the back room. He looked at Nick and smiled. Nick did the same. I could tell they had a great relationship together, they looked at ease with each other and they bantered back and forth.

"Nick, I'm getting tired of seeing your ugly mug around here." Nick put the fag back into his pocket, forgetting all about it and coming back to the counter.

"Ah, Glenn, you're just jealous." He snickered in reply. "Is your daughter tattooing me again today?" He looked hopeful.

"I have a name."

"Cathy." It rolled on his tongue so elegantly. His voice when he said it, all my hairs stood up on end.

"Thanks for clarifying that." I replied, yet my voice came out a little shaken.

"If you carry on flirting she won't even be in the same room as you." The small threat was heard and Nick only laughed in reply. My dad could be quite protective even when he was so easy to get along with. "Cathy?" Glenn asked the unspoken question. I nodded my head.

I didn't know whether I was going to regret this.

"Sure, let me just familiarise myself with the design and then I'll get you seated." I stated. I looked down at the small design and sketched underneath it. It was pretty detailed and I didn't quite have the talent like my father did, but it only took me five minutes and then I was done.

Nick took a seat on one of the plastic chairs by the wall. I could feel his eyes on me. It was unnerving.

"Right, are you ready?" I asked. Nick didn't have to be told twice, he knew this place well, he was seated and ready before I had the chance to tell him what to do.

I carried out the same ritual before I was ready to start. I could smell the musky scent of him even before I had began to sit down. It was going to be a long afternoon, I could already tell.

"Your tattoo addiction is getting out of hand." I stated jokingly. I pressed the needle to his skin after gathering the ink on the end. He didn't even flinch at the sharp pain.

"I like them."

"I can tell." I replied. My father was back in the back room tattooing another customer so I was left alone with Nick. I didn't know whether that was a good thing or a bad thing.

It was hard trying to sit still when your body thrummed and buzzed with Nick's presence, I'm sure pretty much every girl reacted the same. I knew he got a lot of female attention, with a face like that and the body he had, it was inevitable.

"Does this not hurt you?" I asked. He seemed perfectly fine under the needle.

"Nothing hurts me, Angel." His breath fanned across my skin, he smelt like mints and the slight scent of cigarettes.

"What's with the nickname?" He shrugged in reply.

"It suits you." I smiled. Angel wasn't an adjective that I thought would suit me. Nick was a flirt, he probably said it to every girl he had met. I smiled anyway, even though secretly I wished I was the only one. "I want you."

The statement came out so bluntly I nearly choked on my own spit. So long to keeping it cool.

"Pardon?" I almost squeaked.

"I want you, Cathy."

"What do you want me for?" I asked dumbly. My heart was beating so fast I couldn't comprehend what he was trying to tell me. I looked to him and stopped the needle.

Nick looked to me with a twinkle in his eye and an arched brow, as if to say you know what.

Shit.

"Not happening." I replied. I shook my head with emphasis. "Who do you think you are?" I said quietly. I didn't want to attract attention from my father and the others in the building.

"Look-"

"No." I finalised. "I'm not some woman you pick up at the bar and take to your house, I'm not the type of girl who puts out. Christ, Nick." I spun in my chair to turn my back against him.

I didn't know who he thought I was but I was rather insulted.

I could feel his hand against my arm before I had the chance to prepare. My skin arose in goose bumps and I shivered at the contact.

"I effect you." Nick stated the obvious. He did effect me but I wasn't just a notch on his bed post.

"Nick, please, I don't know you, I like dates and things, not this, not like this." And it reminded me of when I was back at home. The thought petrified me. I moved back here for a reason.

"So you're a romantic?" He asked. I turned around, the spark in his eyes gone.

"No, but bloody hell, I'm not that type of girl."

"Shit." He lifted a hand to his face, his muscles bulging.

"What?"

"I don't do dates, I'm doing this in the only way I know how."

"You need a personality change." I tried to lighten the mood, my heart was beating too fast, I wanted to change the topic. This felt all too familiar.

Nick laughed, "its what I'm used to."

"I'm sure other women will be more accommodating to you." More than sure. Nobody else would say no to a night with Nick. He was so hot I wanted to slap myself and tell myself to get a grip, I'd love that too, but no. We were not going to do this.

"Yeah." He rubbed the back of his neck.

I swivelled back over to him trying to ignore the way I felt when I was so close to him. I tried to ignore the nagging thought in the back of my mind telling me to go for it and the nagging thought which told me I was just another body for him to use.

I got back to work.

The atmosphere felt different now. It wasn't light hearted, it felt a little awkward but I could feel the sizzling charge around us growing.

Nothing was said. It felt like Nick was sulking whilst I worked on his knuckle. I could feel his breath still hitting my skin, I ignored it. I got lost in the drawing.

"How's things holding up?" Glenn came into the room. I knew he was doing so to keep an eye on me. He was extremely proud of his place and I knew he trusted me more than anyone to make him proud but he was always still checking.

"Good, I'm almost finished." It didn't take long to do this part of the body and because Nick never asked for colour, it was a lot quicker.

I was glad it was nearly over, I had to keep reminding myself to breathe.

"And you're done." I leaned back to admire the handy work of the small design on his knuckle. I wiped it and put cream onto the hand.

My dad came over to look.

"Wow, good job, Birdie." I squirmed in embarrassment at the nickname when Nick was sat so close to me. He smirked at the nickname, his earlier sulking now gone.

I grabbed the wrap to wrap around his tattoo, by the look of disgust on his face at the sight I knew it would be off by the time he left through the door. I instructed him on the rules but he brushed it off, he knew what he was doing.

"Get back to work then, son." Glenn gave him a clap on the back as he stood up and left through the back door again.

I went to the customer desk and wrote all the details down like usual. I could feel his eyes burning holes in my back and his body was so close to mine I could feel him.

Not this again.

It was so hard trying to keep cool the last time I felt his body against my back.

"Nick, please." I pleaded. I couldn't help the way he had already effected me. He was so intense and he came on so strong. I was a sucker for temptation.

"What's up, Birdie?" He whispered in my ear.

"Don't." I breathed. My body shivered against his touch.

"One day I'm going to put you in the backseat of my car and have my way with you, it will happen, Cathy, believe me." I couldn't get the words up my throat and out of my mouth, my heart lept, my body shivered.

I couldn't reply.

"I will see you again and I'll be looking forward to it, Angel." And with that, he slapped my arse and sauntered through the door leaving me panting and wanting more.

Damn you, Nick.

CHAPTER 3

My body buzzed for the rest of the day. It felt like a charge of electricity surrounded me and I couldn't shift it no matter how hard I tried.

Nick was persistent, I'd give him that but my reaction to him was the only thing that scared me so much. I never was scared of men trying to get me underneath them, I was never afraid of a flirt. I was a very flirty woman myself but I had never reacted to any other man the way I did Nick.

A part of me wanted to charge after him and let him do all the things he wanted, yet another part of me was scared of being used. I never shied away from sex, it was a physical, unemotional thing to me but with Nick I didn't think it would be. I wouldn't be able to stop the emotions this time because he affected me in such way no other man had ever before.

I had only been back a few days and I was already a mess.

"Cathy." My dad came up beside me. "You can take the rest of the day off now if you'd like." He scribbled something in his diary and turned to face me.

"Are you sure?" I asked.

"It's pretty much dead in here today. Go do something fun."

"Like what?" I hadn't been home for years, I had almost forgotten what was here. I guess a tour would be good for me. A walk, so I could try and sort out of fizzled mind after Nick's appearance. "I think I'll go for a walk."

"Sounds nice. Be safe." He kissed me on the cheek before I grabbed my jacket and walked out of the shop. I left my father to draw.

The air was bitter but I valued it today. I needed to wake up, be sharp, I couldn't let Nick affect me. I knew I'd be seeing him, I knew he'd be around more than I wanted as he was so close to my father. Would he try to get me to bed every time he saw me? Would he behave around my father? I hoped he would.

Nick could get any woman he chose, why did he want to have me? Was I a challenge to him? Did he like the chase? The thought left a bitter taste in my mouth. I didn't want to be a part of that at all.

I walked down the street, past the bricked houses and through the small tunnel to town. It wasn't far away and I fancied looking in the shops. It would distract me for a few hours at a least. I hoped.

"Cathy!" I heard my name being called. I turned to the noise and saw the small red head bounding up to me. "Oh my god, I knew it was you!" She gushed.

"Danni?" I looked to her and gasped. Danni and I had been the best of friends in school. She was a natural brunette but had always dyed her head red. She stood out and I was always envious of how confident and sassy she was.

"Girl, you came back!" She pulled me in to a hug and I relished in her touch. She had always been there for me when things got tough. I cried for days when I knew I would have to leave her, it was so hard to leave your best friend at home especially as a teenager and in the middle of growing up. "I thought you would never come back."

"I'm so sorry it took me this long." I stated. I had promised to come back and see her every summer; I didn't, not once. I wanted to see her and it wasn't because I didn't have money to do it, my mother married a rich man who said he'd give it to me if needed. I didn't want that but most of all I didn't want to come home. If I did I'd never want to go back again. I had never liked good byes, they broke me. Doing it more than once was just too much.

"That's okay." She cuddled me closer. The tears were so close to falling. Danni had meant so much to me in the past, I was so happy to have seen her. "Want to grab a coffee with me?" She asked. I smiled.

"That would be nice." I replied. She let me go and linked her arm through mine before whisking me away to the small coffee shop at the end of the street.

You could smell the coffee before entering and once I did I felt right at home. Coffee was my lifeline.

"Go and sit down, I'll order." Danni stated. I looked to her.

"Do you want to ask me what I want?" I asked, her eyes twinkled.

"I know what you want."

"And how do you know that?"

"Because I remembered." She smiled before turning and ordering our drinks. I smiled her way. She always had a good memory. I thought it was nice that she had remembered so easily.

I walked over to the small booth near the window and sat. It wasn't long before Danni came over with our drinks in hand. She put the cups onto the table.

"So, how have you been?" She asked as she took a sip.

"Good. Australia was nice but it's better to be back." I told her. "You've grown up so much." I stated. Her hair was still red but the puppy fat around her face had fallen and her hair had grown long.

"I'm twenty two, darling, of course I have." She winked my way and I laughed in reply. I couldn't believe we hadn't seen each other for five years. It had been so long yet it felt like we had never been apart at all.

"What happened when I left?" I was curious.

"Nothing really. I graduated high school, I did an apprenticeship and then was offered a job, it's good, it pays the bills."

"So no university?" I asked. She shook her head. "Where do you live?"

"In one of the flats currently on my own." She rolled her eyes. "My flat mate left me, it's lonely up there."

"I can imagine. I'm bunking in with my father at the moment."

"Ahhh, Glenn."

"You kept in touch?" I was shocked. Glenn and Danni had always gotten along and even with my mother. After they had split up I hadn't expected my mother to move half way across the world and to take me with her but when it happened my mother had also lost touch with her.

"We did. Not always but I checked up on you as much as I could." She smiled. Guilt flew through out my body. I hadn't kept in touch with her at all once I had moved. It must have hurt her to know that yet she wasn't angry at all.

"Dan-"

"I know what you're going to say." She laughed. "Stop looking so guilty. You're back now, that's all that matters just don't go pissing off again or I will be mad for real."

"You haven't changed." I stated with a smile. She put down her now empty cup.

"I'll kick your ass still even with five years apart, you know that." I laughed.

"I didn't have a doubt." I replied. "But I'm serious, I hope you forgive me for what I did."

"You know what?" She leaned forward. "Come clubbing with me and I'll call it quits."

"Really?"

"Really. We've missed too much time together, let's go clubbing." I smiled with excitement. We had missed so much and I was excited to start getting back into the swing of things.

"Yeah, let's do it."

"Which one?" I held up a small black dress with a low neck line and a small backless, silver dress. Danni sat on my bed with her chosen outfit already in her arms.

"The silver, definitely." She nodded. I approved. It was short, backless and extremely flattering. I took my silver heels and laid them beside the bed.

Danni and I had shopped together and then decided to come home and get ready for tonight. I couldn't help but be extremely excited. I obviously went clubbing back in Australia but it wasn't with Danni and that added to the whole excitement.

My father was still in work so Danni and I had the house to ourselves to get ready. It was already coming to six o'clock in the evening. I wondered when he would finish tonight, I hoped it wasn't late. He already worked so much. I left him a text before I started to get ready.

Danni had used her skills on me until I looked entirely different. My eyes stood out, my skin looked highlighted and my features popped. Danni curled my hair lightly until the dark strands framed my face.

"You look smoking." She stated. I beamed her way. If only Nick could see me now. I hoped I would be able to make him crazy.

"So do you." Her straight hair went past her shoulders and down. Her black dress really showed off her curvy figure. She looked great.

"I haven't told you but those tattoos really look good on you." Danni hadn't seen me with tattoos as I had left before I was legal to get them. "I think I want one."

"You know where to go." I replied. "I'll give you mates rates." She laughed in reply.

We grabbed our things before making our way down stairs. Just as we did, Glenn came through the door. He arched his brow our way just as he came through the door and spotted us.

"Danni?" He questioned and squinted in the dark. He turned on the light and beamed her way once he knew for definite it was her. "Come here." He held his arms out and she went barrelling into them.

Danni had spent so much time with me when we were kids. Danni never had a dad as he died when she was young so Glenn was her only father figure.

"Glenn!" She beamed.

"What a shock to see you here so soon."

"We bumped into each other earlier." I replied.

"And where are you both off to?" Danni came back to stand by me.

"Clubbing." Dad smiled in reply.

"Well, I hope you both enjoy. Be safe, be careful, don't smoke and don't do-"

"Dad, I get it." I lifted my hand up to stop him. "I'm twenty two, not twelve."

"As if I'd let you clubbing at twelve years of age." He rolled his eyes. He took off his shoes and made his way in to the living room. "I think I'm going to order take out. Want any?"

"No, we're going to go now." I replied.

"Okay, have fun, kids." His eyes twinkled. I laughed before we both made our way to the door.

The taxi was already parked on the curb and we ran over to it to get out of the cold. It was stupid of us really wear dresses in this weather.

It didn't take long, only around ten minutes, until we were at one of the hottest night clubs in town. I could hear the music even before we had gotten inside. I was pumped already. I loved dancing, I couldn't wait to get in there.

"Lets go, girl." We both barrelled out of the taxi and were granted access into the club almost straight away.

The floor vibrated as the music pumped from the stereo. The place was dark but it was lit up with the lights circling the dance floor. The bar was illuminated blue so we couldn't miss it. We made our way over to it and ordered the strongest drink on the menu.

"To us!" Danni shouted over the music as she picked up her shot glass. We clinked and began to drink. I grimaced at the taste but welcomed the burn.

"Lets dance." I said to her as I pulled her along. She dumped her empty glass on the side and followed me as she laughed.

The music was so loud it was so easy to lose yourself in the crowd and dance. I let the music take me.

Danni and I danced and drank for hours until we were too drunk to stand up straight.

"I feel great." I slurred her way. She smiled and we made our way to a free table. I needed to sit down, my heels were killing me and the room was slightly spinning.

I let out a breath of relief once I had sat down. I took off my heels straight away and tried to rub the ache away. Heels were a death trap, I was sure of it.

"Woah, he's hot." Danni slurred as she pointed over to a man. I laughed but once I had spotted who she was pointing to, the smile on my face left me.

"Shit." I breathed. Nick was over the other end of the room sat down on one of the tables. Beside him was a big busted blonde. Double shit. Anger flared through my body as I saw him leaning over her. The alcohol wasn't helping. I stood up and wobbled.

"I'll be back in a minute." I stated before rushing over. Danni murmured her protest but I didn't have chance to hear it. The blood was rushing through my ears. How dare he? He said he had wanted me earlier and now he was all over somebody else. She was going to get played if I didn't stop it now. What woman would want to get played. Certainly not me, that's for sure.

The walk over felt like it had taken ages. I had taken my heels off so not getting studded by somebody else's was harder than it looked as I stormed through the dance floor.

As if he could feel me, Nick's head turned and his eyes locked with mine. I faltered but picked my speed back up as I stormed over to him. My body was on hyper aware.

"Nick." I slurred. "I think you're extremely childish." I hiccuped but was too drunk to be embarrassed about it.

The woman latching on to his arm narrowed her eyes my way.

"I would get away from him and quickly too, he's going to play you, you know." I stated her way.

"I'll do what I like, thank you." She replied over the music and smirked. My anger grew.

"Nick." I looked over at his stormy eyes. "I need to talk to you." Without his reply I took hold of his hand and pulled. He stood up with me. The blonde protested but I didn't care. Nick took hold of my hand and pulled me outside of the door at the side of the building.

The air had gotten colder and I shivered as he walked briskly infront of me. He took me over to the side of the building where it was almost dark.

"What are you doing, Cathy?" He asked. I could feel the tension radiating off of his body.

"Clubbing." I stated back childishly. Nick sighed.

"Are you trying to ruin my night?" I snickered.

"I don't even want to be a part of your night. You're disgusting." I spat. "I hate people like you, you think you can have any girl you want but the truth is, Nick, nobody takes you seriously, you're a disgusting, horrible-" I was suddenly slammed up against the wall. I gasped as my back touched the cold and rough wall behind me.

"Don't say things you don't mean, Angel." He whispered venomously into my ear. "What do you want, hmm? Do you want my attention?" I shivered at his contact. I gulped.

"Get off me. I don't want anything from you." My voice sounded weak even to me.

"I've really angered you haven't I? What can I do to make it up to you?" He smirked against my neck and I used my hands to try and push him off of me. I wasn't going to be taken as a joke.

"Get the fuck off me, that's what."

"Cathy, you're turning me on." He stated. "I've never seen you this angry."

"You haven't seen nothing yet, Angel." I spat the word out. He took my hands and held them up against the wall. The breath left my throat in a rush.

"Enough." His voice was like a whip. It broke through the air and I stopped in his grip and stopped struggling. I huffed and puffed as he held me against the wall. My skin felt alive. "What the fuck's going on?"

"I don't know." I let my head fall forward. The drink was getting to me more now I was outside. My anger left me in a rush. "You can go back inside with your blonde."

"I don't want to go back inside with her. What's your problem, Cathy?"

"There isn't a problem." I had made a fuss over nothing. Nick could fuck who ever he wanted to fuck even if I didn't think it was right. Jealousy stabbed through me selfishly. I hardly knew the guy, I didn't have some stupid pretend hold on him.

"You've really wound me up tonight, Angel." His body was restrained through his shirt. He looked so handsome in a white button up shirt and black jeans. He smelt so good too.

"Good." I huffed. Feeling vulnerable I crossed my arms over my chest. I knew I looked like a defiant child. This is what drink did to me.

"Fuck, Cathy." He whispered before chucking two hands into his hair. I watched him and my body reacted the only way it could in the state I was in. I wanted to put my fingers deep in his hair, my tongue deep in his mouth. God, I wanted it all. "You have no idea how-"

Before he could reply I grabbed his head so hard and pulled it straight down until his lips were on mine. He gasped but I swallowed it as soon as I opened my mouth against his. His tongue was so strong yet gentle and it dominated me almost straight away.

He pushed me roughly back up against the wall until I had no room to breathe. I pulled his hair, I yanked his top and kissed him so hard it hurt.

"I'm taking you home." He growled. "Say good bye to your friend, we're going."

"She can't go home on her own." I gasped. "Wait, how did you know I was with my friend?"

"Because I've been watching you all night." His eyes were the darkest they had ever been. He wasn't playful anymore, he was ready to mate, ready for everything I could give him. "I'll take your friend home on the way back. I'm taking you home and that's that, Cathy, go and get your stuff and your friend." I looked to him with wild eyes, panic only starting to set in. I didn't think I would cave so soon. "Now."

"Nick-"

"I need to have you or so God help me I will go insane."

"You're so dramatic." He looked down at me.

"Don't play games with me, Angel, you won't win, believe me."

"Who said I was playing games?"

"Look, I don't care what you do, as long as you end up in my bed tonight." He came forward until I could feel his breath again. "You like playing with Fire, Cathy, you knew you were going to get burnt."

CHAPTER 4

The place was extremely empty today, I didn't know why, yet, I was grateful. I wasn't ready to converse with the public, not when my head was in the wrong place.

I couldn't get Nick off of my mind, especially after last night. I didn't know what happened but I had left his house way before he could get me into his bed.

I freaked out.

I moved back home, one, because I wanted to see my dad and two, because I had enough of men trying to take advantage of me at any given time; especially a certain man.

I shook my head. I needed to banish these thoughts.

There was no doubt in my mind that Nick was effecting me but I wasn't ready to give him everything just for me to be hit to the curb straight after. That wasn't me.

As soon as I had gotten to Nick's apartment, after a very steamy make out session in the back of a taxi, my heart was beating and anxiety decided to creep in. He got out of the taxi and I got back in. "I have to go, I'm sorry." I stated, and then I left him there on the curb with his hands in his pockets and the face of a man who was not going to get laid any time soon. Not by me anyway.

That was the last time I spoke to him or seen him since last night. I half expected him to walk in to the parlour today and demand another tattoo, or to demand a reason as to why I left him high and dry last night.

I was glad he didn't.

The phone rang and I picked it up. I was alone today working, dad said all I had to do was phone him and he'd be up to help. Today, however, I made him take a day for himself. He mumbled and grumbled but finally decided to take the day off.

The man on the other end of the phone booked an appointment for next week. He wanted half a sleeve on his arm which would cost quite a bit. As soon as the phone was put back into its cradle, I was bored and alone once again.

I could literally hear crickets cricketing the place was so dead. It was weird, dad said the place was always busy, and it was, I saw that, but some days the place was empty.

I was so excited when the clock hit four in the evening. With hardly anyone making appointments today and no customers I was happy to be locking up the place and going home.

As soon as I was home, I dumped my coat on a hanger and my other items in the bowl in the hall and made my way into the kitchen.

"Dad?" I shouted as I walked through the living room and on to the modern floor boards.

"I'm trying to make fried chicken." Glenn stood infront of the oven with the frier in his hands. He looked comical in his apron and perspiration on his brow.

"What the hell are you doing?" I laughed. The grease in the frier was sizzling to the top. He was struggling to control everything going on in the kitchen. He had never been the best cook.

"I just said what I'm trying to do." He replied as he wiped his forehead with the back of his hand. "Your mother used to make fried chicken. I thought I'd give it a go as we have company tonight." Glenn wasn't in love with my mother anymore but he looked up to her a lot, even if they didn't talk.

"Company?" I sat down on the barstool behind him. I turned around to keep an eye on his cooking.

"Just a few of the old pals." He stated. I sighed, old didn't mean Nick. I was grateful.

"Sounds nice." My eyes narrowed as I watched him shaking the frier in the hot grease. "For god sake, dad, leave the frier alone, I'll make dinner."

"You'd do that for me, Birdy?" He whipped around and gratitude was evident on his face. I laughed at him before nodding my head. He let out a huge sigh of relief and chucked the apron on to the dining room table. "I doubt you'll need an apron, you're too good."

"Even professionals need an apron." I rolled my eyes and picked it up from the table. I wrapped it around my body and had to tie a bow at the front.

I ditched the disaster my father had made and decided to start from scratch.

My dad hustled around me as I made dinner. I didn't know who was coming tonight but I was glad my father socialised with his friends regularly. Glenn was an extremely sociable man and could talk to a brick wall and still make friends.

"You remind me more of your mother every time I see you, you know." I smiled at his statement. I loved my mother, she was always so genuine, sweet and soothing. I, however, hated her new husband, with a passion. I shivered a little.

"Is that a compliment?" I asked jokingly.

"It is." My father replied. "You do take after me in the sense of humour department though. I'm just funnier." I scoffed.

"I'm not too sure about that." I started to dish out the chicken. I put the chicken legs into bowls and placed them on to the dining room table. I had also cooked wedges and plated them up next to the chicken.

"Ahhh, you're a star." Glenn came up to kiss me on the cheek before rushing off to the living room and sitting on his arm chair to watch the beginning of the football.

I went upstairs and decided on showering. I heard the door knock and his friends enter the house just as I turned on the shower.

I striped out of my clothes and got in to the piping hot shower. I let out a sigh of relief.

I was only in the shower for two minutes before I decided to leave. I got out of the shower and wrapped a towel around my body.

Just as I opened the door, I nearly screamed at the figure before me. A hand clamped around my mouth so the sound wouldn't travel further, that was hard to do as my father had the football on extremely loud anyway.

"Fucking hell." Nick's voice was rough and deep as his burning hot eyes raked my body from head to toe. "You're a dirty fucking girl, Cathy."

"I've not done anything." I trembled as I spoke. Nick stood before me in black jeans and a white top got me all kinds of crazy. His tattoos were on show, from his muscled arms and up his neck. Fuck, he was too hot.

"Coming out in just a towel, dripping wet." He gruffed.

"I didn't know you were going to be here." I rolled my eyes. "It's my house, my shower, my privacy. Get the fuck out." I hissed as I pointed to the stairs. My skin was full of goosebumps at the close touch from Nick.

"You know, it's not exactly, what's the word..." he trailed off as he looked up to the ceiling. I leaned against the door frame and watched. "Satisfying to be left high and dry."

"I don't care." I pushed past him and made my way into my room. He followed. I went to shut the door in his face but he held it open with his hand. He was so strong. I huffed in annoyance.

"I know you wanted it too, you know."

"Fuck off." I muttered. Before I could say anything else, my back was up against the wall. What was with him slamming me on to hard surfaces? "Get the hell off me."

"No." His face cake close, until his nose was touching my neck. I started to pant. "No." He repeated.

"I'm not doing this with you again." God knows it was so hard to get out of the moment once I was in it. I said I was going to be strong, I said I wasn't going to let this happen. "Get off of me, I won't tell you again."

"Or what?

"What?" My eyebrows crossed on their own accord.

"What are you going to do about it?" He pushed his body closer to my body, his white t-shirt now a little wet too. I couldn't help but flicker my eyes down to his abs. He had such a stocky and powerful body. He was too sexy for his own good.

"I could scream blue bloody murder, believe me."

"I would like it." He smirked. Nick's eyes twinkled as he took on his boyish charm. He opened his mouth to reply, but a voice came travelling from outside of the door. I hadn't realised Nick had closed it.

"Cathy? Do you know where Nick has gone? I swear to God, if he is in there with you I am going to grab his balls and chuck them under the wheel of my car." His voice was twinged with a tiny bit of humour but the evidenence of threat was still there.

"Tell him I've gone for a fag." He whispered in my ear. Goose-bumps arose again.

"He will try to find you."

"He won't. Go on, tell him." I couldn't speak. Nick's finger touched a spot on my thigh before it moved higher and higher. My mouth went dry.

"He's gone for a-a fag." I stuttered. His middle finger joined his other, my body shivered as they moved up my inner thigh.

"Good girl." Nick rasped. I heard footsteps move away from my door but I couldn't relax, not with his hands on me. They were so dangerously close, so close.

"Stop it." I breathed. "Please." I was going to cave, I was going to jump his bones any second now. I couldn't stop, I didn't want to, but I needed to.

"Your tattoos."

"What about them?" I could feel his breath against my skin.

"They're so bright."

"I like colour." I couldn't breathe.

"Why?" His fingers touched me, it was so feather like and soft, I wanted more.

"Nick." I moaned.

"Yes, baby?" He moaned against my neck. "Beg for me."

"No."

"Beg for me." He demanded more firmly.

"Please, Nick." I couldn't help it, I wanted to kick myself so hard in the face. But as soon as his touch was there, it was gone. "What the-"

"Not so satisfying, huh?" Nick's body backed away from mine. He continued to walk backwards, leaving me breathless and empty until he was by the bedroom door.

"You're a prick." I let out.

"I like it that way." He winked my way before leaving the bedroom. I looked at the now closed door with bewilderment. For God sake, Cathy, Jesus. I couldn't have just kept my bearings could I? I flopped onto the bed and sighed.

After ten minutes of feeling sorry for myself, I decided to get dressed and face the music. I wanted to stay upstairs forever and never leave, but I knew that wasn't ever going to happen. I took a deep breath and I went downstairs.

I could hear the men shouting and cursing from half way down the stairs. The football was on and it was a very competitive sport, especially in this house. I wonder what team Nick supported?

As soon as I opened the door, my father turned around to face me with a grin.

"We're winning." I laughed at his childish happiness but it made me happy within to see him this way. My eyes flickered over to Nick.

He was sat on the chair. I half expected him to be watching the TV, however, his eyes were trained on me. He looked so relaxed, his ankle crossed over his knee and his arm outstretched over the back of the arm chair. I swallowed and turned my attention back to my dad.

"Have you all eaten?"

"We have."

"Did you enjoy it?"

"Best fried chicken I have ever had." A man from beside my father spoke. He had salt and peppered hair and looked older than my father. "Glenn did good." I laughed loudly.

"Oh, dad, come on." I bent over as I laughed. "He didn't make them, guys. I did." Still laughing, I made my way in to the kitchen.

I could hear their voices from within the living room.

"You're a liar, you sneaky bastard." Laughter filled the air.

"You didn't tell me Cathy could cook." Nick's voice stopped me in my tracks.

"I didn't need to." I could hear my father reply.

"I'm going for a fag." Shit. I moved over to the sink and began to wash up, making myself look useful instead of listening in.

"You're lungs will be black soon, my boy, you need to give up."

"Fuck off." Laughter filled the air once again.

I could feel his presence before he even spoke.

"What do you want?" I asked as I washed the grime off one of the China plates.

"Many things, darling, many things." I turned around with soapy hands and took in his figure leaning against the counter. He was always so laid back and relaxed.

"You need to get over yourself." He shrugged in reply.

"You're quite the cook aren't you? A woman after my own heart, tattoos, good cook, what more?"

"You're never going to find out." I turned back to continue the washing. I heard his laugh from behind, it made my toes curl.

"What did it feel like last night when you left?"

"How did I feel?" I asked.

"Yeah?"

"Happiness." His snicker made me turn around to watch him again. He was smirking. God, that damn smirk.

"Do you want to know why I'm asking?" He started to stalk towards me. I couldn't move back. I followed him with my eyes, my heart racing.

"Not really."

"Seeing you in just a towel, knowing I was so close to getting what I wanted yet still so far. Knowing I could have had you, I had your permission, your consent, I could have made you begged until you were on your knees, but I left." Arrogant twat.

"Lucky me." His body was pressed up against mine for the second time that night.

"Do you know what it took to walk away from you?" His breath, so warm against my skin. "A fucking miracle and a raging-"

"I get it." I cut him off, not wanting to listen to him anymore. "I get it, I really do. You wanted to show me how it felt to be left wanting."

"Not quite correct." I looked to him, his blazing eyes. They were captivating. "I wanted to teach you a lesson. Naughty, dirty girls get punished, don't they?"

"Do they?" I quivered. I didn't know why, but I liked his dirty talk.

"One day, I'll show you." And a part of me, the stupid, annoying part of me was excited to try.

Chapter 5

My father had given me the day off and quite frankly, I needed it. I had been working long hours this week as a group of bikers had wanted various tattoos which couldn't all be done in one day.

Also, I hadn't seen Nick for days.

A part of me was missing him, the other part was quite happy I hadn't seen him. He messed me up, in more ways than one. I was having a breather, but I wasn't sure I was enjoying it.

Danni had phoned me up during the week and we had planned a day out. I didn't know what she had in mind but I was excited to hang out with her.

Once I was dressed, I made my way to the front door and left, locking it behind me. Glenn had gone to work early this morning so I had the house to myself.

I jumped into a cab I had called earlier in advance and made my way to the cafe Danni had planned to meet me at.

It didn't take long before the taxi was pulling up towards the curb. I passed him a note before leaving the car and making my way in to the cafe. It smelt of freshly baked cakes and freshly brewed coffee. Yum.

I made my way up to the counter and ordered before Danni arrived. I then grabbed my stuff as soon as it was done and went to sit down in a small booth.

It didn't take long before Danni was bounding her way up to me, a small bobble hat laying cutely above her head.

"Hey, cutie." She smiles before sitting down opposite me and grabbing on to the drink I had bought her in advance.

"Hey, how are you?" I asked in greeting. I took a sip of my coffee and sighed. It was nice to get out and to have company with somebody other than the biker crew and my father. It was nice to be occupied from all thoughts of Nick.

"You know what? I'm doing okay. My stupid neighbours are pissing me off lately though." She rolled her eyes. I laughed at her bubbly personality.

I had always wanted a personality like Danni's. She was always so happy and bubbly, I was envious. Sometimes, it felt like half of me was missing and lost. I wasn't the girl I used to be.

"It's okay, I'm still living with my dad." I stated. I loved my dad but I was definitely old enough to have my own house, that was for sure.

"My little two bedroom flat is always open to you, darling, you know that." I nod my head in reply. I didn't know if I was ready to leave my father just yet. I had missed him so much.

"Thanks, Dan."

She waved me off with a smile.

"Okay, anyway, first of all I want to know where you went the other night when we went out clubbing. You're a secret dirty stop out aren't you?" Her eyes twinkled with curiosity and amusement as she looked to me. "You know I won't judge."

"I wouldn't say dirty stop out." I replied sheepishly. "We didn't do anything, I was going to but I stopped short."

"Why?"

"I was scared." I was being honest here. I saw Nick as any other man on this Earth, yet, he didn't feel like just another man.

"Tell me about it." Danni said as an encouragement to continue. I sighed. I had a girl friend now, I could tell her anything.

"He's a bit of a play boy, you know, a ladies man and me? Well I'm just an average girl with a fuck load of tattoos on my skin and I maybe or maybe not might have a small crush on him." I looked down at my cup of coffee. "I don't want to be used by him."

"If he's using you then he doesn't know what he's missing." Danni stated. "In fact, to me, he'll be labelled as a dick head. You're hot stuff."

"Thanks." I laughed. "He's so handsome and he's got tattoos all over his body." I dreamt of him more than I should have. He was more than just handsome.

"Still, he needs to be brought down to his knees." Danni stated. I looked to her with confusion. "You know what brings a sexy man down? A sexy woman. Come on, we're going shopping."

We didn't just end up shopping.

I've had my nails done, my makeup done and now I'm on to my hair. I didn't know how much money I was forking out and to be honest, I didn't really care.

I already felt more confident than I did before. I felt like a polished woman and I felt good.

As I sat there in the leather chair with a black cloth wrapped around my neck, I relaxed. The Italian man who had a pair of scissors in his one hand and my hair in between his two fingers whizzed around my hair like a professional.

I guess he was really.

He styled my hair and cut it into a way that looked glamorous. My hair was naturally an inky black so it was hard to dye it or colour it in any sort of way. I didn't care, I just wanted to look good.

In my mind, I wanted to look good for Nick.

When he was done, I looked at myself in the mirror and I wanted to gasp. My hair looked full of life and voluminous. My makeup was done so nicely and precisely. Everything stood out.

"Wow, hot." Danni said as she came up beside me.

"Very very nice." The hair dresser admired his work and smiled proudly. I got up to pay.

Before long, Danni had dragged me to another store and we were trying on dresses.

Passing the mirrors, I felt so good. I had never been treated this way, this thing was never my thing.

I tried on many dresses but I fell in love with just one. It hugged my curvy figure in the best way possible and felt so good against my skin.

I could never wear colourful clothes too much as I felt the colours contrasted against the tattoos I had on my skin. This dress was black but was made of fine silk. It was short and tight against my body.

I took the dress off my body and held it in my arms until I was at the counter. I was going to buy this, most definitely.

My card felt heavy in my hands as I paid for the pile of silk.

"Are you ready to go?" Danni asked straight after I had paid. I nodded. Luckily, I had black heels at home. I didn't know when and where I was going to wear this, but I was hoping this effort wasn't going to be wasted.

In fact, I wanted to see Nick tonight. I felt good about myself and for the first time ever my makeup was done perfectly.

Danni and I shared a taxi back to our homes. Danni left first with a hard kiss to the cheek and then I was the next one to be dropped off.

As soon as I opened the door, I was greeted to silence again. With a shrug, I went upstairs to try on my outfit again.

Ten minutes later, I heard the door downstairs opening and closing.

"Cathy?" I heard my father's voice.

"Hold on, dad." I shouted back. "I bought a new dress, I'm just trying it on."

"Come down and let me see it." He replied. I smiled. My father was a masculine man but he loved to see me dressing up. As a child he would help me dress up in consumes and we'd play for hours. I know he misses how things used to be.

As soon as I was ready I opened my bedroom door and made my way downstairs. I emerged into the living room to see my father.

"It looks amazing." Glenn said, his eyes twinkling and a large smile upon his face. "I wish you didn't have to keep growing."

"I'm an adult, dad." I laughed.

"I wish you were still my baby." He stated almost tearfully. He was always so sensitive when it came to me, his only child.

All of a sudden, I could feel Nick before I saw him. I turned around to face him emerging into the living room from the kitchen. I hadn't realised he was here.

His confident steps faultered as he took me in. Satisfaction swept through his gaze and I stood there proudly. He almost came to a stop.

"She looks good doesn't she?"

Nick nodded slowly as his eyes continued to sweep my body.

"I'm going back upstairs." I stated as I started to blush at their stares.

"I'm going for a piss." Nick said and followed quickly behind me. I didn't have it in me to tell him to stop following me. In fact, I was glad when he pulled me back by the elbow and laid his nose against my neck.

"Fuck." He whispered as he pushed me to my bedroom door. "That dress..." he trailed off.

"Do you like it?"

"I more than like it." He growled. "What's it going to take for me to get on top of you?" I rolled my eyes.

"I'm not that type of girl, Nick."

"What type of girl are you?" I shrugged.

"I've never been the romantic type, Nick, but I like going out for dinner and-"

"Come out for dinner with me."

"What?"

"Have dinner, with me." He sighed as he caged me between his rock hard body and the wall. His eyes looked straight to me. "It's crazy, I know. I don't usually do this but I can't stop thinking about you and quite frankly I'd rather take you out for dinner than not be around you at all."

"Really?"

"Babe, I wouldn't be able to get the image of that dress and your body out of mind even if I tried." He closed his hooded eyes slightly. "We might as well give that dress some good use."

"I'd love to go out to dinner with you." I replied.

"I'd rather that dress on my bedroom floor, but beggars can't be choosers." He winked my way. I slapped his chest hard before moving away from him.

"Don't make me change my mind." I looked to him. He lowered his head for a minute and smiled my way.

"I'll try my hardest." He looked like a vumernable little kid and it made my heart melt. "I'll pick you up later tonight, how about that?"

"Sounds good to me."

"I'll see you then." And he left my room without a glance back. I smiled triumphantly.

I didn't know what his intentions were and how far this would go, but for now, I wanted to live life to the fullest. And finally, a part of my old self was starting to make it's appearance.

Once I had stripped out of my dress and back into my jeans and my t shirt, I laid the dress carefully out on the bed, making sure it wasn't going to crease and get ruined.

I then made my way back downstairs. I could still hear Nick and my father talking so I decided to walk past them and in to the kitchen. I could feel Nick's eyes burning holes in to my back as I moved.

"I swear to God, Nick, stop staring at my daughter's arse." My dad never missed a trick. I laughed loudly.

"Dad, I'm feeling violated."

"I know, Birdy, don't worry, I'll kick his arse." Glenn replied. I laughed again and made my way back in to the living room after grabbing a bottle of water.

Nick sat in the arm chair with his ankle laying on top of his other leg. He looked so casual and comfortable, it made my heart race.

"I'm always getting ganged upon when I'm here." Nick muttered solemnly to himself. "You couldn't hurt me with that crusty arm anyway, Glenn."

"You're a twat." Glenn replied and I laughed again. His voice was full of humour and deep down I knew Glenn loved Nick a lot. They were like best friends and Nick obviously adored my father. Who wouldn't?

"A twat who's taking your daughter out tonight." Nick replied. Glenn looked to me with a shocked expression.

"Is that why you keep going upstairs after my daughter?" Glenn looked back over to Nick. "If you hurt her, I'll hurt you, I swear to God."

"I'll look after her, Glenn. You don't need to worry." And for once, Nick looked serious. I did trust him.

"You're a police officer, that's your job you donut, please, just do your job properly in the care of my child."

"I'm not a child." I replied but he didn't hear me, if he did he chose to ignore it.

"I swear to you, Glenn." Nick stated. Glenn finally nodded his head with approval but I could see the warning signs in his eyes.

Nick looked over to me and smirked. I smiled his way.

"I best get going." Nick got up from the chair and clasped his strong legs. "I got a hot date tonight."

"Don't push it." My father muttered.

"I'll let you out." I rushed over to Nick and pulled him in to the hall way before closing the door behind us.

"Steady on." He chuckled. "Have you come to give me a goodbye kiss?"

"I will punch you in the face." I said back. He chuckled again.

"I'll see you tonight, darling. Seven o'clock."

"Seven o'clock." I nodded firmly. My heart flipping at the word darling. Jesus, why did he effect me so much?

"Wear that dress." He demanded. I nodded my head.

"I was counting on it."

"Good girl." Nick bent over to kiss my forehead before retreating and moving to the front door. "Seven o'clock, don't forget."

"I'm not going to forget." I laughed. His kiss making me tingle.

"See you later then." He said. "I'm looking forward to it."

Chapter 6

The silk dress was back on my body at quarter to seven the same evening. The silk was cool against my warm skin yet it didn't stop or calm the nerves that began to over take my body when I thought about tonight.

Okay, it was obvious I had a crush on the guy, yet, I knew I had to keep a certain distance between us. It felt already too soon, but it was a date, where was the harm in that?

The thing was, it was hard to say no to Nick. He was handsome and just my type. Where was the harm in living a little? Not many girls could say they went out with a blue eyed, tattooed beauty.

Well, that was depending on how many girls Nick took out on a daily basis. It was clear to see that Nick had a way with the women, and there was a high chance I was just another conquest. A very high chance.

My father must know this too, he was a little apprehensive about the whole thing. He knew what Nick was like with the ladies, knew what he was like full stop. My father couldn't stick the fact he may want to do the same thing to me, too.

My father, however, was a sincerely nice guy and when it came to Nick, he'd do pretty much anything for him. The bromance between the two was unreal. I came first, obviously, but my dad was way too easy going to ever say no, even when he wanted to.

I looked in to the mirror again. I had decided to keep my hair the same style and my makeup, however, I did redo the eye shadow and my lipstick. My lipstick was now a deep red and my eyeshadow a nude.

I was ready physically, mentally, not so much.

"Are you ready yet?" Glenn knocked the wood of my painted white door. I opened it and stepped outside, closing the door softly behind me.

"Yeah, I don't know why he wanted me to keep the dress on." I stated whilst looking down at the silk. Where was Nick taking me? He didn't seem the romantic, so why was I dressed so nicely?

"That boy has weird fantasies and fetishes." Dad replied.

"And you know that how?" I asked, disgusted. I didn't want to know what they talked about whilst braiding each other's hair and telling each other their secrets.

"I'm not even going to say, love." He shook his head even though the smile on his face showed me he was remembering back to a time in the past.

I really wondered what went on around here before I moved back home.

"He obviously likes silk." Glenn shrugged. "Just be careful okay?"

"I will." I stated. Could I ever be careful around Nick?

"I love that boy but he has some series issues. If he asks you for sex, say no. He has charm and if you're anything like your mother then you're going to fall for it."

"That's disgusting, dad." I replied, torn between wanting to laugh or gag. "I don't want to know about your past sex life to be honest."

"Yeah, well, your mother fell for the funny ones and Nick can be bloody hysterical sometimes, when he hasn't got his head up his arse, and I just need you to be careful."

"I will, stop worrying. If anything, I think I'm the funny one." I replied with a smile. Glenn chuckled before taking me in to his arms.

"When your mother took you to Australia away from me, I missed out on all your first dates. You're here now and I want to do it right." I snuggled further in to his body. I had missed being away from him every day. Phone calls were never enough when you were a daddy's girl.

I hated it in Australia, I hated my mother's new husband more than anything.

"You're a soppy git." I replied, even though I felt the soppy one. Tears welled up in my eyes, but I didn't let them fall. I was happy now with my dad. I wouldn't ever have to go back to Australia. "I'm going to tell Nick."

"I don't care what that fucker says about me." I laughed at his statement. "I feed the greedy fuck."

"You do?" I asked as I moved away from his body.

"Nick can't cook and he's too tight to pay for his own food so he usually comes over here begging for some of my bolognese."

"Bolognese?"

"I know, it's like looking after a sixteen year old teenager." He shook his head. "Funnily enough, he hasn't come here for food half as much as he used to before you came. I don't know whether it's because he wants to look independent or he just doesn't like you." Glenn winked my way.

"And I'm going on a date with the fucker." I replied.

"Exactly." We smiled in unison. "Have a good time tonight, text me or ring me if you need-"

"Dad." I held my hand up to stop him. Did he forget I was twenty one years old, not seventeen. "I'm an adult. I can survive without my daddy."

"I wish you didn't have to." He shrugged. "But I mean it, anyway."

"I know." I mouthed. I grabbed my small bag and moved around my father to descend down the stairs.

All of a sudden, I could hear a loud exhaust and rattling coming from behind the front door. I turned to my father.

"That, lovely, is called the monster truck." Glenn replied.

"What?" My face twisted in confusion. What in the name was the monster truck? The noise had stopped outside regardless.

"Nick's banged up truck."

"I thought he drove a cop car?"

"On the job and when he can get away with it. He also has a motorbike but probably doesn't want to give you the shits." My father walked down the stairs behind me, before he was beside me. He opened the door wide.

"You know, I can ride a motorbike." I stated. I had learnt to ride in Australia with a few of my friends. I had picked it up pretty quick and the next thing I knew I was buying one out of my savings.

It was a sleek black and red motorbike which hit a top speed in under ten seconds. It was way too much for me to begin with but I loved it so much it was all I rode for years.

"Jesus Christ, and your mother let you ride the thing?" Glenn's face was painted with shock.

"I'm not made of glass." I laid a kiss to his cheek before walking out of the door. As soon as I did so, Nick jumped down from his side of the truck.

He sauntered up to me. My mouth watered at his figure. He was dressed in tight black jeans, a white shirt and black converse.

He looked so casual against my silken dress. I felt way too over dressed.

However, the gaze that landed on me was more than welcoming. He racked my body from head to toe as he walked towards me.

"Riding in style are you?" Glenn shouted from the entrance of the door making Nick remove his eyes from my body.

"Fuck off." Nick shouted back, a small smile on his face. Soon, his body was so close to mine I could feel his breath on my cheek and his warmth radiating off of him. I shivered.

"I don't know what to say about your monster truck." I stated honestly. It was white and rusty and it obviously rattled when it was driven. It was a death trap.

Nick moved his eyes back up to Glenn who had now closed the door on us both.

"Bloody Glenn." Nick muttered. "It's not called the monster truck." Nick wandered off over to the truck. I followed him.

"What's it called then?"

"I haven't named it anything." Nick responded. He went over to the other side of the truck and opened the door. I followed after him. "Let's get you up."

"I'm sure I can do it." I said as I looked to the small step which would lead me up to the leather seat.

"Fine." Nick left to get in his side, easily jumping up into the seat and starting the engine.

I lifted a foot up on to the step and tried to jump. However, my legs were too small to get there.

"Do you need help?" Nick asked, his brow lifted sardonically. His face was painted in to amusement. Bastard.

"No." I tried again to jump, but this time I nearly fell flat on my arse.

"Are you sure?" His annoying voice came out again from above me. I huffed in annoyance.

"Fine you bloody bastard." I let out as I couldn't seem to hoist my leg up.

"I was hoping you'd say that." Nick jumped out of the truck, it swayed as he did so. I felt him behind me before I could say a word.

The next thing I knew, his hand was on my arse.

"Nick, I swear to fucking God, get your hand off my arse."

"Fine." He huffed. He then laid a hand to the back of my thigh and pushed until I was able to hoist a foot on to the floor and pull myself up on to the leather seat.

As soon as I was sat down, I let out a breath and closed the door in his face. I saw him walk around the truck until he jumped back in to his seat.

He was smiling largely.

"Why are you smiling?" I asked as my brows furrowed. He set the truck in gear as he looked to me out of the corner of his eyes.

"I saw your panties." Oh my god. He looked so smug too as he drove the truck out of the small drive way.

"Get a grip of yourself." I demanded. I wore black lace trimmings and I tried to pretend I never wore them for him. That wasn't the point however, he shouldn't have been looking.

"I would but I've got female company." I looked to him with wide eyes. "And as I'm on a date, I've got to be a gentleman." He smiled my way. My world stopped for a second as I saw his pearly whites. God, he was so fucking handsome.

"Who told you that?" I asked. The truck was now in full motion. The radio stopped the rattling being so loud, yet I could still hear it clearly. He really needed a new car.

"Glenn." I burst out laughing. "Don't laugh. He made it perfectly clear I was to treat you like a lady tonight."

"And you're going to listen to him?" I didn't believe that, not for one minute. When did Nick ever listen to anybody? He didn't strike me as the type to jump when demanded to.

"Would you rather I didn't?" He asked, a smirk playing on his lips. God, he was so arrogant and confident. It, however, didn't do anything to put me off him. It made me want him all the more.

The electricity in the banged up truck sizzled between us. I couldn't help but shift in my seat as I felt the palpable energy over take me.

"I'd rather you do as you please." I managed to let out. It was hard to concentrate when I could smell him, that musky male smell coming from his body.

"We'd be in my bed if I were to do as I pleased." He muttered back, like a sulking teenager as he couldn't get what he wanted.

Nick drove the car with ease, you wouldn't think a man so muscular would have so much grace, but he did. He looked so in demand of the car, his body powerful and ripped. I couldn't stop staring at his biceps as he tore through the gears up the highway.

"You disgust me." I breathed. I had to get a grip of myself. I was already running low on oxygen and the night hadn't even started. I had at least two more hours left with Nick tonight, I needed to stay in control of my body.

Nick looked to me through the corner of his eyes as he kept facing towards the road. A small smile lit up his face.

I hope he didn't see the blood stained blush on my cheeks, or the tenseness of my body.

"You're a liar, a pretty shit one too."

"No-"

"I can feel you from here, you know." Nick stated, driving the car around a tight bend.

"Feel what?" I asked, my heart leaping. Was I really that open? Could he see everything I thought and felt? God, I hoped not.

"Your body, it's rigid and warm. You're more effected by me than you think." No, I knew how effected I was by him.

"Don't flatter yourself." I muttered. He chuckled in reply.

"I would love to go on about you and your tendencies to lie, however, we're here." And for once, Nick fidgeted in his seat. He looked nervous as I took a look at the building in front of us.

"The burger shack?" I questioned. My mouth watered. I loved burgers, and even though I was dressed up to eat somewhere a little more expensive, I was so happy Nick took us here instead. This was more me, more comfortable especially whilst I was dealing with Nick.

"Yeah, look, I don't have a lot of money on me at the moment, pay day is quite a long way away and I'd love to say I was a rich billionaire but fuck that. If you're not happy-"

"Shut the fuck up, Nick." Jesus Christ, the man could babble. "Lets go." I could barely hold my excitement as I jumped down the truck. I ditched my heels before the night had started and relied on some flat shoes instead. That meant I wouldn't twist my ankle when I jumped so far down.

I didn't even bother waiting for Nick to walk along side me, instead, I went straight in to the small little diner.

It smelt so good.

Before long, Nick was behind me. I could feel his warmth, his presence way before I could see him.

"I didn't know you liked burgers so much." Nick stated with humour as he came to stand beside me. We joined the queue.

"Nick, I just like food to be honest." I replied honestly. No harm in anyone liking food too much. "You need to stop worrying, I'm not Queen Elizabeth, you know. A burger shack will do me just fine."

Nick didn't reply. I looked to him as he looked down at me. He looked at lost for words. Well, well, well, I had redeemed the man speechless. This was a first.

I didn't have time to ponder on the fact I had left Nick speechless, or the fact he seemed shocked that I preferred a burger shack over a posh restaurant (honestly, who wouldn't?) as the queue had died down and it was our turn to order.

I stalked up to the counter with Nick hot on my tail.

"Hi, I would like the double bacon cheese burger with fries please." I stated. I turned to Nick, waiting for him to place his order.

His eyes were planted firmly on me. He snapped out of his trance before turning to the man on the counter and ordering too.

"I'll have the same."

The meal came to under twenty dollars, which to me was great. Nick offered to pay, and even though I didn't feel entirely comfortable with it, I still let him.

I then followed him over to a small booth in the corner of the room. It was quite secluded and peaceful as we sat on the red leather benches.

Nick went to pick up the food from the counter a few minutes later. He carried the tray and laid it softly in front of me. He then sat back opposite me.

He reached out to grab his drink first. His hands were so large, they smothered the cup snuggly. I never found hands so sexy until I saw his. The small smarter of black hair on his arms and his hands were enough to make me tingle; everywhere.

He was just pure masculine.

The tattoos didn't help either. They were everywhere across his body, leaving nothing but imagination to see where the rest of the tattoos led.

"I kinda like it." I took my eyes away from his arms and swivelled them up to his eyes.

"Like what?" I asked through a mouthful of food, which, by the way was amazing. Seriously, a burger this good was uncanny.

"You, in that dress that really isn't meant for a burger shack."

"I feel over dressed." I stated. Truly over dressed. The other customers here were dressed in hoodies and warm clothing. Not that I was cold or anything, but still. I was way too over dressed for the occasion.

"You could always just pretend we're somewhere fancy." He shrugged as he took hold of about ten fries and laid them in his mouth. He leaned back on his bench and laid one arm across the length of it. The tattoos on his under arm were now visible.

"Would Sir like a sip of my Pepsi?" I batted my eyelashes his way as I joined in on the game. Having demolished his drink in one sip, he was always welcome to mine. Anyway, even if Pepsi wasn't exactly what you would order in a fancy restaurant, I had never drank wine and liked it so I redeemed it unacceptable to say.

"Say Sir again and I'll be forced to take you home." Nick growled. It didn't stop him from diving over the table to take my drink. He drank it all in a few seconds flat.

"You were meant to join in on the game." I groaned whilst biting another part of my burger. I grabbed the drink back from Nick and frowned in to the empty cup.

"The only game I'm willing to take part in is the one where I undress you." I hoped it didn't show how much his words effected me. His eyes were intense as he took a hold of my body. I wished I could give in to temptation, really wish I could.

Nick oozed sex appeal, he owned it. It was obvious he was amazing in bed. However much I wanted to see for myself, I was still worried I'd be humped and dumped, not something I really wanted happening to me right now.

"I thought you were being a gentleman tonight." I retorted. I knew it wouldn't last long.

"All thoughts of being a gentleman flew out of my mind as soon as you started playing games and calling me Sir." He replied.

"It was only the once."

"Once is all it takes."

"And will you use that motto even after you've had your way with me? Once is all it takes?"

"Cathy, once isn't even going to be in my vocabulary with you." His voice was deep, laced with an internal battle to lose control and come at me. Laced with a hunger. Laced with a need.

I couldn't help but think back to the conversation my father and I had earlier. Nick knew how to play his words, he was definitely charming and I was falling for it, just like my father knew I would.

"Say something funny." I demanded. Nick looked to me with confusion.

"What?"

"Say something funny." I repeated. It come to a time where I hadn't seen my father for years, yet he knew me more than I knew myself. I was exactly like my mother, I knew I was.

"Why?"

"Because dad said I'm just like my mother and I'll fall for the charming and funny men and leap in to bed with them without a backwards glance." I stated. I looked to him, his eyes set with a type of determination. "I don't want to be used. I don't want to jump in to bed with you so soon."

"Fucking Glenn." Nick muttered. "He's the biggest cock block known to man." Nick leaned back again in his seat. I started to clear away the table.

"I've had such a lovely evening, honestly. Thank you." I said to him. He looked up at me.

"You want to go so soon?" He asked, it looked as if he was disappointed at first, but that went as soon as I saw it.

"Well-"

"How about I come back to yours?" Nick asked. I stared at him wide eyed, he caught on to my expression. "No, not like that, I mean I come back to yours and we can just hang out?"

"Why not yours?" I asked curiously.

"I thought you'd feel more comfortable at yours considering you think I'm a walking sex addict or something." Nick sighed. "And truthfully? If I took you back to mine I don't think I'd be able to control myself. I'm respecting your views on the whole thing, but it still doesn't stop me from being horny when I look at you."

"You have such a romantic way of words." I replied. Even though his comment made me smile. "But okay, that sounds good I suppose."

"Good." And Nick stood up from his seat.

"Oh, oh." I started to clap excitedly. "Guess what I've got on DVD?"

"What?" Nick asked as he led me out of the door. We made our way over to his truck.

"Mean girls." I said with a large smile. I wasn't a huge fan of chick lits yet mean girls was ducking hilarious. Plus, a part of me just wanted to piss off Nick.

"Brilliant." He replied back, sarcasm dripping fromhis tone. "I can't wait."

CHAPTER 7

As soon as Nick and I were back home, my father was on him like a leech.

"I hope you treated her well, Nick." Glenn said as soon as Nick had stepped through the front door. I almost felt sorry for him, yet I was extremely amused by the whole situation. I was happy somebody was giving him a grilling and so I didn't have to.

"Glenn, give me a break." Nick huffed as he flopped on to the arm chair in the corner of the room. It faced the TV on a slight diagonal but it seemed to be his favourite place to sit.

"You want a beer?" Glenn asked as he made his way to the kitchen. Dad already had a bottle in his hands bed was nursing it between two hands. Nick grunted his reply before Glenn went to the kitchen to grab him a bottle.

"And me." I shouted back as I flopped down on the leather sofa beside of the arm chair. I lifted my legs up until they were tucked under and leaned my body against the arm of the sofa.

Nick instinctively reached over until his hands were in my hair. He began to play with the ends.

I looked over at him, but I only found him watching the football with entertainment. Did he even realise what he was doing?

Right now, I didn't even think I cared. With my head so near his arm, I was itching to lay on it, on him, and I was beginning to unravel beside him as he toyed my strands.

Without even realising it, I made a noise in the back of my throat. With that, Nick whipped his head to the side and his eyes landed on me.

"Cathy." Nick rasped. His voice sent a tingle throughout my body. His tone made my body jolt with desire. God, how much I wanted him. I had wanted him all night. Why did I have to promise myself I wasn't going to sleep with the guy?

"Nick." I couldn't help but breathe back. Who said this was going to be easy? In fact, this was harder than I ever thought it was going to be. He looked better than ever as he leaned against the arm chair, as his hand was in my hair.

Okay, I really wanted him.

He just looked pure male, his hairs coming out from under neath his shirt, his legs spread in a suggestive way, his eyes trained on me.

Shit. I was weak, I was as weak as my father knew I was going to be.

All thoughts flew out of the window as soon as Nick's grip on my hair tightened. I gasped as the small amount of pain jolted downwards.

"You have no idea how badly I want you." He said lowly so my father wouldn't hear us. I shivered at his words. He didn't know how badly I wanted him either.

"Have me then, Nick." I replied quietly. I could barely get my words out as excitement shot through me like wildfire. His eyes widened before darkening into grey cold storms.

"Don't tease me, Cathy, I haven't got that type of control with you." He grunted. I could see the strain in his face, the strain in his large body. I knew he wanted to touch me, I wanted to touch him too. I wanted his touch.

"I want you." I said, my breath coming out in short pants.

The night had turned drastically. It wasn't even an hour ago I was adamant I wasn't going to sleep with him, now, I wanted nothing more.

Nick did this to me, he effected me so greatly without even trying.

"Fucking hell." Nick groaned. He shot up from his chair. "Get in my truck." I looked to him, my heart beating so hard against my chest. "Now."

I didn't think twice before getting up on shivering legs.

"Glenn, don't worry about the drinks, I'm taking Cathy out to get some dessert." And I could hear the underlying innuendo in his tone. If I wasn't so turned on, I would have laughed.

"I swear to God, Nick, if that is a metaphor for something else I will castrate you-"

Nick pushed my out of the front door and slammed it shut behind us. I could barely think before he had me in his truck.

"Where are you taking me?" I asked as Nick started the truck again. The familiar rattle gave me a sense of comfort, even though comfort was the last thing I should be feeling right now.

"There's a hotel close to here, we can go there. I can't wait any longer, I've never wanted anything more than I do you, Cathy." He stated as he squeezed my knees tightly. Before he could put the truck in to gear, I stopped him.

His eyes were wild, his hair a mess from the countless times he's laid a hand in to it. His lips were wet and I just wanted to kiss him senseless.

With my hand still on his, I pulled him forward before grabbing a fistful of his white shirt. With that, I brought his face down roughly on to mine, his lips wet and soft.

He was shocked at first before it had even began to register. As soon as he had a hold on himself, his lips began a bruising rhythm against mine.

I moaned loudly against him. I couldn't help it. His kiss made me feel everything from desire to excitement.

I touched him everywhere I could without a second thought. I didn't care about the consequences, the punishment or the fact I could be physically dumped tomorrow by Nick. I didn't care about anything but right now.

"You need to fucking stop or I'll never get us off of this drive." Nick panted before sitting back in to his seat and reversing the truck so fast out of the drive, my back pressed firmly against the seat.

It didn't take us long at all until he had pulled up outside of a small hotel. I was pulled out of the truck and led over to the elevators.

"Don't you need to book a room?" I asked as we stepped inside the elevator. The door man had only nodded his acknowledgment.

"Shut up." Nick demanded before pressing me firmly against the elevator wall and smashing his lips to mine. I couldn't think of anything else but Nick.

It wasn't long before the elevator pinged and Nick had led me over to a brown wooden door. He opened the door and led me inside.

Before I could even take my shoes off, Nick had me up against the door as soon as it was shut. His body pressed firmly to mine.

"Aren't you going to offer me a drink?" I asked teasingly. Even though, I didn't want a drink, I wanted Nick.

"I would love to wine you and dine you, Angel, but I need to be inside you." Without a second word, his lips were back on to mine.

It didn't take long before his hands were confidently on my clothes. He slowly undressed me, until I was left panting all over again for him. He stepped away from my body and raked his eyes up and down, from head to toe.

A low rumble came out from his chest.

"You're killing me." With a surge of excitement at his satisfying gaze, I leaped at him.

I'm sure Nick had the stamina of a horse. There was no stopping the man, and as soon as he had started, he hadn't wanted to stop.

That was fine by me, I hadn't ever remembered feeling so good.

As I laid there sweating, Nick breathed loudly beside me. His arm laid across my stomach and his face stayed in the crook of my neck. His breath tickled my skin, but my heart beated loudly as he cuddled me close.

"I didn't peg you as a cuddler." I panted. He had worn me out, well and truly.

"I'm not."

The statement made me smile brightly. Maybe he had wanted to make an exception with me?

Soon, Nick leaned up on an elbow and smiled down at me. He kissed me lightly on my forehead. I couldn't help but revel in all of this now.

"Do you want a shower?"

"Sure, you can go first if you want." I stated as I stared in to his eyes. They were so amazing. So bright yet experienced. I'm sure he saw things not many people have at his age. I admired him.

"I meant with me." Nick chuckled softly to himself before getting up from the bed. His body was now on display for me, it just made me want him again. God, how could I still want him? "Stop." Nick demanded.

My glassy eyes focused sharply on him as I looked to him with confusion.

"Stop thinking them thoughts or I'll be forced to take you again." That sounded nice, to be honest. Nick chuckled again before slapping my arse firmly and walking in to the bathroom. "Come in when you're ready."

"Let me just recover." I replied before taking in a deep breath. Well, things had turned out better than expected. He hadn't turned cold on me, and he seemed pretty happy. How long was this going to last? I wondered. Maybe tomorrow was the day he was going to say he didn't want me anymore and that last night was a mistake.

The thought made my heart twist painfully.

I got up from the bed, my legs shaking and weak. I hadn't expected Nick to have taken my soul out of my body tonight. This wasn't even planned. I should have felt disgusted in myself, I was a disgrace to all the women who promised not to have sex with the play boy, yet, I didn't feel like that at all. I felt womanly, proud and sexual.

If Nick could go around talking about how badly he wanted a girl, why couldn't I act upon it too?

Suddenly, a noise came out from the small kitchen area opposite me. I turned my head to try and find the noise. I got up from the bed and made my way over to the phone which laid in its cradle on a small end table.

"Nick, I couldn't reach you at your house so I decided to call your fuck pad instead. I need to talk to you." The message came out from the phone. I moved backwards as if the phone had burnt me.

Fuck pad?

Anger flared through my body at the words. Fuck pad? Nick had taken me to his fuck pad? God, that hurt so much.

But what more did I expect? I knew he just wanted to use me. He had fucked so many girls here too. I felt dirty, used, disgusting. How could he?

I grabbed my clothes quickly and chucked them on to my body. With that, I found a small piece of paper and wrote him a note:

You're a bastard. I hope you find a willing woman you can fuck next time in your 'fuck pad.' Prick.

With that, I left his apartment just as he called my name.

I felt embarrassed, my face heated up as I had to walk past the door man at the reception area. I bet he knew, I bet he knew what Nick was up to. To him, I was just another one of them girls.

I didn't know why I was so angry. This was why I promised myself I wouldn't do this, not until I knew Nick was being genuine.

I had already had enough of men thinking they could use my body. I had that back in Australia. God, I wanted to cry. I was weak, and I fell for his charm.

My anxiety began to rise as I remembered what had happened back at home. This wasn't like that, but I still felt the same, and that was enough for me to break down.

I walked down the street as tears fell from my eyes. Why did I have to cry? Why did I have to cry over a tattooed play boy who I had only known for a few weeks.

Instead of wanting to go back home, I continued down the road until I saw a street full of shops and small cafe's. I was lucky that one was open at this time.

I would rather sit in there until I gathered my bearings than go back home to the man who knew me more than I knew myself. He was right and I hadn't listened.

Well, I had tried, but Nick just made me forget about everything else but him. I wish he didn't have to effect me, I wish I didn't like him after all.

I hated that I still liked him. Hated the fact I still wanted him. And after tonight, however angry I was at him, I still craved him.

I ordered a small coffee as soon as I had entered the cafe. I didn't fancy eating, hopefully coffee I could stand.

All in all, I needed to woman up. This was a learning curve for me. Mistakes had been made but hopefully no more.

But even as I thought it, I knew it wasn't true. Nick didn't feel like a mistake, even though he should. I didn't want this to be the end, but I wasn't in control of that. I knew Nick would never want to see me again, not after tonight. Had he known I was so easy after all?

My phone rang in my pocket as I grabbed my coffee. I made my way over to the table and fished it out. On the screen was Nick's number. I looked to it and sighed. Did I want to pick up?

I wanted to hear his voice, I wanted to see what he had to say, but I was scared it wasn't going to be something that I liked.

With that, I let it ring on. He didn't deserve my time right now anyway. He deserved nothing from me.

I drank my coffee slowly, but it tasted like shit. It was not because the coffee was horrible, it was just because I had a bitter taste in my mouth already.

The phone began ringing again. It was Nick.

This time, I picked it up, longing burning throughout.

"Cathy, I'm sorry. Where are you? Please, I need to explain." His voice came out rushed and panicked. I could hear the rustling of wind down the phone as he moved.

"I don't want to be a part of your fuck pad gang." I stated. "I never asked for this."

"Where are you? I'll come for you, I'll explain I swear." His voice was crushing to hear. I sighed.

"I'm in a cafe somewhere-" as soon as I had said those words, he walked in to the cafe. He was only wearing his jeans, a thin t shirt and his converse. He looked freezing cold but the only thing that made me shiver was the desperate look on his face.

He sauntered up to me, his face full of guilt and sorrow.

"Cathy-"

"I don't know whether I'm just being stupid or if I've actually got a valuable reason to be mad." I stated truthfully. I had the right to be mad as hell with him right now, but if he wanted to explain, I would let him.

"No, you have every right to be mad, if you took me to your fuck pad where you fucked men all the time I would be going out of my fucking mind." He sighed as he sat down opposite me. "I hadn't meant to take you there, I didn't want to see you where I see every other girl because you're not just every other girl to me. I was just going crazy for you and I wasn't thinking." He looked down.

"I get it." I said. I knew what he meant. It was hard to think when we were so wrapped up on each other.

"I know we've only had one date, and I know I don't do dates or anything like this, but I want something to work with us."

"You do?"

"I don't know what, but I want something. You're too addictive, I can't keep away." My heart leaped at his words. Everything I had thought about Nick had flown away. He wanted something to work? God, I did too.

"I want that, too." I smiled.

"Will you spend the night with me? At my place, not back there." His eyes were hopeful as he took me in.

The Nick that had ended the night was not the Nick I had started with. I couldn't help but smile his way. I liked this side to him, the soft side, the side that you couldn't help but fall for.

"This is going so fast." I muttered. It was, so many things had happened tonight with Nick and I was feeling extremely over-whelmed.

"I know but I don't know what to do with us. I've never wanted to try with anyone else, so I'm out of my depths. I just want to be with you, I can't leave like this, I want you to spend the night with me, I can't take no for an answer."

"Okay." I smiled his way. His answering smile was just as breath-taking. I would give him another chance if this was what he want-ed.

Truthfully, this was what I had wanted too.

CHAPTER 8

Once we had gotten back in to the truck, Nick seemed fidgety and nervous.

"You don't have to take me back to your house." I said. If he was going to react like this, maybe it was better he dropped me back home. I didn't want him to feel nervous and unready.

"No." He gruffed. "I've just never taken a girl back to my home. It's nothing much, so don't get your hopes up, I don't live in some golden trimmed apartment with floor to ceiling windows."

"Neither do I, you dick head." I rolled my eyes but smiled. Who cared where he lived? I was already honoured that I was the first woman who was going to see his home.

Nick chuckled. I enjoyed the sound, especially when he had been the way he was tonight.

"I'm just warning you, that's all."

"Is that it?" I questioned. He couldn't have just been worrying over the fact he thought his house wasn't good enough for me to see.

"Yeah."

"Is it?" I pushed further. He looked to me through the side of his eyes and sighed.

"This is a big step for me. You've quickly turned in to something more than what I've had with anyone else."

"In a bad way?" I had to ask.

"No. It's just going to take some time getting used to. I'm twenty eight, I should have had at least one serious relationship by now, but truth is, I haven't."

"Why?" Nick shrugged.

"Because I haven't wanted to spend more than one night with anyone else." My heart wanted to burst with joy. I had spent more than one night with Nick already, and here he was taking me back to his home.

I know I shouldn't let my hopes run too high, there was always a chance Nick was keeping me around for his sexual benefit rather than anything else, however, I had made it further than any other girl who spent the night with a Nick. To me, that meant something, at least.

"Lots of broken hearts, then." I replied. I hoped I wasn't another broken heart he could add to his jar. I hoped it would never get that far.

It was way too early to say I loved Nick. However, I really liked him and he was so easy to love. So so easy. I knew I wasn't the only one who wanted to spend more time with him, to want his attention.

I knew Nick had broken a lot of hearts. It was inevitable with him being the way he was and looking the way he did.

"They knew what they were getting in to. I never signified to them that I wanted more." He gave out a small, harsh laugh. "Not until I met you, anyway."

"Are you regretting wanting to take me home?" I turned in my seat to see him. He turned his head to gauge my reaction, to see how I felt.

All in all, I was just curious. It wouldn't hurt me now if he had told me we were going too fast for his liking.

"Sit back in your seat properly." Nick demanded as he drove through the country lanes. The car swerved as he sped down the narrow lanes.

"You haven't answered me, officer." I rolled my eyes again as I sat properly in my seat, like instructed.

"Don't call me officer." He growled. "Or I won't be accountable for my actions. You want to role play, Angel, I'll only be more than happy to oblige." With the thought of role play and seeing Nick handle the truck with control, I didn't think I had wanted anything more.

"Yes, please." Nick's hand shot out to squeeze my knee gently.

"No. You're too fragile for that at the moment. Besides, I thought we could just watch TV and eat?" He looked to me, his lip stuck in between his teeth. I couldn't stop looking at him. I wanted him, I wanted him more than I had before.

"What are we going to eat?" I asked.

"Cathy." Nick growled. I laughed.

"I was actually being serious this time." I giggled. He turned to me, his pearly whites on show as he smiled. He kept his eyes on me a little too long. I worried he'd crash the truck in to a tree if he wasn't careful.

"You're too beautiful." My smile dropped at his compliment. He had said things, but he had never complimented me so... naturally, without being sexual. My stomach flipped. I couldn't talk.

Nick laughed nervously as he scratched the back of his neck, something I realised he did when he was nervous or uncomfortable.

"Don't worry, I think you're pretty handsome yourself." I replied, wanting him to relax. He was always so confident in himself, it was different to see him so self conscious and nervous as he sat beside me.

Maybe I effected him more than I thought.

It wasn't long before Nick pulled his truck up along side the pathway. Beside us was a small block of flats. The flats seemed in the middle of no where, only trees and other cars parked around the building.

I hadn't noticed we were home until he started getting out of the truck.

"Wait there." Nick demanded. A few seconds later, he had opened my door and had helped me down from my seat. I looked to him and he shrugged. "It's never too late to be a gentleman." And I knew he had only been feeling guilty for what he did.

Still, the thought was there and I loved this side to him.

He then led me over to the door which led us to the inside of the building. There were lockers for your mail lining the wall beside us and a door that led us to the stairs on the other. In front of us was a small elevator.

Nick pressed the button and we waited for the elevator. He obviously lived on the top floor, or near to it, otherwise we wouldn't be using the lift.

A part of me was really excited to see Nick's place. It didn't help that I was kind of smug about the fact I was the only female to see it.

We entered the elevator a second later. The elevator was filled with mirrors which enclosed me as soon I stepped inside. I looked at myself and mentally cringed. I looked like shit.

Still, Nick didn't seem to agree as I caught him staring right at me. His eyes were full of appreciative satisfaction, something I hadn't really seen until now.

"Stop staring at me, you creep." I said to him, a huge smile on my face.

"Come here." And I didn't have to be told twice. I walked over to him and he enclosed me in his arms as the elevator began to move upwards.

"Nick." I sighed. I took in his scent and sighed again. He smelt so good, so masculine.

"I want to kiss you." He gruffed.

"What's stopping you?" I asked. I wanted him to kiss me, I wanted him to show me that he wanted me here.

Suddenly, before I had time to think, I was being pushed up against the wall. Nick's arms bracketed my body and I went limp against him.

Then, without another second going by, his lips were upon mine. His lips were soft against mine, and now he took his sweet time as he kissed me.

"I love kissing you." He stated. I felt the same, most definitely. There was something about kissing Nick. He knew exactly what to do and there was no denying that I could do it all day without tiring.

When the elevator pinged at it's stop, he left my body feeling bereft as he walked forward.

I followed him until we were in front of his front door. He opened it wide and led me inside.

I was surprised at his apartment. I half expected his apartment to be messy or at least a little untidy but the flat was spotless.

The sitting area was relatively medium sized, and was designed incredibly. The walls were a bright white and everything inside was a grey. It was modern and quite homely considering the colours.

"I love your place." I stated honestly. It wasn't big, yet he had done a lot to make it look so good. I truly did like it more than any place I had before.

"I'm glad you do." He shut the door softly behind me before taking hold of my hips between his hands. He pulled me towards him with force and I barrelled into his chest with a gasp.

"What are you going to do?" I asked. A part of me wanted to him to have me again. God knows I wanted him. Yet another part of me wanted to just spend time with him, to get to know him. I just wanted to get closer to Nick. There was nothing I wanted more.

"There are plenty of things I'd love to do with you tonight, Cathy, but I think we'll just settle for a film or something, what do you think?" He looked down at me, his eyes twinkling.

"That would be lovely."

Nick led me over to the sofa and I sunk down in to the grey material. Nick sauntered over to the open kitchen where I could watch him as he moved.

"Would you like a drink?" He asked.

"What have you got?"

Nick bent over to look in his fridge which was half the size of a normal one but still looked full. He then straightened up and looked to me.

"I've got beer."

"And that's it?" I asked. I was happy with a beer but I'm sure he couldn't just live off that. Didn't he have milk or bottled water?

"Uh...yeah." He looked sheepish as he flickered his yes back down to the fridge. I laughed.

"I'm happy with a beer."

"Ah, a woman after my own heart." He moved back to his fridge and grabbed two cold bottles of beer. He opened them with a bottle opener and sauntered his way back to me.

Nick sat beside me and laid his feet on the coffee table in front of him. His arm instinctively wrapped around my shoulders and I snuggled in beside him.

"Are you hungry?" Nick asked as he grabbed the remote and turned on the TV infront of us. It was a flat screen TV which was quite big and on top of an electronic fire place.

"I'm half and half really." I stated. He turned to face me and smiled.

"What does that even mean?" Nick chuckled. I shrugged but a large smile played on my face.

"It means I'm half hungry and half not." Nick chuckled again.

"Do you want me to order you something?"

"Will you think I'm greedy?" I had already had a burger and fries not so long ago, however, we had burnt off a lot of energy. It wasn't my fault I was peckish again. "I don't want to put you off."

"For eating? Babe, nothing could put me off you, especially you eating."

"Go on then." I smiled. "I'll have a pizza."

"I'm glad you said that." Nick got up from the sofa and picked up his mobile phone. He called the pizza delivery place and ordered a large pizza between us.

Once he was done, he came back to sit beside me. A crime series played on the TV infront of us. Nick went to turn it over yet I stopped him from doing so.

"I like this."

"Do you? I knew you had a thing for police officers." He stated as he looked to the tele with entertainment.

"I have a thing for one police officer." I smirked his way.

"Oh, yeah?" I placed my hands on his chest.

"Mmmhmm." I mumbled. Nick took a hold of my hands and held them still. I tried to move them, yet his grip was strong on mine.

"Don't." Nick growled. "Please."

"Why not?" I pouted. Nick let go of my hands and pushed me gently backwards. He laid on top of me.

"Because I'm trying to be good." Nick replied.

"I don't like you good."

"But it's what you deserve." He sighed. "I'm trying not to fuck this up before it has even started."

"I think you're doing fine." I smiled. More than fine. I hadn't expected this, not at all. Nick was completely different from the one I've seen before. I loved them both, but this one made me buzz with excitement and warmth.

"Well." He smiled his shy smile and I could have melted in to a puddle beneath him.

"Now, get off me you fat lump." Nick gasped mockingly at my demand.

"I have you know, I am muscly, not fat." He sat back down softly and I sat back up beside him. I snuggled back in to his warm body. It really was muscly. He had a typical, well shaped, police officer body.

I loved it.

We sat in silence for a few more minutes until Nick shifted beside me. The series was getting intense by now and I had finished my drink in minutes.

Once the pizza had arrived, we ate in silence again. The silence wasn't awkward, far from it as well. I felt comfortable with Nick, like we had known each other for years, not a few weeks.

Nick ate almost all of the pizza without giving me chance to eat even a quarter. I looked to him with annoyance, he just smiled back sheepishly.

"You've eaten all the bloody pizza, Nick." I moaned. "You're selfish." Nick laughed loudly.

"A man's got to eat, darling."

"No, a real man would make sure I ate, too." I crossed my arms and huffed.

"I'm sorry, baby." Nick pinched my cheek like a baby and I slapped his hand away. He chuckled but I didn't speak to him for at least ten minutes.

However, once we had made it to bed, my good mood had been restored. His room was small and cosy and once he had me cuddled up in his bed, his smell surrounding me, I was as good as new.

Once Nick had his head on the pillow, he was sleepy.

"Night, Nick." I whispered. I didn't think he would hear me. The lights were out and I felt his breath against my neck, now slow and even.

"Night, love." He mumbled.

Nick took me home the next morning in his rattling truck. He had woken up happy and with a smile on his face... I felt the same as he looked.

It was amazing to wake up next to him, even with all the sexual tension.

I wanted to wake up like that more often.

Nobody had gotten under my skin like he had, and the way he treated me all night and morning, I'm sure I was crushing on him a little too hard.

But who could blame me?

I unlocked my front door slowly, feeling slightly embarrassed that I spent the night with Nick. Surely my dad was going to know.

Usually, I wouldn't be so embarrassed, but my father hadn't seen me for years, and Nick was his best friend. Things were going to be weird, I knew. But I couldn't stop myself from wanting to be around him.

I tiptoed in to the house, hoping Nick didn't catch on to what I was doing. However, I didn't think he did as he walked loudly in his police man boots.

So long to keeping quiet.

Anyway, Nick was already for work. It was deeply satisfying to dress Nick in his uniform even when I wanted to take it all off. However, I knew Nick still wanted to show me that I meant more to him than just a fuck.

I was grateful.

The next thing I knew, my father was walking in to the hall way. He smiled my way and I couldn't help but blush.

Did he know what I had been up to?

"Nick, you bastard." Glenn flicked his wrist and the tea towel in his hand whipped against Nick's face. Nick didn't even flinch.

"Glenn, so very nice to see you." Nick smirked. "I hope you had a wonderful evening last night."

"Don't give me that bullshit. What did you do with my daughter?"

"Treated her right, Glenn, you know me."

"Yes, I do know you and that is what worries me."

"Well, you needn't worry, I got her back in one piece." Glenn looked towards me again and then flickered his eyes back to Nick.

"Come in then."

Nick and I made our way inside of the living room and Nick sat down in his usual chair.

"Is there any coffee going?" Nick shouted as Glenn moved around in the kitchen.

"Come and make it yourself, you lazy fuck. You know where everything is." Nick chuckled before getting up. He passed me with a soft hand to my back before going in to the kitchen.

I followed him, not quite knowing what to do with myself.

It seemed Nick felt more at home here than I did yet. I was hoping that would change soon.

Nick moved around the kitchen and made himself a cup of coffee. I watched his body move with grace around the area.

Once Glenn had moved out of the kitchen, Nick flickered his eyes to me. He laid his coffee cup back down on the counter and sauntered his way up to me.

He pulled me to his body and grinded himself up against my front. I gasped.

"I've got work in ten, what are you going to do all day?" He asked as he continued to grind against me. I could barely breathe.

"I'll probably help my dad out at work." I stated back. Nick kissed my forehead.

"You'll think about me?"

"Nah." I joked. Of course I was going to think about him, I had since I met him.

"You will." Nick demanded. "Because God knows I'll be thinking of you."

CHAPTER 9

S prawled out on my sofa I sighed. Danni sat in the arm chair Nick always occupied and I sighed again. I wished it were him sitting there beside me.

His words this morning played around my head on repeat.

God knows I'll be thinking of you.

Whether it were true, the words still shook me. I didn't really know what was happening or how it had even started with him. However, there was no doubting I wanted him.

Did I regret sleeping with him so soon?

To be honest, no. Things happened and I didn't regret them, not with Nick. I wasn't one to dwell on something that was not changeable.

Danni slurped on her can of coke and took a bite of her chicken burger. I had eaten mine on the way back from the burger shack Nick took me to last night.

"I thought you were vegetarian." I stated as I mindlessly flicked through the channels. Work had finished earlier again today, it seemed when Nick wasn't there, business wasn't booming. I bet all the women came to get a glimpse of him.

Currently, Glenn was out and about and Nick hadn't made contact since he left this morning. Danni was my only company.

"Don't even talk about it." Danni moaned.

"Why not?" I questioned. Danni laid her Burger down on the arm of the chair and flopped backwards.

"I'm a bad person." She replied. I chuckled quietly before diverting my attention back to the TV. Nothing was on, and quite frankly I was bored.

Even though it was turning half five, the skies were still light and the air warm.

In Australia, there was always something to do as we lived near the big city. Here, we lived near a town but the city was quite a while away. I loved it here, but there wasn't all that much to do, especially on a day like this.

"Do you want to go out and do something?" I asked. We were twenty one years old, we weren't some bored teenagers on a weekday. Even though, that's exactly what I felt like.

"Like what?" Danni asked. Suddenly, she shot up from the chair she was sat in. "I have the perfect place, actually. Come on, I'll show you." Danni got up from the arm chair and grabbed my arm before I had the chance to question her.

Where were we going?

Danni led me over to her small beatle which was situated on my drive and we both got inside.

"It's a pretty warm day and you remember that place we always used to go to? Where we sat on the grass and got pissed until morning?" My eyes widened at the memory that overcame me.

Of course I remembered. That place was the only place Danni and I spent our summer at the age of 16 when I came back from Australia one year.

I hadn't realised that would have been the last one we would ever spend together.

"Green fields?" I asked. My heart fluttered with excitement. Hell, that place was the only place that ever kept me sane that year, and Danni of course.

Things got easier, but that year was the hardest.

"Green mother flipping fields." Danni bounced in her seat as the car started to move and we set in to motion.

It didn't take long before the metal iron gates came in to view. In fact, it wasn't any longer than a ten minute drive.

The iron gates surrounded the field because the furled was a part of a large factory building which situated on the side of the field. However, the field was huge and the factory was being greedy.

Before, the iron gates would be left open and anyone could treck the field with no problems. Many young kids spend their summers on green fields and nobody had a problem with it.

Danni parked her beatle on the gravel and she led us over to the big iron gates.

"I haven't been her since you left." Danni muttered. She turned to look at me with twinkling eyes. "So this a special moment for our friendship."

"It's like being sixteen all over again." I stated back. Even though it was a tough year, I would love to go back in time where things were less stressful and a little more peaceful.

Nothing could touch you at sixteen.

"This times gonna be better, trust me."

The skies had suddenly turned a darker shade of blue, and I knew night was going to be upon us soon, in the next couple of hours. That made the experience all the more exciting.

Danni tried to nudge the iron gates open, however, they were firmly locked. Her brows furrowed at the offending lock hanging from the slider.

"It seems to be locked. They must have cracked down on teenagers using their field."

"Kill joys." I muttered.

Danni seemed to remember something, and before long she was circling the iron gates.

"What are you looking for?" I asked.

"There was a hole in the gates before, I'm trying to find it." Danni replied. Suddenly, she hit a spot in the iron gates and a little part of the metal flew backwards and the hole was formed. "Paid to get it locked but not fixed. School boy error, I say."

"Are you sure we should be going in?" I said. I hated to be boring and a kill joy myself, but I wasn't going to be happy if some alarm went off and I was shipped off to jail.

"Stop bitching and get in." Danni held the metal open and I crouched to move forward. Danni followed behind.

The factory was dark and still beside of the field, and infront of us vastly was the green field.

It looked exactly the same but with no beer cans and vodka bottles.

Danni led us over to the spot near the centre of the field and we sat down. Luckily, the air was still warm and it wasn't windy at all. I laid beside her.

"Just like old times." Danni sighed. I nodded, hoping she knew just how much this meant to me too. I hadn't meant to leave her and never return when I promised I would. I hadn't meant to stop everything.

Danni was my only friendship back then that meant something. She was the only person who didn't judge me for anything. And even though I let her down and left her lonely, she still forgave me, because that's who she was.

We were twenty one now and I didn't think I'd ever want to leave her again, not the way I did at sixteen. Not when she needed me.

"I'm sure creepy Steve was sick in this exact spot." Danni stated. I couldn't help but giggle.

"He probably did." I replied. "Creepy Steve was really..."

"Creepy?" Danni replied. I laughed. Steve was proper creepy. He'd do anything to get with anyone, and had no shyness about him. I wondered if he were still around this village, I wondered what he was up to now.

Danni and I stayed quiet for a while. We took in the surroundings and relaxed.

Danni sat up on her elbow to look at me. She wore a smile on her face.

"So, how's your boyfriend?"

"My boyfriend?" I spluttered. "Darling, I wish." We weren't that far yet, hopefully one day we would be, maybe.

There was no doubt I was petrified. I had never expected to like Nick as much as I did. I knew things were only going to get worse. Hopefully, things would work out, and even though I was as petrified as I was, I never gave up on something I wanted.

Nick was hot, charming and just...Nick. I wasn't scared to try. I wasn't going to pretend I didn't want him or I didn't like him. Maybe things were rushed, maybe I liked him more than I should have, but you can't put a timer on things like this. And pretending didn't make it any less real.

People really had to stop playing and tune in to their emotions.

"Things getting serious?"

"I wouldn't say serious, but we're getting somewhere. I like him, I think he likes me, for now." I shrugged, not knowing what else to say. I liked him and I think he liked me. It had only been a few weeks so nothing could be certain.

"You're hot stuff, why wouldn't he?" She laid back down on her back. "I want to meet him."

"You will, I'll introduce you properly." I stated truthfully. Maybe Danni would fall under his spell, too. I hoped she did in completely different ways.

Danni and I talked for hours in green fields. We talked about our past memories and our new ones that we were hoping to make in the future. We talked about everything we could think of and caught up in all of the gossip we missed out on.

Suddenly, however, when the clock struck 10:18, police sirens were heard outside of the iron gates. The lights flashed around the field and on the factory walls. My heart sky rocketed.

"What the fuck." I whispered as we both shot up from the floor. We walked towards the iron gates and was greeted head on with a police officer.

At first, I hoped it was Nick, yet instead stood a fourty year old woman.

"Excuse me girls, this is private property and we've had complaints from the security guards of the factory." The lady stated. "I'm not going to arrest you for trespassing, however, I need you both to come to the station."

"Shit." Danni muttered under her breath. The lady led us over to her car and led us both inside.

Once my back touched the sticky leather of the back seat, I turned to Danni with wide eyes.

"My fucking beatle is still on the drive." Danni let out.

"I think we have more important things to be worried about. For God sake, we're going to jail!"

"She said she wasn't arresting us. We're not hand cuffed, we're not going to jail." Danni stated as she looked longingly to her car. "I swear if she doesn't take me back here afterwards, I'll cut a bitch."

"Do you have to say things like that in the back of a police car?" I hissed her way.

"Shut up. Girls will love you in jail, you'll be fine."

"They'll love you, too. I heard they love rebellious red heads who state their vegetarians but eat chicken burgers." I retorted.

"Don't bring my misdoings in to this." Danni turned to look at me. "I'm happy I ate it before I go down for life."

I couldn't help but laugh.

The lady who drove us to the station flickered her eyes in to the rear view mirror. She shushed us and even though I was busting to laugh again, I controlled myself before we really did go down for life.

When the car pulled up at the police station, my heart started to pound again. It was all fun and jokes, however, this was serious.

I was outside a police station for trespassing. She said she wasn't arresting us, but what the hell was she doing? Taking us back for coffee? I didn't think so.

The lady led us in to the station. The reception area was full of blue plastic chairs and a massive desk with glass windows stood before us. It took up most of the room.

Danni and I looked incredibly innocent as we walked through the halls in to a back room. In the room was a table and three chairs. It looked more like an interrogation room than anything else.

What was going on?

The lady left without a second word and the door closed firmly beside her. Danni and I stood in the middle of the room not quite knowing what to do next.

"Where did she go?" Danni asked.

"I don't know." I shrugged. "I hope she doesn't leave us here all night."

"You can take the floor I'll have the table." Danni stated.

"I don't think so, lovely. You take the floor and I take the table. It's only fair as this is all your fault."

"My fault?" Danni spluttered. "Girl, I was just trying to have fun with y'all." Danni walked over to a plastic chair and sprawled out across it.

As I paced the floor, my ears perked at the sound of heavy boots on the floor and a masculine voice. I could just about make out the words as they walked closer.

"I don't want to be dealing with stupid little girls getting in to a spot of trouble. Just let them go." The voice came out. Another was a girl's.

"They're the orders, come on, it won't take long." She replied.

Suddenly, the door creaked open and my eyes adjusted to the light outside of the room.

My heart began to speed up as I locked eyes on Nick. I didn't even realise he was working so late. I hadn't spoken to him all day.

His face took my breath away, and suddenly I felt safe in his presence. He wouldn't take me down in to a cell. He'd get us out of here, I knew he would.

As soon as Nick caught sight of my form, his eyes widened. His small smile was easily seen by me, but easily misleading to others. His eyes twinkled my way, and I was so happy to see him.

"Nick." I breathed. And the sight of him in his uniform did things to me I wish they didn't. I didn't even know I had a thing for uniform until I met Nick.

Nick's eyes darkened to a dark blue when I breathed his name. He easily recovered himself, especially in front of his work colleague who looked comical next to him. She was blonde and mousey, so very small next to Nick's large frame.

And weirdly, she couldn't keep her eyes off him.

"Oh, so this is Nick?" Danni came up beside me to take in an eyeful. "When I said I wanted to meet him properly I didn't mean like this." She stated. "I've literally just been arrested."

"We didn't get arrested." I rolled my eyes. "Police officers don't lie."

Nick smirked largely at us both. He took my body in, a sudden look of worry casting over his face. As soon as he knew I was okay, his smirk returned.

"You know, trespassing is against the law." Nick stated. The girl beside him went to talk, but Nick held out his hand to stop her. "Cathy, I need to talk to you."

"Yes, officer." I walked forward and Nick led me out of the room. He continued to lead me down a hall until he opened the door to another back room. Luckily this time, it wasn't an interrogation room, but a small and empty staff room.

He flickered on the lights and as soon as the door was shut, he took hold of my waist and pushed me back on to the wall beside it.

"You were the last thing I expected to see tonight." Nick stated as he laid his lips to my neck. I sighed and relaxed against him.

"I hope I made your night."

"You really did, Angel." He breathed. "You were the best gift I could have received tonight."

"Aren't you mad I did something illegal?" I asked. "You're a police officer, you're meant to be against all this stuff."

"You trespassed, it's not exactly murder is it?" He laughed. I let out a breath of relief. I had never been in trouble much, so this was out of the ordinary. I felt more panicked than I should have been.

My heart lifted and I decided to play.

"So I'm not getting punished?" I asked mischievously. I laid a hand to Nick's chest. "That's a shame, officer." Nick's eyes turned dark again, and the smile on his face fell.

"Angel, stop playing."

"I've been a very naughty girl." I batted my eyelashes his way. He growled before pulling me away from the wall and pushing me on the sofa that laid across the opposite wall.

"Didn't I tell you? I love naughty girls."

"Aren't you lucky?" I stated with a smile.

"Luckiest man in the world." He laid his body across mine. He was so heavy and full of muscle. Masculinity shot through his body like a wave.

"Didn't I tell you that I love a man in uniform?"

"Ahh." He smiled. "I guess you're the lucky one."

"You could say that." I shrugged. He smiled down at me, his eyes bright.

"You know, I hate that room."

"What room?" I asked. Nick grinded above me, I couldn't help but moan.

"The interrogation room." He replied. "But seeing you there, it made it a whole lot better. Even in a room full of black, you make it full of colour."

"It's my tattoos." I stated as I looked down at my colourful arms.

"It's the way I see you, bursting with colour and happiness. You're not like me, you're not all black and white, bleak and dark. You've got something I haven't, you're everything I'm not."

"Don't be silly, Nick. Don't put yourself down. You've given me more in these last few weeks than anyone else has before."

"Only because I'm trying." Nick stated. "It's hard not to when I feel the way I do about you."

And little did he know, I felt the same way about him, too.

CHAPTER 10

Nick didn't finish work until midnight but I didn't mind staying with him until his shift ended. In fact, there was nothing I wanted more.

It was quite a turn on to see Nick doing his job and doing it so well. He demanded the room with quiet authority and a deep voice to match. Not only that, all eyes were on him.

Especially mine.

Nick had sat me down on his office chair, which was also in a room full of other desks and officers. They were open but spaced out quite nicely.

He demanded "stay here, I'll take you home later." And that was the end of it. It was flattering to know he just wanted to look after me.

In terms of Danni, she got picked up earlier by one of her old friends. She had no one else to call really. I offered for her to stay with me, I think it would have been funny, especially with Danni, to be let loose in a police station. Yet Danni had other plans. She had always been a night bird.

Nick had his team around him and he spoke to themwith calmness and authority. They listened intently as he spoke about a man on red alert around the city. It was interesting to hear him, even though I kept getting side tracked at the naked women calendars on his wall.

I didn't know whether they were serious or some kind of office prank present. Either way, they were funny in my eyes. Even though I was a jealous person when it came to the people in my life, they were still pictures and Nick had taken a liking to me. He could have any girl he wanted, mousey Alice or the blonde with big fake boobs in the waiting area. However, Nick had stated he wanted me.

I didn't know how that was humanly possible, however, I wasn't complaining.

"Just keep an eye out for him, he will usually be around the small lanes in the city." Nick stated as he paced the floor, his fine muscled glory on display for all of us to see.

I kept an eye on Alice. She seemed to take a liking to Nick. I was a woman myself, I could see it in her eyes how much she fancied him.

Tough luck, Alice, he's mine.

I hadn't meant to let my cat claws spring free from my hands.

When Nick had finished his speech, his team assembled out of the room and some in to their own office cubicles. Nick came sauntering up to me, my body slouched in his chair and my feet kicked up in to his desk.

"Hey, handsome." I flirted. He smirked my way, his eyes bright as he took in my form.

"Getting comfortable there, sweetheart?" My smile broadened his way.

"The naked women on your wall really help with the settling in." I stated, my tone mocking and joking. His eyes flickered up to the calendars on his wall and back down to me. He smirked again.

"Jealous?"

"Just merely an observation." I shrugged.

Nick suddenly grabbed a hold of my hips and hauled me out of his chair. I wanted to shriek with shock, but didn't want to disturb his work mates, so I decided to keep my mouth shut.

Next thing I knew, Nick was slouched in his own office chair and I was upon his lap.

"This isn't appropriate, you know." I stated. I didn't want him to put me down, however. His legs kept a good balance on his desk and were used as a good seat beneath me.

"Fuck it." Nick let out as he breathed in my scent. I wiggled on top of him as he began kissing my neck silently. "Stop wiggling." He demanded.

"I can't help it when you're kissing my neck." I hissed his way. Nick stopped what he was doing with a smirk and kept a hand on my thigh as he booted up his computer.

He rolled further to his desk and I had no choice but to lean back on to his chest.

"Quite the compromising position." I stated. Nick chuckled quietly.

"I could think of better positions to put you in."

"That's not very community friendly."

"I don't do community friendly." Nick gruffed.

"You're a police officer."

"I'm a police officer when I'm a police officer. The real Nick isn't community friendly. You should know this by now." Nick replied. I sat up and turned to look at him.

"Then what are you when you're the real Nick?" Nick shrugged in reply. "Well, what's your favourite thing to do?"

"I like to draw." That was the last thing I expected to come from his mouth. He obviously loved his tattoos and the art work on his walls were one of fascination and passion. I, however, hadn't expected him to be in to that stuff himself.

Nick was always so uptight, so brooding and mysterious. It was hard to imagine him sitting there drawing, letting his thoughts and feelings out on paper.

I admired him for having a passion.

"What do you draw?" I asked. Nick moved his mouse around as he did things on his computer. They looked too confusing to even comprehend.

"Anything really. Abstracts, usually with no colour."

"Why no colour?"

"There's no point painting colourfully when you're not thinking and feeling with colour." Nick stated. My heart sank at his words. I knew he was battling something inside, it was hard to tell but something about him was there. This, this told me definitely that he was battling with his demons.

I wouldn't push him, I'd never push him for information. If he wanted to tell me, when the time was right and he was ready, I'd be all ears to listen to him.

"Maybe the colour will shine bright if you let it." Nick sighed.

"Cathy, nobody paints in colour if they're just going to blacken it with their feelings. Even if they do, I don't lie that good."

"Well, you haven't blackened my colour yet."

"Give it time." Was his response. He was quite a pessimistic person when he wanted to be. Sometimes he was all so sure of himself, others he was ready to be negative.

Before I could respond, the office door opened and everybody stood at the man who barged in. Nick didn't bother standing, I stood glued in his lap.

The man seemed highly respected and he was obviously high up in the hierarchy around here. I was confused as to why Nick hadn't stood up, too, like the rest of his team.

"Abel." The man snapped. His voice was low and lethal. Nick turned in his chair and gently pushed my off of his lap. He stood gracefully from his chair without attitude.

"Yes, sheriff?"

"There's been an emergency up north of the city. We need you to lead tonight." He stated. His chubby body leaned against the door frame in a relaxed posture. He didn't seem at all intimidating anymore.

Nick nodded before shutting down his computer.

When he came back up from bending over his desk, he whispered in my ear.

"I'll be back in fifteen minutes. These jobs won't take long. Sit at my desk and do not wander around, there are dangerous people around here at night." His voice sounded stern. I rolled my eyes. "Cathy, I mean it."

"Yes, yes. Go and do your job." Nick stood up straighter and eyed me effectively. I sat back down in his chair and gave him the sweetest smile I could muster. He narrowed his eyes.

"Behave."

"Yes, sir." Without another word I moved towards his desk and started messing around with his equipment. He was going to have to let me if he wanted me to stay entertained and sane.

He sauntered off, Alice hot on his tail. What was up with that girl? If I wasn't in his work place, I'd have been telling her by now that Nick and I had a thing going on. However, I wasn't really that petty.

She could have her silly crush. God knows I had mine.

The office cubicles were dead after ten minutes. Many people had gone home, many more were coming to work at 11:50.

Nick was meant to be finishing in ten minutes. I doubted that was even going to happen if he was out on the job. I sighed.

Feeling bored and extremely advernturous, I decided to get up from the desk. Fuck Nick. Nothing was going to happen to me here, police were everywhere.

With that thought, I left the offices and made my way down the hall. I passed the interrogation rooms and nearly shivered. They were horrible places. So dark and scary inside.

With the female toilets to the left, I decided I did indeed need to pee. With that thought, I went to the toilet.

The toilets were small and I wasn't sure if they were for the staff or for the public who needed to come to the police station. With that said, they weren't very nice.

The paint was chipping off from the walls in all directions and it smelt strongly of cheap soap.

After I released my bladder, I made my way to the sink to wash my hands. I looked at myself in the mirror and sighed. I really did look like shit.

My hair was a mess and most of my makeup had washed off. I didn't know how. It was maddening how much you changed throughout the day and during your activities.

After a few minutes in the toilet, I left.

Suddenly, my body smacked into a soft belly. I grunted at the contact. As I was pushed backwards a touch, I looked up at the figure infront of me.

"Why, aren't you a pretty thing?" The man stated as he raked suggestive eyes down my body. I cringed in disgust.

The man was lanky, tall and looked extremely greasy. He wore the uniform Nick wore. I shuddered at the look of him.

"Hi." I said. Not really knowing what to say or how to say it. I tried to push past him, but he shot out an arm and pushed me backwards gently.

I swear to God, I was going to kick this man in the balls.

"Where are you going?" He asked with lust clear in his voice. I shivered. Not again.

My chest began to tighten as my memories collided in to me with force. I had spent so long trying to forget everything that had happened. I had tried so hard, and this man had to come and fuck everything up for me.

I heaved a large lungful of air.

"Away from you." I spat. "Leave me alone."

"Don't be that way, petal." The name caused me to take a step back with shock. He was using the pet name he always used. I couldn't breathe.

"Fuck off." I hissed. I laid two hands to my head.

"Now, now." He hushed. He went to touch me, I recoiled at the gesture.

Please, don't touch me.

I pleaded. I pleaded in my head. I needed someone to help me, anyone. I needed to get away from him.

"I'll scream blue murder if you touch me." I hissed. He chuckled loudly.

"Nobody would hear you here, petal. Only you and me." He winked. I choked on the air I was meant to be breathing.

The memories felt all too much. They over took my mind without a backwards glance. I couldn't stop them. On shaking legs, my memories came back to me.

It was a windy night in Australia, Sydney. The winds pushed the metal bins around he garden and the small trees held on strongly to their roots as they were pushed in all directions.

My mother had left only an hour ago to her work party. She went every year, and every year I hated it. I hated it when she left, when she had to go and leave me with her husband.

When I was sixteen, I pleaded and begged her to stay. I did at seventeen, too. At eighteen, I stopped begging her to stay when she left. I accepted my faith. I couldn't tell her, she wouldn't believe me. Not when she was completely in love, not when she was head over heels. She wouldn't hear me, she wouldn't listen.

The thing was, he hardly ever touched me, he hardly ever hurt me. It was his words that were my undoing. The way he used to tell me all of the things he would love to do to me, maybe next time, maybe the time after that, he didn't know and he didn't want me to know, either. He was the master of mind games, a monster under the bed.

I hated him with every fibre I had in my body.

Tonight, he was watching the rugby game in his study. I wish he'd stay there all night, but I knew him. He'd be up soon. He called it tucking in, I called it hell.

I used to sit on my bed and cry whilst I waited for him. There was nothing I could do. He reinforced curfews when my mother was out, he used them religiously to keep me indoors and in hands reach.

Why couldn't she see what he was doing to me?

I heard the familiar footsteps I heard every night. Sometimes he'd leave me be, sometimes he wouldn't. Tonight, I knew he was coming my way, I knew by the way his breathing quickened as he approached my room. I knew by the way his feet rocketed the house.

He wanted me to know he was there. He could smell the fear a mile away. He loved it.

The door creaked and it seemed like hours until he was beside me. I hid under the covers. At eighteen I was hiding under the covers like a three year old girl. I was hiding under the covers like I was scared from the ghost.

"Catherine." He purred. I could feel his hands running down my body as I shivered. "Let me see your face."

I ignored him.

The next thing I knew, he grabbed the top of the blanket and ripped it away from me. Now he could see my tears, he could smell the fear radiating off of my like a wave.

"Don't touch me." I sobbed. Maybe tonight was the night he would do it. Mum wouldn't be back for hours yet. He could, he had the chance.

"Come on, petal, you know I wouldn't hurt you." I looked to him, not being fooled. I could see by the sadistic look in his eyes that he would. He wouldn't think twice about it.

"Please." I pleaded. "I don't want this."

"Of course you do." He chuckled loudly. His sounds vibrated off of the walls. "I can see it in the way you look at me. Your mother would be very, very angry if she found out."

"Go away."

"You're eighteen now, Catherine. Old enough to follow your desires. Old enough for me to follow mine. You know I want you, I have since your mother introduced me to you."

"You're sick." I spat. His words infuriated me. Why couldn't he just leave me alone? Why couldn't he just jump off the face of the Earth and let me live?

"That's enough." He grabbed my thigh tightly. I tried to push him off me. He was too strong, he wouldn't budge. "Be a good girl, Catherine."

He leaned in closer to my mouth. I screamed and screamed and screamed.

Until everything turned black.

"Cathy!" I heard a voice so thick and deep. They sounded panicked and frightened. I couldn't open my eyes, they were too heavy.

I really wanted to open them. The voice sounded familiar. I wanted to see the person talking to me, I desperately wanted to open my eyes wide.

"Get the fuck away from her!" The voice bellowed. "I'll break your fucking neck."

"I was just talking to her, Abel. You fuck off."

"Don't push it, Dixon. I swear to God, I will fucking kill you. Never, ever touch her again." I felt hands upon my face. Arms around my body as I was rocked back and forth. "She's mine." The voice growled.

I couldn't help but sob. I wanted to open my eyes. I wanted these memories to leave me. I was just so tired, so washed out and tired.

"Come on, Angel. He won't hurt you. I've got you." The voice hushed. In that moment, I knew who the voice belonged to. It was Nick. I sobbed more once I knew he had come to save me.

"Don't go." I croaked quietly.

"I'm not going any where. You're okay, you just panicked and blacked out for a few minutes. Open your eyes now, Angel."

"I can't." I sobbed. "They're too heavy."

"You can fall asleep, I'll take you home. You're safe, I've got you." His arms tightened around my body. The pressure and the warmth coming from him relaxed my beating heart.

"Thank you." I whispered, before I stopped fighting and let myself fall asleep.

Once he was done, he left me sobbing in bed.

This was the worst he had ever been. He touched me, he did all of the things he said he would. I knew it was only a matter of time.

He broke me, left me in two pieces in my bedroom with a smile on his face and the eyes of a winner.

In reality, it wasn't the monsters under the bed or the ghosts you were meant to be afraid of. Not when the man under your roof was the devil and was insistent on dragging you to hell.

Chapter 11

I woke up with a frightened start.

The darkness was meant to help with the mind. If you were sleeping, none of the memories could touch you like they did when you were awake. The nightmares were just nightmares, the thoughts were the one's which kept you up at night. Real memories; real pain to feel.

As my heart beated harshly against my chest, I looked over at the time. It read three in the morning. With two hours sleep already, I felt groggy and my eye lids were heavy with the need to sleep.

I could smell Nick surrounding my senses. It calmed me down enough to gather my thoughts, however, all I wanted to do was sleep. Every time I closed my eye lids, the memories of what had happened came flying back.

I had spent years trying to forget and only one night had set me off in to space.

I didn't ever want to feel the way I did before.

With a new set of panic to the little girl I was before, I quickly scrambled out of bed in search for Nick.

I didn't know where he was or why he wasn't in bed asleep with me. I felt relieved I had him right now, he had taken extra care with me tonight especially when he was working.

Nick was like that, he didn't care what he was doing, he'd do anything for the people he cared about. Surprisingly, with the worrying thoughts in my mind, I still managed to smile. The thought of Nick caring for me when he really didn't have to made me feel all kinds of happy and giddy.

He didn't know how much it meant to me.

I padded through his hall and down to the living room. I couldn't hear a thing but the quiet background noise of the TV.

Finally, I saw Nick. He was sat on his sofa with his feet kicked back on to the coffee table; his usual position. He looked so relaxed from behind but as I rounded the coffee table, I came face to face with the haunted face of Nick Abel. The eye bags were prominent even through the human eye, his face contorted in to a frown.

A small note pad laid on his thighs and his hand moved quickly as he scribbled notes down on to a page. He hadn't realised I was there.

"Nick." My voice came out to gather his attention. He didn't stop his writing, but his eyes flickered to mine. His bright eyes were dull with tiredness, his eyes telling me just how shaken up he really was.

Was it because of what happened earlier?

"What's the matter?" I asked. I stood there in only one of his T-shirts and he hadn't even suggested anything. Even though the thought made me frown, I was secretly glad. I didn't think I was ready for that yet, especially when the memories were so raw.

With that, I slowly approached him, gauging his mood. His eyes followed my body around the coffee table and he leaned back in his seat as soon as I was perched on to his lap. I laid my head against his chest and curled in to a ball.

After a few seconds, Nick sighed and two large arms came around to wrap around my body.

"You're not acting like yourself." I stated. I wanted him to talk to me. I wanted to know what was really going on throughout his mind.

"You shouldn't be worrying about me." He came back. His voice was rough but it still held that authority and power it always did. It was also gentle, too, like he was talking to a child.

"I'm worrying because you're never this quiet." I stated. "I'm worried I've put you off me." It couldn't be all that sexy to see the girl you was dating on the floor panicking the way I did. Nothing was sexy about that, I couldn't help that. I hope Nick understood.

"Don't be fucking stupid." Nick snapped. I jumped at the boom of his voice. "I'm a lot of things but I'm not heartless. What I saw earlier broke my heart, that doesn't mean I don't want you anymore."

"Nick, I'm-"

"I'm going to stop you right there." Nick stated as he pushed me off of his body. I sat up on the sofa and he kneeled on the floor. He took hold of my hand and looked straight in to my eyes. His eyes were so gorgeous, I couldn't help but get carried away in them. "I'm not going to let you feel guilty for what happened."

"It hasn't happened to me since I was nineteen." I explained. I had snapped out of it after a few months of getting them all the time. It became my life for many years, what he did to me, I didn't have the chance to feel after a while.

"Cathy." Nick breathed. He squeezed his eyes shut and re opened them again. I saw the pain there, the pity I really didn't want.

"Don't, Nick, don't look at me like that." I pleaded. I couldn't stand the sympathy. What had happened had happened, I didn't want to think about it anymore.

"Will you tell me what happened?" He laid his head against my hand on the sofa. He still looked at me, watching, waiting.

I knew he was all ears, he'd listen to me and he'd understand. I hadn't told anyone, I didn't want to say the words and make it real.

"I can't." I whispered. I'd never had to, both my mother or my father didn't know. Nobody. I couldn't say the words, couldn't get them past my lips.

"Cathy, I think I know what happened to you." Nick stated, my heart started beating frantically. "You can tell me if I'm wrong or stepping out of line. I have spent the last two hours trying to figure out what had caused that breakdown, it wasn't easy because you didn't say much to give anything away."

"Don't." My voice was barely a whisper.

"You were raped weren't you? As a consenting adult, but still too young to know any better. He fucking touched you and had you without-fuck!" Nick shouted as he pushed the glass lying on the table across the air. "Tell me I'm wrong Cathy, tell me what I have said is wrong."

"Nick-"

"He ruined your life." Nick snapped. "I'll fucking kill him, Cathy."

"Nick." Tears rolled so quickly down my face. I began to sob as I laid my head in both of my hands.

"I'll break his neck in two for ever touching you, I swear to you, Cathy, he will never get the chance to hurt you again." Nick came quickly to my side. He pushed my hands away from my face and took it in to his larger ones.

The tears still ran down my cheeks, he wiped them away without force. Kissing my cheek, he murmured sweet nothings.

"I'm not scared anymore." I whispered.

"You're scared of your own memories." Nick stated. "You're not scared of him because he's not here and you left, you're just scared to fall asleep at night because the memories are so real in the dark. Your memories are your worst enemy, they're the devil and the devil never sleeps."

"Maybe I'm the devil." I stated. I never slept when I was younger, too afraid he'd come in and hurt me whilst I was asleep. It was only since I had moved back to America where I ever felt safe.

"You know you're my Angel." Nick exclaimed. "I've never said anything less."

"Thanks for everything you've done for me." And I meant it to the point I would tell him every single day. Him being here was enough to help me feel safe, even from my memories. Nobody would ever want to cross paths with Nick.

"You don't have to thank me, it's in my job description."

"As a police officer?" I questioned.

"As your boyfriend." He stated.

"Nick-"

"I know what you're going to say. It is soon, it's only been a few months, but let's be fair, it's inevitable. I've never brought a girl back to my apartment, never slept with one in my bed, never let them see me working. You're the only one and I care about you. What happened earlier isn't going to push me away, believe me, there's no running." He explained. "I'm all yours and I want you to be all mine."

"I was yours the minute I met you." I stated. "There's no escaping them eyes."

"This will be easy for you then." He smiled. He took hold of my hands and pulled me up from the sofa. I stood before him in only his shirt. "I don't want to do anything tonight, even though you're looking fucking hot in my top."

"You're still in your uniform." I said. "You should take it off."

"You'd like that wouldn't you?" Nick smirked. "Maybe one day I'll give you a strip show."

"In your uniform?" I asked with hope.

"Of course, I heard my girl loves a man in uniform." His words made my heart flip. He took my face in to his hands again and brought my lips up to his. "Please don't worry about anything, anymore. I'll take good care of you."

"I don't doubt you for a second."

"It's in my job description."

"Which one?"

"Both." I giggled and he smiled broadly my way. "I missed that. Seeing you earlier really hit home. I know what it's like to feel so out of control and seeing it from you made it really hard for me, you know that don't you?"

"You're such a softie." I stated. "Who knew that Nick Abel, the village's biggest play boy could say such beautiful things." I winked his way as I joked. I didn't want to spend anymore time moping around, I wanted to go back to normal, to feel normal.

"Stop messing." Nick chuckled. "I'm giving up my play boy ways."

"That's going to be tough." I mentioned.

"Not so tough when you've got what you want at home."

"You're too cute, Nick." I blushed, I couldn't help myself. He was on fire tonight, I knew he just wanted to see me happy again. It was working, I was glad. He pressed all of the right buttons even when he didn't necessarily know which ones would work.

"Don't tell my work mates you just called me cute. I'll allow it, because it's you who said it, but let's keep it between me and you, I have a reputation to uphold."

"Don't you have a play boy reputation, too? Don't you want to keep that one?"

"Fuck that reputation. I'm whipped, so what?"

"I like you whipped." I replied. Nick chuckled again.

"Are you tired?" He asked. I nodded my head. I was exhausted, however, I didn't want to sleep. I didn't want to lay my head on the pillow and let my thoughts cascade me. Nick was right, I was scared of my own memories, especially now. "Do you want to go to bed?" I shook my head.

"I don't want to sleep." I stated.

"Want to watch a movie?" Nick asked.

"Can we watch something funny?"

"You want to watch a comedy? Good choice, babe. I like that idea." Nick grabbed the remotes from the coffee table, sat down and kicked his feet up. He patted his thigh and I sauntered over to him and resumed my position from earlier.

I loved being on his lap, cuddling close. He was so manly and warm, so muscly and cosy. I could live on his chest and on his lap forever.

Nick put on a film and we cuddled in close. It was so late but I didn't care. Being here with Nick was everything I needed tonight. Knowing he was there for me, knowing he was going to take care of me, look after me and keep me safe, I was grateful.

It was crazy how much things changed the more you got to know someone.

I feel asleep on Nick's chest around half an hour in to the film. I was warm and the sound of his heart beating against my ear was everything I needed. His arms kept me safe.

And I slept with no demons.

I woke up disorientated and every part of my body felt achy and sore.

I sat up straight and realised I was still on Nick's lap. I stretched out slowly and quietly without waking him up. He slept so peacefully and his hands were still on my body.

Suddenly, my phone started to ring. I heard it from the small side table beside the sofa. I quickly reached over to grab it, Nick's hands gripped my hip tighter.

With my vibrating phone in hand, I answered it and laid a hand to Nick's face. I stroked it gently. He sighed and relaxed again beneath me.

"Hello?" I greeted.

"Cathy." Glenn's voice came out from the speaker. "You haven't been home for a while, are you okay?"

"Yeah, I've been with Nick." I stated. "What's up?"

"Has the fucker been good to you?"

"More than you'll ever know."

"Okay." I could hear him grimace. "I don't need to know."

"Not like that." I laughed. "I missed you."

"You've only been gone for a few days, Cathy."

"No, I mean when I was in Australia. I missed you more than words could ever explain." I wish he could have helped. I wish I never left him. I needed him.

"I missed you too, Birdie." He replied back. "Not that I'm complaining, but what's brought this on? A few days with Nick and you're kissing my arse. What's he said?" I laughed again.

"He's been totally fine, dad, stop panicking. I was just thinking that's all."

"I was getting worried then. Unless he's high there's literally no depth to him." Nick, high? I couldn't even imagine it. He was a police officer, for God sake, and dad took it with humour.

"Dad." I scolded. "Don't be mean." Nick had more depth to him than anyone would ever care to admit or to find out. Nick was very reserved and totally different on the first glance.

"The fucker knows I'm only kidding." Glenn replied with a chuckle. "What's he doing anyway?"

"I thought you rang to see how I was, your daughter."

"I've had enough of you. Put Nick on the phone." His tone was full of humour.

"You're on fire today, aren't you?"

"You know me, Cathy, full of surprises."

"Hold on, I just need to wake him up." I stated. He was still snoring softly beside me. I didn't have the heart to wake him.

"Lazy bastard." I heard Glenn mutter before I laid the phone down on the arm of the chair. I started to gently kiss Nick's cheeks. I went down his neck and back up again. He moaned.

"Cathy." He hissed. "What are you doing?"

"Waking you up." I stated. I continued kissing him and biting him gently. He flinched every time.

"You need to stop."

"Well, are you awake?"

"I'm awake and I've got morning glory." Nick replied. I chuckled as I looked to the bulge in his pants. I patted it gently as he growled.

"There's no time for frolicking. Dad's on the phone." I stated. Nick groaned again, this time not in pleasure.

Nick held out his hand. I picked up the phone and laid it in his hands. He put it to his ear.

"Glenn." He greeted.

With that, I decided to move to the kitchen. Considering what happened last night, I felt on cloud nine. Everything seemed to be looking up with Nick and my family in terms of my father. I had my best friend back, my father and now Nick. Best of all, the devil was away and I didn't have to worry.

I grabbed a few frying pans and decided to make Nick breakfast, as a thank you for last night. He was a man, he'd love a fry up.

"I swear to you I'm looking after her, you know I keep my promises." I heard Nick state down the phone to my father.

"That lifestyle is over. I haven't wanted it since meeting your daughter." He replied to Glenn.

"It's not my fault I like your daughter, Glenn. I care about her, I'm looking after her and you need to stop worrying."

"I know I'm Nick Abel, but I'm a changed man."

I couldn't help but to smile. My father was just too cute sometimes, he'd look after me too, always.

"Glenn, I'm too fucking manly to be doing pinky promises with you." Nick sighed. "Fine."

After a few more minutes talking about the football scores, Nick hung up the phone.

I couldn't stop smiling.

Nick caught on to my mood as soon as he sauntered in to the kitchen after me. He wrapped his arms around my waist.

"A fry up. God, you really are the woman of my dreams." I giggled but the idea made me smile even more. "I like you happy." He stated.

"I like me happy, too." I stated back.

And with Nick in my life, it was hard to be anything but.

CHAPTER 12

O n Saturday, I had almost fully recovered mentally from the trauma I had experienced earlier this week. Luckily, I felt back to normal, all thanks to Nick.

And as I was so thankful, when he suggested I help him shop for groceries, I agreed, even though I hated shopping with a fiery passion.

A part of me was happy he was finally going to get some decent food in his fridge. How could any man just live off takeaway and beer? I swear he was a typical, lazy man and it wasn't even fair when his body looked like God had carved it himself.

"Babe, want to shower with me?" Nick asked. I had just woken up and I wasn't a morning person. Nick had woken me up earlier than necessary on a Saturday morning and I wasn't in the slightest bit pleased. Now he wanted to shower? It wasn't even eight in the morning yet.

"Go fuck your self."

"What's the point when you could do it for me?" Nick smirked my way. He took off his top and as I slouched over the kitchen counter, I couldn't help but look at his body. He smirked even larger.

"Like I said, sweetie, go and fuck yourself." I smiled sweetly his way. I needed more coffee. As I filled th coffee machine up to the brim, I felt a warm presence behind me. "Nick." I warned.

"Come and shower with me." He demanded. I shook my head.

"I need to wake up first and-"

"Shower, now." His voice rasped my way with authority slicing through the air.

"You police officer voice will not work with me." I stated. Before I knew it, Nick's hands came around my waist and I was lifted in to the air and over his shoulder. I didn't even both squealing.

"I swear to God." I huffed. "Don't you dare put me in the shower."

"I like dares." Nick replied back, humour in his voice. I hugged loudly again. Without a second word, I was dropped in to the shower and cold water spurted along my body. I screamed.

"Nick!" I shouted. "You're a fucking twat-" Nick's lips smashed to mine before I could let out another word. He pushed me back until my back was hard against the tile of the shower wall.

His lips were bruising against mine, his hands digging in to the raw flesh of my hips as my wet shirt rose above my chest. Nick roamed his hands along my body, up my neck and back down. I moaned against him.

"How long has it been?" Nick gasped. I shook my head in mis-understanding. "How long has it been since I was last inside you?"

"Too long." Was my only reply. I looked in to his eyes, they were dark and needy with desperate pleasure. He wanted me, I could tell. I wanted him, too.

"I knew I was losing my mind." Nick gruffed. "Even an hour feels like three weeks."

"That's because you're a man slag." I replied. I said it as a joke but my voice was so breathless and needy I didn't know if he'd take it as one.

"I'm now your man slag." He stated. "Now shut up and get naked."

"Nick!" I huffed. After I second I smiled. He really was romantic in his own little way. "That was cute."

"It wasn't meant to be cute." Nick huffed. "You're ruining the mood. I just want to feel you."

"Feel me, then."

"Get naked, then." Nick jerked back. I rolled my eyes before ripping the soaking wet top from off of my skin. I pulled it over my head and let it drop to the ground with a thud. Before him I stood naked.

He raked his eyes up and down my body, from head to toe. His eyes turned darker, a dark, dark shade of blue. He pushed me against the wall again with a punishing force.

"You're too fucking hot." Nick stated. "Where've you been all my life?"

"Australia." I breathed.

"Too fucking far away, that's where." He laid his nose to my neck. His tongue came out to lick the ridge. I gasped. "You're not going back."

"I wouldn't want to." Never again.

"What would you rather?" He pushed his hips forward until I moaned. He was hard in all of the right places. "An Australian geezer, or me?" He ground his hips again my way. He took hold of my chin until my eyes were looking straight in to his.

He dared me with his eyes to say anyone but him. He dared me, he gave me the choice and I would never take it. Not now. He pushed in to me again as a warning.

"You, Nick." I breathed.

"Good. I'd choose you, too." He breathed as he lowered from my neck down my belly and down my thighs.

"Well, I didn't think Australian geezers were really your thing." I stated. I moaned again as he kissed his way back up my body.

"I only have a thing for one person." Nick stated.

"That better be me or you're not getting any sex."

"You know it's you." Nick replied. "Look, my eyes are on you." He looked to me, made me look at him again. "They're not on anybody else."

"Let's keep it that way."

"Pretty hard not to when you're naked."

The shops were on nearly every single corner of the village. They were so easy to get to, therefore Nick and I decided to walk.

The sky was clear of any dark clouds, even white ones too. The sun was out in full beam today and the weather was hot. It was the perfect day to get some fresh air, so I was jumping when Nick suggested it.

As we walked down the cobbled streets, Nick took my hand and wrapped his fingers possessively around mine. We kept our hands linked as we walked and I couldn't keep the smile off of my face.

He didn't even let my hand go when we made our way in to the store. He kept us linked, my smile stayed.

"To be honest, I haven't been shopping for a while."

"That's because you live off everyone else." I rolled my eyes his way. "You're eating my dad out of house and home."

"So?" He pouted. I laughed his way and smoothed the wrinkle on his forehead. He pulled my finger down and kissed it before getting too preoccupied with the scented candles in aisle three.

He picked nearly everyone up in turn and smelt them. I stood there and watched his fascinated look on all the homeware.

"That one doesn't even smell like apples and cinnamon." Nick huffed as his looked to the candle with disgust.

"Which one do you like?" I asked. I came closer to him and picked up vanilla. He snatched it out of my hand to sniff.

"This one reminds me of you." Nick stated. "I'm going to buy it."

"Since when have you ever had a candle in your house?" I mused.

"Until now." He smiled. "I'm also trying to impress you."

"By buying a candle?" I asked as my brow cocked up high.

"Isn't that what women like?" He asked as he turned towards me. "I even stated it smelt like you."

"I smell like vanilla?" I asked.

"Not really. You smell better." He smiled again. I laughed before taking the candle and throwing it in to our basket. He could have the sodding candle if it made him so happy.

Suddenly, just as I was about to turn, a voice came out from behind us.

"Nick!" The voice was high but sultry. It made you do a double take, that was for sure. I turned around to the girl shouting out his name and found a long legged blonde run towards us.

Kitted out in sports gear, she smiled brightly Nick's way. Nick stiffened infront of me.

"I knew it was you." She breathed. Her hair was long and golden, her skin bright and her body with curves in all of the right places.

"Sarah." Nick nodded. I could see him flickering his eyes to me from the side of him. I looked to him. "This is my girlfriend, Cathy." He introduced.

Sarah looked to me as if she had only realised I was here. I could see the small frown on her face and the disappointment in her eyes at the world girlfriend.

Who was this woman?

I held my hand out.

"Cathy." I greeted.

"Sarah." She sized me up.

"Nice to see you again, we're going." Nick went to grab my arm but Sarah shot her hand out to stop him.

"Don't you remember me?" She asked. Nick shrugged without a care. I don't think he did remember her. I wanted gasp in shock, but it in fact didn't shock me at all. It was wrong, but I felt satisfied at the thought of it. "I spent the night with you and I woke up and you had left."

"I must have been busy." Nick stated. He went to pull me away again but Sarah stopped him.

"Is that all you've got to say?" She scoffed. "I wanted to see you again."

"Look, Sarah, I'm just trying to have a nice day with my girl-friend." Nick replied. His demeanour was calm, his voice sounded irritated and annoyed.

"You slept with me no longer than three months ago. That's not a long time in my eyes." Sarah replied. I looked down as the reality hit me.

I knew he was a man slag before he met me, he even admitted it. I wasn't going to be childish about this, I couldn't change Nick's past and quite frankly, I wouldn't want to.

We've all done things we're not proud of.

"Can you just leave us the fuck alone, please?" I shot out. She obviously wasn't getting the message from Nick. I wouldn't ever have talked to somebody like I just did but I was trying to be mature even when jealousy surged my body. She wasn't helping.

"I'm just trying to have a conversation with Nick." Sarah replied, her eyes alight with fire.

"You're trying to have a conversation about sex with my boyfriend." I rolled my eyes. "Fuck off."

Without another word, Sarah stormed off, her basket hitting the back of her legs as she walked away with anger.

I didn't even care that I sounded rude. I didn't care when she was blatantly saying things to Nick that she knew would hurt me.

"Oh, Cathy." Nick let out. I turned to face him.

"What?"

"You've got a foul mouth." He stated. He smiled my way and I couldn't help but laugh.

"I'm sorry if that was a turn off." I apologised. I had never been like this, lately, I had had enough of people's shit.

"The only thing that was, was a turn on." Nick stated. "If we weren't in broad daylight I would be taking you out in to that alley."

"We're in public."

"I wouldn't give a fuck about that."

"You're a creep."

"Yet again, I don't care." Nick shrugged. "You're not mad at me?"

"Of course not." I replied. "You had sex, so what? Don't we all?"

"I only have sex with you now."

"I believe you." I stated. I believed him because I knew he wouldn't do that to me. I wouldn't do that to him, either.

We had that respect for each other.

When we got home, I helped unpack all of the food and put them in to suitable compartments in his fridge and cupboards. He was stocked up now with food and drink.

I mentally thanked the lord.

I loved takeaways and fatty foods but fatty foods always went to my hips. I didn't need that kind of negativity in my life.

When the clock struck half ten, Nick and I went off to bed. It didn't take long before I was deep in to sleep.

I woke up with a start. Nick wasn't beside me.

Suddenly, I heard music flowing in to the room from the living room. With that, I rolled out of bed and followed the sound.

The sound of a guitar playing brought me out of my half asleep state and I stopped at the door ledge as I watched Nick play.

He swayed slightly to the music and strummed with peace and harmony. The song was sad but his body was strong against the guitar. His back was towards me, he didn't know I was awake.

What surprised me next was the fact he started the sing softly to himself. The tele played quietly in the background but all I could hear was his voice.

It took me high up in to he sky and brought me back down again without another thought. It was truly mesmerising. Goosebumps arose across my skin and I started to walk towards him.

Without his acknowledgment, I sat behind him and wrapped my hands around his back.

He relaxed at my touch as if he knew I was there all along.

He stopped singing as soon as I touched him, but he continued to play the strings of his guitar.

"You're so good." I murmured. My heart was beating wildly.

"You're meant to be asleep." He stated as he played.

"You weren't there."

"I can't sleep."

"Are you okay?" I asked. Nick stopped playing and I frowned. He laid down his guitar and turned towards me.

"Of course I am. I just can't sleep sometimes that's all." He explained. "I watched you sleep for hours, you look so beautiful I wanted to touch you, I always want to touch you. I had to leave before I woke you up, seems like I did that anyway."

"I don't like it when you're not beside me." I pouted. Nick took my face in to his hands.

"I don't like it either." He stated. "You know I'm never far away."

"I know." I replied. "Are you sure you're okay?" I asked again as I took in the bags under his eyes. He hadn't been sleeping at all lately.

"To be honest, Cath, I've been feeling things I've never felt, lately. I'm petrified I'm going to ruin things before they've really gotten started. I've rushed things, I know that, but I like you and I want you, you know that. I'm just a fool with no idea what I'm doing."

"You're doing fine to me." I stated.

"For now." He replied.

"You need to stop worrying about us. What happens, happens. Let's have fun together."

"I like you." Nick said again. I smiled at his words.

"I like you, too." I replied with a twinkle in my eyes.

"You're the only person I like." Nick stated. "I don't like many people."

"I can tell." I replied. "But that's okay, as long as you like me." I joked. Nick chuckled.

"Come here." I flew in to his arms without a second thought.

And that's where I stayed all night.

<h1 style="text-align:center">CHAPTER 13</h1>

"It's time, bitch." Danni said to me as she spread across Nick's sofa. Nick was currently working so I decided to invite Danni up to Nick's (with his permission) so I wasn't on my own.

Glenn closed the shop today as he went on a road trip to visit his brother. He would be back tomorrow evening and therefore I had two homes to myself.

"Time for what?" I asked as I cleaned Nick's kitchen. I had spent days with Nick and not once had we cleaned and tidied. The place was a pig sty.

"We're going clubbing again."

"When?" I asked again. I hadn't been clubbing since Nick and I had been together, in fact, the last time I went clubbing, Nick was with another girl.

"Tonight!" Danni exclaimed. "I need to get pissed."

"Tonight?"

"Don't do this." Danni moaned. "You've got a boyfriend, I'm proud of you, okay? But do not say no to a night out. You're all I have."

"Dan." I sighed. "I'm coming out, stop moaning." I laughed her way, she decided to laugh with me.

"Will lover boy mind?" She asked. I rolled my eyes. We were in our twenties, we weren't childish. Of course, I knew Nick would worry, especially as he worried so much about us already, however, we didn't have that kind of relationship where we got so protective of each other both of us were not allowed to do anything a part.

"He won't mind." I stated. Danni chuckled.

"Ring him and tell him."

"He won't mind." I repeated.

"He's a sexy, possessive God who has the hots for you, you never know, he might mind." She replied with a smile. I rolled my eyes again.

"Stop stirring shit." I replied with humour dripping from my voice. She laughed again.

"Go on, ring him."

I picked up my phone and dialled Nick's number. The phone rang and I hope he picked up even if he was in work.

Nick picked up the phone after three ring's.

"Cathy." He breathed, his voice sending shivers down my spine. "Are you okay?" His voice sounded worried.

"Yeah, yeah." I waved his worry off. "Danni and I are going out tonight." I stated.

"Where?"

"Clubbing in town." I replied.

"That's okay, love." Nick sighed. "Please, just behave yourself."

"You know me."

"I do and that's why I'm worrying." Nick replied. "But I trust you just like I know you'd trust me."

"Of course."

"I'll be in work all night so I'll be up for you. Make sure you ring me or text me if you need anything." Nick said.

"I will."

"Promise?"

"I promise." I stated.

Nick and I put down the phone after a few more minutes. I turned to look at Danni with a smug smirk on my face.

"You've got yourself a keeper." Danni stated as she let out some air. "I need me a Nick Abel. Sexy police man and let's you out clubbing. You don't see that in a romance novel nowadays days."

"You're so dramatic." I replied as I continued to clean. "We're not seventeen, you know, Nick has past that stage and so have I."

"Still, you're one lucky girl."

"I think so, too." I smiled. If I thought about it, I really was a lucky girl. I didn't think Nick had it in him to be in a stable relationship with anyone, not when he told me about his past with women. However, Nick was proving himself and everybody in the village wrong.

People spoke, Nick was a well known play boy around here, but he was changing right in front of everyone around him.

I knew leapords never changed their spots, but it's not the physical part of him that needed changing. A soul can change, no matter what anybody said.

Of course, I was still worried that in a couple of months Nick would get bored of me and go back to the way he was before.

My past showed me, however, that time goes by too fast to change a thing. I was so grateful for leaving Australia and being away from him, I'd do anything to be happy at this moment no matter the cost.

My past showed me that my happiness is almost as important right in the moment than anything else. I didn't give a shit about tomorrow or a day past it, right now was what I lived for.

"You want to start getting ready?" Danni asked. I looked to the time, it was nearly half five in the afternoon.

"It's a bit early isn't it?" I replied. I didn't usually start getting ready until half six/ seven, as we usually left the house around nine to get in to town.

"Not when you want to look smoking. I'm on the prowl tonight, Cath, trust me." She winked. "I haven't woken up in a man's bed since the last time we went out. It's been too long." She mused.

"Use protection."

"No, I thought getting knocked up would be a fun thing to do." She rolled her eyes. I knew where I got it from now.

"Sarcasm is the lowest form of wit." I pulled the gloves off of my hands and put away the cleaning materials.

"I'm the lowest form of everything else, I might aswell use the lowest form of wit, too."

"You're so hard on yourself."

"It's a good job I like hard things."

The music was so loud I couldn't help but smile. I loved the way the music blasted through my veins and through my ear drums. I loved the way everybody felt connected as they danced to the beat on the dance floor.

There was never anything better.

Danni stood tall in her sky scrapers and her mini dress. When she said she wanted to look smoking, she wasn't kidding. Her hair was long and wavy down her back and I'm sure her legs sparkled.

I wore black, again. I'm sure I could live in black. My mini dress came just above my knees and even though my heels were big, they still weren't as big as Danni's. I had never mastered the art of heel walking.

And I really didn't fancy a broken ankle tonight.

Danni pulled me up on to the dance floor the second we entered the club. She grabbed us two drinks from the bartender and pulled us in to the tightest spot on the floor.

It was so hot and tight, but I didn't care. I started to dance with Danni and the night was under way.

After two more hours, it was fair to say that I felt drunk. I was way past the point of tipsy.

Sadly, I hadn't heard a thing off Nick and even though I was missing him strongly, I was having such a good time. I thought about him, in fact, the drunker I got, the more I thought of him.

I wanted him, I always did. But right now, I wanted him more than anything. Alcohol was just no good for me.

As I wobbled to the toilet, I got my mobile out of my clutch and dialled his number. I hope he wasn't busy, I just wanted to hear his voice.

Nick picked up with fast speed.

"Are you okay?" He asked. I giggled. "What is it, Cathy?"

"I missed you." I slurred. Even though I slurred, the passion was still in my voice. I did miss him, it had only been a day and I missed him.

"I miss you, too, baby." Nick sighed. "Are you drunk?" His question made me giggle again.

"A little." I laughed. Nick chuckled quietly.

"I hope you're behaving."

"I promise I am." I couldn't keep the smile off my face.

"As long as you're happy." Nick stated. "Then I'm happy too. Just make sure nobody puts their hands on you but me."

"They won't, I won't let them."

"Good girl." Nick breathed. "Go and have some fun, you don't want to be talking to me all night. I'll see you tomorrow morning."

"Bye, Nick." I breathed. "I like you." Nick chuckled.

"I like you, more." With that, I hung up the phone. I held my phone tightly against my chest and closed my eyes tight. It didn't matter where I was or who I was with, I would never get him out of my head.

I wobbled out out of the stall I was currently in and went back to the booth Danni and I picked up throughout the night. Danni sat on the black leather chair next to a blonde headed boy who was wrapped all around her.

Men in clubs didn't pull me to them anymore. Even if they did, I compared them to Nick no matter how good looking they were. None of them would ever compete with Nick, not with my feelings towards him already.

As soon as Danni saw me beside her table, she left the blonde headed boy and came barrelling over to me. He couldn't keep his eyes off of her, I smiled over at him and he winked when he saw me looking.

Danni latched on to me as soon as she came over. She was so drunk, she couldn't stand straight. I wasn't that bad, but it was still hard to keep us both up. The room was spinning and my legs felt like jelly from all of the dancing.

Suddenly, I felt a hand grab on to my arse. I sat Danni back down with a small push and turned around until I saw a red shirt before me.

"Excuse me." I shouted in to his ear. He smirked down at me, but he didn't look like Nick. I looked to him with disgust. It was never okay for a man to just go up to a woman and touch her without permission.

The aggravating thing was, he was smirking like a proud little boy.

The red shirted man touched my arse again and I lost it. Without another thought, I pushed him forcefully backwards. I wanted him to leave me alone, I didn't want him to ever touch me the way he did. However, the man tripped over the chair standing behind him and he went straight in to the round metal table. It collapsed beneath him with a thud.

The thud was so loud, people from all angles of the room looked our way. Without another though, two strong arms came around my waist and I was hoisted upwards and outwards.

"Get off of me!" I screamed at the security guards holding me up. "Let me go!"

The arms wouldn't budge and the movements wouldn't stop. I tried to wriggle free, I tried to get out of the strong gasp but the strong gasp was just too strong. I started to panic, I started to panic as this man held me up above his shoulder.

"Let me go!" I pounded his back harshly as I breathed heavily inwards and heavily outwards.

"I'm calling the police." His voice was loud and strong as he dumped me down on to the concrete outside of the club.

Once he said police, I mentally cringed. Even though I was still drunk, I still knew who was on the job tonight and Nick was one of them. I hoped to the high heavens Nick wouldn't be here to see me like this. Not like this, not again.

"No, please." I pleaded. The man shook his head.

"They've already been called, Miss. We don't tolerate assault."

"He was grabbing me!" I stated.

"We don't tolerate assault." He repeated. I looked to him and shook my head with disgust his way.

"But you tolerate sexual assault?" I questioned. The security guard looked down at me, his brows furrowing.

"Miss, just be quiet."

"You're a pig, you're all pigs." I spat. "He was touching me up without my permission, all I did was push him."

"You can explain yourself to the police."

"This is a joke. You're a joke." I stated. Just I was about to open my mouth and have a go at him some more, I heard the sirens of the police car before I saw the flashing lights.

Fuck.

The car came speeding up to the club, which was totally unnecessary. I wasn't some kind of serial killer who had been on the wanting list for decades. I pushed a man for touching my arse and I get treated like some sort of criminal.

And that man was still let free to enjoy his night.

Once the police car stopped on the curb in front of me, I lowered my head and prayed Nick didn't get out of that car.

Firstly, I saw Alice come barrelling out of the car like she was some sort of wizard in the police force. I knew what was coming next, Nick always worked with Alice.

Nick bounded out of the car, the air charging with electricity around us. As soon as he got out of the car, as soon as he felt it too, he looked my way. His eyes binded on to mine, I looked to him with apology.

"What's going on here?" His voice came out. It boomed and caught everybody's attention around him, especially mine.

"Assault, sir." The security guard stated matter of fact. He obviously respected Nick as he bowed his head at his figure.

"That's bullshit." I let out loudly. Nick pointed his eyes my way, his forehead crinkled with a frown. He was basically telling me to shut up. My anger boiled.

Why isn't anybody listening to me? Why can't anyone see that I wouldn't hurt him on purpose. It wasn't even assault, I just pushed him away from me. Nick should understand, why is he angry with me?

"I'll take her." Nick stated. Alice had a smug smile on her face and I wanted nothing more than to pull her down a peg or two.

"Nick-"

"Shut it." His voice came out. I stepped back in shock. Why would he even think about talking to me like that? He watched me as I moved, but his face didn't change. He swallowed loudly, his eyes were still dark as he watched me with irritation.

I hope my anger showed his way too.

"Come on, Nick, let's take her to the police station." Alice said. Nick turned to her but turned back to me straight after.

"I haven't done anything wrong!" I exclaimed. Nick bounded over to me and took my arm in to his hand.

"Alice, prowl the streets whilst I take her back."

"Abel-"

"Do it, Alice." His voice sliced through the air with demand. I'd do anything he said too with that kind of voice.

Nick pulled me in to the police car, not in the passenger seat but in the back seat. Nick buckled me up but there was no soft gentle touches involved, in fact, he felt aggressive, too rough and harsh as he touched the belt.

Nick buckled himself up and got the car in to motion. There was a silence.

"Nick, you have to believe me." I said. "I didn't assault anybody-"

"Cathy, just be quiet." His voice still sounded irritated.

"You're a bastard." I gritted. "Get me out of this fucking car."

"Cathy-"

"Get me out!" I shouted. "How could you? How could you speak to me like this? Like you're irritated with me when I've done fuck all. You can go and fuck your self."

"Cathy, shut your fucking mouth." He hissed.

I took my seat belt off my body. Nick looked to me in the rear view mirror with anger.

"Put your seat belt back on." He demanded.

"Stop this car and let me out, right now." I demanded back.

"I have to take you to the police station, you've been charged with assault, Cathy!" He boomed. My teeth gritted harshly.

"I didn't assault him." I gritted. "Let me out of this car right now or I swear to God, Nick, it will be the end of us." I was so livid, so angry I didn't know what I was saying. I wanted him to do as I told him, I wanted to get out and away from him.

The car came to a quick halt. The doors weren't unlocked but at least the car had stopped.

"Cathy." Nick's voice turned gentle, his voice sounding almost worried.

"Let me out." I said harshly.

"Just come to the station with me, we won't be there long and I can take you home." I shook my head.

"I said let me go."

Nick turned to me in the back seat. His face was one of worry. I knew he was pleading with me to stay, to do as I was told but there was no way I could. I was so angry I couldn't even think, I just wanted to be on my own.

Nick sighed and the doors unlocked. I gave Nick one last look before leaving the car.

"Cathy-"

"Leave me alone." I let out. The streets weren't dark and I was only a minute away from my home.

Nick's car stayed with me until I was at my house, he didn't once leave me to walk on my own. Even though the gesture was nice, I was just too angry to care.

I got home and as soon as the door was shut, I let a tear fall from my eye. I stayed there with my back against the door and fell asleep with the clothes I wore tonight.

My sleep was troubled and my back ached, however, I was too tired to move.

Anger really pulled the energy out of you.

I woke up with a startled start as I heard pounding on the front door. My body vibrated with the sounds and my head pounded.

"Cathy, open the fucking door!" I heard Nick's voice and my heart shot in to action.

"Go away." My voice gruffed and I coughed the grit away from my throat.

"Just let me in." He demanded.

"I don't want to speak to you."

"I haven't been able to think straight all night. I was just doing my job."

"No, you spoke to me like fucking shit. I'm your girlfriend and I didn't assault him. You should believe me, why would I do that?"

"I do believe you!" He exclaimed. "I believe you."

"He was touching me, Nick." I let out. I could hear Nick's breath through the wood of the door. He took an in take of breath.

"Cath-"

"He was touching my arse and all I did was push him away from me. The real assault that went down in that place was him and his assault on me. The security guards only cared because the table broke, but I didn't mean for that to happen."

"Oh, Cathy." He let out quietly. I could barely hear him.

"You knew I wouldn't do that to anybody." I sniffed. "Just leave me alone, please." I pleaded.

"I can't." Nick said. "I'm sorry, please let me in and we can talk."

"No, I don't want to talk, I just want you to leave me alone."

"Don't do this." He pleaded.

"Go." I demanded.

"I'll make it up to you, just don't give up on us." Nick pleaded some more. "Of course I believe you, I always will."

And even though I knew he was telling the truth, I just wanted to be on my own for the time being. I was tired, pissed off and hungover. I didn't need him pounding on my door and pleading.

"I'm coming back later and you'll let me in so we can talk." Nick stated. "I'm not staying away for any longer than that."

"Fine." I whispered.

"I'm crazy for you." Nick stated. "I'm so crazy for you I've never felt so alive."

CHAPTER 14

It was seven in the evening and Nick hadn't come back to talk just yet. The truth was, I didn't really want him to come back. I didn't want to talk to him.

Of course, his job was his job and I totally understood that, however, he out of all the people on this Earth should have understood what I was feeling last night. I had grown up with men taking advantage of me, that one man who was meant to be a parental figure, he took advantage of me in ways I never thought possible.

Yes, maybe it was just a touch but at the end of the day, I wasn't to blame.

Some men would never understand, as I saw from the security guard, but when that one person you though understood you and cared for you did the same thing, that was what hurt. What hurt the most was how Nick knew everything about my past and he still made that man the victim.

Well, I wasn't going to stand for that.

My phone pinged with an incoming text. Sat in my pyjamas whilst I felt sorry for myself, I opened it.

Just going to the pub with the boys for a quick drink. Should be home about 11 ~ Dad.

I texted him back with a simple okay and laid my phone back on to the table in front of me.

I continued to look at my phone, kind of hoping that it would light up with Nick's name. I was furious with him, but I couldn't help but miss him deeply. The last few days had been so perfect as we built our relationship, however, now it took the turn for the worst.

Was this really the right thing?

I was so cautious about this relationship. I didn't want to get hurt, I didn't want to feel so lost and hopeless ever again. I knew Nick had the power to hurt me more than anyone, he would always have that power because I couldn't control how I felt when it came to him.

I was feeling things so fast and quick.

Our connection was strong, our sexual tension so undeniable. I didn't want us to end before we had the chance to get started.

With that thought, I sighed deeply and got up to get myself a beer. My head was still pounding with the after math of last night and I still felt sick to my stomach. I didn't know if that was because of Nick or the alcohol. Maybe it was a bit of both.

I decided to have a beer anyway. I was totally on edge tonight, waiting for Nick's call or a knock on the door. I couldn't relax, no matter how hard I tried.

Glenn had just come back from his road trip and decided to go to the pub until later. Did that mean Nick was going, too?

Maybe it would be easier for me if he didn't come here tonight to talk, I just didn't really feel like it. A big part of me wanted to see him, I mean, I wanted us to be okay again, but another part of me was just too tired to try tonight.

But even I knew, Nick wasn't like that. He promised he'd come over tonight to talk, I knew he would because he'd want to make things right.

With a beer in my hand, I switched the TV on, hoping the noise would drown out all my thoughts of Nick.

It didn't.

When the clock struck half ten, I wondered if Nick would ever bother coming tonight. He said he wanted to make things right, so why hadn't he come?

This wasn't like Nick, not since the day I met him. He valued our relationship too much to leave me hanging. Even though I didn't feel like talking to him just yet, I still knew that it was for the best. Communication was key in a relationship and I knew we would have to talk soon, so we could continue to build and grow.

With a frown marring my face, I fell asleep an hour later, a little pissed off and a little sad he hadn't wanted to make things right after all, even when he had said he did.

I woke up with a start. Shit, this felt like deja vu.

The door pounded, it was barely light outside. I cradled my head as the pounding continued, I squeezed my eyes shut. Who was making all that noise?

I ignored the pounding, not even sure what planet I was really on. I was so disoriented and still half asleep, I didn't know who could be at the door.

I barely even heard the pounding over the noise of the TV.

Suddenly, my phone rang. It vibrated loudly on the table and I groaned. There was too much noise.

I picked up the phone but I didn't have the chance to say anything.

"Cathy, open the God damn door!" A voice boomed from the other end of the phone. It was like cold water had splashed strongly across my face.

Nick.

I knew his voice a mile away, I knew it was him by the way the hairs on my neck stood up and the way my heart began beating strongly.

I was still pissed off at him, more so now because I knew he hadn't come back to talk when he said he would. If he really wanted this relationship, why didn't he try to help it? The thought was beyond me. I was just left feeling confused.

"Go away." I croaked. Sleep was still evident in my voice.

"Open the fucking door, Cathy." He growled. I sat up straight, anger washing over me like a wave.

"Who the hell do you think you are?" I hissed. He had the audacity to come over at my house and talk to me like I was in the wrong. Who did he think he was?

"I need you to let me in, we need to talk." He pleaded. I scoffed his way.

"You said you'd come back last night, it's now nearly four in the morning and you think now's a good time?" I scoffed again. "Are you brain dead?"

"I can explain!" He let out. He continued to pound on the door.

"You had your chance and you blew it." I replied. "And stop pounding on my fucking door!" I screamed as the pounding got louder. It was making my head thump against my skull. I really didn't need this right now.

"Let me in." He demanded.

"Just go away."

"Stop running away from me."

"You're pushing me away!" I let out. "You're being a dick." And with that statement I couldn't help but let a tear fall from my face. I begged myself to stop crying, because he didn't deserve to see me like this. I so desperately wanted to sob, to sob and cry and just get it all over with. I didn't want to bottle my emotions up, but I thought it was for the best.

"Just let me in and I'll explain."

"I don't want to see you."

"Fuck!" Nick shouted in irritation. I then heard him rustling around on the end of the phone. The rustling lasted a few seconds before I heard him make a sound of victory. The next thing I knew, a key was going in to the lock of the door and the door opened loudly.

Shit. He had found the key under the plant pot, one my father and I always left incase we were ever locked out.

It didn't take long before he stomped in to the living room with wild eyes and his hair sticking up in all directions. He looked rough, really rough. His eyes were swollen with the bags underneath and he was still wearing the same clothes as yesterday.

"Why do you never do a damn thing I tell you to do." He hissed as soon as he saw me. His breathing was strong and his eyes were dark with anger.

I could smell the alcohol on his body before he had the chance to move any closer. Had he been out all night drinking? Nick hardly ever drank to this kind of state. In fact, I had never seen him drink more than three beers. Right now, he wasn't drunk but I had no doubt that a few hours ago he was.

"You don't control me." I stated. I got up from the sofa, but continued to keep the distance between us. I couldn't let him touch me, I knew I would cave in. I always did, his touch was too much.

"I know I don't but I wish you'd just fucking listen." He let out. He stood before me, his legs spread apart and his hands laid strongly beside him. His hands were rolled in to tight fists, either out of anger or to stop him from lunging to touch me. Maybe it was a bit of both.

"Listen? Why would I ever want to listen to you?" I pointed. Nick's brows furrowed in reply.

"I'm a dick, I know I am but I just need to explain." He sighed as I looked to him. "I need you."

"Maybe you should have thought about that before, one; speaking to me like shit last night after I had been touched up by somebody else and two; for not coming back to talk. Instead, you come home half cut and at four in the morning." I huffed. I didn't want to shout but he had to see that he was in the wrong. What he did was not on, I needed him to see that.

"Listen, I fucked up, I knew I would. I'm trying, I really am and I know what I did upset you, I know that. You have to forgive me." He pleaded. His angry eyes had vanished and now he was looking guilty and upset. Good, it served him right.

Even though it pained me to ever see him so upset, I knew that this was what he needed. He was going to fuck up and so was I, but that doesn't mean we both should get away with it. A little hurt and pain never hurts, I think it really did help.

However, I was still so super pissed.

"You fucked up." I stated and he sighed. His shoulders went slack as he looked to the floor. His hands dived in to his hair and he tugged gently.

"Forgive me, Cathy, God dammit." He pleaded some more. His face lifted until his pleading eyes were looking in to mine. "You can't break up with me, not now. I need this, I need you. You're the first girl I've ever wanted to spend time with outside of the bedroom. I couldn't stand to see girls the next morning because I never felt anything for them. I had pointless sex and that was it. With you, though, you're the only girl I've ever looked at in the morning and thought shit, I could do this for the rest of my life. I wouldn't tire looking at you, I couldn't tire being with you. You make me want to change, you make me want to be a better person."

"Nick-"

"No!" He shouted. "Can't you see? I'm a fucked up fool who's caught feelings for a girl who deserves the fucking world and more. Don't you see what it's like? I'm living my life so messed up. I'm twenty eight and I don't even know how to treat a girl. I especially don't know how to treat you, you're too good for me and I don't know how to make you stay." He stepped a little closer. His chest was heaving and his eyes turned dark as he drank my body in. I shivered at his look of appreciation.

"All you have to do is be on my side." I sniffed as tears began to fall. I couldn't stop them this time, no matter how hard I tried. "Aren't we supposed to be a team?" I questioned. "You know what I've been through, you know who I am." I stated.

"You're the most perfect girl in the whole world." Nick breathed. "I want to get to know you better, I just need you to stay. Tell me you forgive me."

"I forgive you." I sobbed. I ran over to him so fast I crashed in to his body. I clung on to him so tightly. "Don't be a dick again."

"I can't promise anything." Nick stated. "But I'll try my hardest for you."

"That's all I could ask for." I sniffed against his shirt.

"Stop crying, I can't bare to see you cry." His voice sounded pained. He grabbed a hold of my body until I was in his arms. He started to walk upstairs and I clung on tightly to his neck.

Nick opened my bedroom door and laid me down gently in my bed. I sniffled loudly.

"Where's my dad?" I asked. I hadn't thought about him since Nick had turned up and I was thrown out of my sleep.

"You don't want to know." Nick chuckled. I narrowed my eyes dangerously his way. He was already on a clear warning, he better tell me right now where my father is.

"Nick." I warned. He rolled his eyes gently, but the smile on his face made my heart melt.

"He found a woman in the pub. He's pretty smitten already." He winked. I looked to him with wide eyes. I groaned.

"What the hell?"

"I've never seen him with anybody else since he split up with your mum all them years ago." Nick stated. "I don't really know where they went but he's been gone for bloody hours."

"So you came here?" I asked. "You smell of beer." I crinkled my nose up in disgust. Nick's head fell in shame. He rubbed the back of his neck in an uncomfortable gesture.

"I went to the pub with your father and his friends. I was so pissed off with myself I guess one beer led to two and so on so forth." He sighed. "I should have came here sooner to see you. I'm so sorry for everything I've done." He looked so sincere, I had a hard time ever trying to stay pissed off at the guy.

"It's okay, I suppose. Do it again though and I'll knock your brain about in that thick skull of yours." I tapped his head gently. He grabbed my wrist and brought it to his mouth. I gasped when he kissed my skin.

His kisses went further up until he was kissing my neck. His body leaned over mine and I giggled loudly as he did so. He chuckled in to my neck, his happiness coming off of him in waves.

"I missed you." He growled against my neck. "And I've now discovered I hate doors."

"Why?"

"The amount of pounding I've had to do to get you to listen. They stand in the fucking way. I hate them." He pouted as he looked to me. "Nobody stands in the way of you and me."

"They're just blocks of wood." I stated. "I'm sure if you were that desperate to get to me you would have knocked the thing down."

"Trust me, I was so close to knocking the fucking thing down." Nick gruffed. "You have no idea how much it angered me to know I couldn't see you or touch you. I just needed you to listen to me. I couldn't bare the thought of you knowing how shit I had treated you without letting me have my word."

"Well, you deserved it." I stated. Nick smiled.

"You put me in my place, don't you, Angel?"

"Of course I do." I smiled back. "Would you have it any other way?"

"I could think of a few more ways to have you." He smirked. With that thought, I jumped on to his body and started kissing my way down it. He had the nicest body known to man.

He groaned.

"Are we going to have makeup sex now?" He asked, his voice sounding hopeful.

"We are, but we're doing this my way."

"Lead the way, Angel, take me with you."

"Always."

<h1 style="text-align:center">CHAPTER 15</h1>

As I laid on Nick's chest panting, he stroked my hair gently. I listened to his harsh breath ease, and his heart beating against his chest so frantically.

We didn't talk, we couldn't. The simplicity we laid in right now was worth more than a million words. Things were getting way too intense, too much, too soon. I felt that; I wondered if he did too.

The fact he had fought for me, stayed with me even after he had gotten what he wanted spoke volumes. He stated that he'd never see the girl again after their night together but he had me.

In fact, he kept on coming back.

Even the thought made me ecstatic. There was no lie that I was falling for Nick and way too fast, too. There was no lie that he effected me in so many ways. The fact that he may also feel the same way about me gave me so much hope and faith. Maybe things could work out for me, maybe I did deserve this.

I lifted my chin up and took in the face that was Nick Abel. He was absolutely gorgeous, there was no doubt about it. His chin was strong and sharp, his nose so small and cute. His brows were dominant and black, just as dark as his hair. His eyes shone so brightly you couldn't help but stare.

He truly was gorgeous and all mine.

Suddenly, his eyes flickered down to mine as he caught me staring. I smiled.

"What are you looking at?" He asked.

"You." I replied. Nick smiled down at me, his shy smile that did wicked things.

"Do you like what you see?" Nick asked as he smirked my way.

"You're not bad." Nick chuckled in reply.

His deep chuckle made my toes curl. God, I could never stop listening to it. I tingled all around.

"Stop." Nick growled out. I looked to him again in confusion. "You've got that look on your face." He stated. "And I know exactly what you want."

"Don't look at it then." I rolled my eyes with a cheeky smile. It wasn't my fault I wanted him again. I always wanted him, in anyway I could.

"You know I could never do that, Cathy." He replied seriously.

In silence we laid again. Nick held me close in his arms and I revelled in his touch. He was so warm and I snuggled closer to his body.

Luckily, my father was out but he could always come back. The thought didn't even cross my mind as I laid with Nick. I was content and happy in his arms, a place I wouldn't mind staying in forever.

"Oh, I forgot to tell you, we're going up Xavier's for dinner tomorrow." Nick stated. He looked to the clock and sighed. "Well, technically today." It was almost half six in the morning and I hadn't been asleep at all.

I didn't even feel that tired, not when I was high on Nick.

"Your cousin Xavier?" I asked. Nick nodded.

"Emily invited us up for dinner this evening. I told her you'd come with me."

"Sure." I replied. It was the first time I was ever going to meet a part of Nick's family. He didn't talk about his family much, the only people he did talk about was Xavier and Emily, and of course their baby boy Dean. Other than that, he hadn't mentioned anybody else.

I was nervous to say the least. Was this the first time Nick would be taking a girl to meet the family? It probably was. I just hoped they liked me, because I wanted to be with Nick more than anything.

"Don't panic, they will love you." Nick stated. It was easy for him to say. Of course I was going to panic.

"I'll try not to." I replied back. With that, I lifted my hand to touch the outline of one of Nick's chest tattoos. He sighed under my touch.

"Your touch does things to me."

"Oh yeah?" I breathed as I continued to touch him. The contrast between the two of us was striking. My tattoos were colourful and bright whereas Nick had no colour on him at all. We stood out together and I think for all of the right reasons.

"Yeah." Nick replied.

"Did you mean the things you said earlier?" I asked as I thought back. The things he said were everything I needed to hear from him.

"With every part of my body." He explained. "And you have absolutely no idea." Nick sighed. "In fact, I have absolutely no idea, no idea what's going on, what I'm feeling or why. I just know that I go out of my mind when you leave and I'm at peace when you stay. All I know is that you make this beat." He laid my hand to his chest, right where his heart is. "And this hard." He laid my other hand down below.

I gasped as I felt him.

"Nick." I moaned. His blazing eyes met mine.

"Believe me when I tell you I like you." Nick demanded. "Because I do. I fucking do."

I woke up as soon as the front door slammed against its hinges.

"Fucking hell." Nick moaned as he laid his forearm over his eyes. "This damned house is loud."

"I think it's dad." I mentioned. Nick's arm that was currently around my body squeezed tighter.

"Tell him to be quiet. I'm not used to anyone else being in my apartment but you so I don't get these kind of disadvantages." Nick removed his arm from his face. He looked to me with sleepy eyes. "Besides, I'm pissed off now."

"Why?" I asked as I sat up in bed. I looked back to him and yawned. He went to stick a finger in my mouth but I swatted him away with a scowl. He chuckled.

"I wanted morning sex." I rolled my eyes.

"You always want morning sex."

"Yeah well, I never got it before so now I keep wanting it with you." Nick sat up too as he stretched. My mouth watered at his muscled body. "Besides, I don't think your dad will mind." Nick smirked as he looked to me.

Just as I was about to open my mouth, Nick's body leaned over mine. He pushed me back down and laid his lips to mine. He was so soft, I couldn't help but moan.

And just like a bucket of cold water had splashed over the both of us, my dad spoke from outside my door.

"Cathy? You in?" His voice was soft and gentle.

"Yeah I'm in." Just as I was about to tell him that Nick was here too, the door opened.

My father barrelled in to the room and stopped short at the sight of Nick. It didn't help that he had nothing on under the covers. My face blushed so badly, I could feel the heat in my cheeks.

"Nick's here too." I mentioned, even though we all knew it was too late. I was old enough to have men in my bedroom, I knew, but it was still so embarrassing to have my father come in when both of us had nothing on.

I didn't think my father was used to it. I was an only child and my father had been without me for years.

"I'll count to five and if you haven't got clothes on in that time then I'm leaving to South Africa and I'm never coming back." Glenn mentioned. "I'll also have to change my name. How does Pablo sound?"

"Dad." I couldn't help but laugh. Nick frowned as he looked to my father.

"I don't know what you're frowning at, my boy. Get a move on." Glenn snapped his fingers.

"Fucking hell, Glenn." Nick mumbled under his breath. My father looked to him. "I can't get dressed if you're still here."

"Right." Glenn mumbled before leaving the room and closing the door behind him.

I let out a sigh of relief as soon as he was gone. I laughed nervously, but I was still blushing red.

"Red's a good colour on you." Nick smirked my way as he jumped out of bed. He took a hold of his clothes and chucked them on to his body in record time.

"Do one." I replied back. Nick laughed loudly but I was still in shock.

I got out of bed and made my way in to the bathroom. I did everything I needed to do before getting dressed. I chose denim shorts and a cropped t shirt.

"What time are we going?" I asked from the cupboard.

"Around three." Nick replied. He came up behind me to touch me on the arse as I bent over to grab my shoes. I looked around and glared at him. "I'm only touching what's mine."

"Get your hands off my bum." I demanded. Nick sighed but he did as he was told, even though he looked like a child as he pouted.

At three o'clock, Nick and I got in to his van. He hoisted me up and I sat in the passengers seat. We said good bye to my father, even though I felt so embarrassed, and then Nick started the engine and we got on to the bustling roads.

Nick turned on the radio and plugged in his phone. Music filled up the car.

"I didn't peg you as an Oasis fan." I stated. Nick smiled my way but he didn't say anything more. I didn't know whether he was remembering something or whether he just wanted to sit in peace.

I looked out the window as he drove. I took in the scenery before me. The trees, the fields and the many people and children around.

The van rattled as it drove, but the noise gave me comfort now rather than fear of the thing breaking. That said, he still needed a new van. Maybe I could get him one for his birthday. I didn't even know when his birthday was. There was still a lot Nick and I didn't know about each other, but I couldn't wait to find out more about him.

"I haven't told you this but you look hot." Nick's voice came out to snap me out of my reverie. I looked to him.

"Thanks, Nick." I replied. "That was so romantic." I winked his way.

"What can I say?" He shrugged arrogantly. "I'm a man of many talents." He said it as a joke, but so far I realised he was good at everything. He could sing, play guitar (which was hot) and he was amazing at his current job. I didn't doubt there was more he could do.

"You're an arrogant human being."

"If I make you think I'm good at everything and that I can give you everything, you won't want to leave me." Nick explained. The comment made my heart shatter. Did he want me to stay that much? It didn't help that his face was so serious.

"Pull over." I demanded. Nick looked to me as he steered the vehicle. His eyes went dark.

"Cathy-"

"Pull over, now."

"Shit." Nick whispered as he pulled over down a lane and came to a halting stop.

Before I even had the chance to talk or do anything, Nick took hold of my body and planted it on his lap. His nose found my neck and he breathed.

"You're a demanding little thing." He whispered as he kissed me. I moaned against him. "You're turning me inside out, for fuck sake." He growled. "You come in to my life, the tattooed beauty, you demand things and it turns me on, you talk and giggle and it turns me on."

"Nick." I moaned as he touched me. His kisses went up and then back down my neck.

"I can't get you out of my head, every time I close my eyes I see you. I'm going out of my fucking mind. It's killing me but saving me all at the same time."

"And you're saving me." I breathed. "I don't want to leave you, no matter how much you piss me off or how little you have. No one else can make me feel the way I do about you."

"Cathy, fuck." He squeezed his eyes shut and his nails dug in to the skin of my hip. I gasped at the slight pain but it only made me want him more.

I gripped on to his hair and I smashed his lips against mine. He moaned in to my mouth so loudly.

"You're never fucking leaving." He growled against my lips. "We've gone past that now. I'm in too deep."

"Me too." I breathed.

"You're not leaving." He repeated. "And if you do I'll find you. I found you once and I'll find you again and again and again. Believe me, Cathy, you're not getting rid of me."

"I wouldn't want to." I hissed out as I squeezed my eyes closed. Nick grinded below me. I let out a shaky breath.

"I want you." He said as he continued. "But not here. After this dinner I'm going to take you home and show you just how much I want you."

"Please." I moaned. Nick took my body off of his and sat me back down in my seat. I groaned again at the loss of contact.

Nick didn't speak as he reversed the car and we made our way back on to the road.

"I swear you're going to make me crash my car one day." Nick grumbled. "Damned girl making me fucking crazy."

I couldn't help but smile.

It didn't take long before Nick had parked up on the small drive way outside of a small home. It looked homely from the outside with dark brown brick and a red door. It was something I envisioned living in. Somewhere my thoughts were plagued with as I lived with Nick.

All those things were a bit too soon, but it never hurt to imagine them. The thoughts made me happy.

Nick got out of the van and came around to help me down. I loved being in his arms so this was my favourite thing about his van.

He took a hold of my hand and we made our way to the door. I was nervous, still, but what happened in the car left me relaxed anywho. No matter what happened, Nick wouldn't leave me.

Nick knocked on the door with the same strength and authority I've always known him to have. It was exceptional how he did things, and so very hot.

The door opened in two seconds, the beaming face of a blonde haired woman answered. She took my form in before wrapping her arms around me and pulling me in to a hug. I giggled and wrapped my arms around her. She was petite and small but so very beautiful.

"You've melted the ice king." She let out. I couldn't help but laugh some more.

Nick grumbled but the grip on my hand tightened. It was hard to hug and hold a hand at the same time, but Nick wouldn't let go.

As soon as Emily let go of my body, she took my form in again.

"I'm so excited. I can't believe this." She whispered to herself before grabbing my hand and pulling me inside. Nick let go of my hand just as soon as a little boy came bounding up to us.

"Uncle Nick!" He screamed as he launched his body in to the arms of Nick. Nick took hold of him and snuggled him close.

Shit, my ovaries were exploding.

If there was something more of a turn on than seeing a hot man with a baby then please let me know because God, I was ready to combust.

"Hey, Deano." Nick chuckled. "I hope you're still behaving."

"Yes, Uncle Nick, I want to be a police officer just like you." He giggled. "So I have to be good."

"Good boy." He kissed his forehead and then set him back down on the floor. Still, Dean didn't stray far as he took hold of Nick's hand and Nick walked him on to the decking out in the back.

I followed Emily until another man came up to us. He wore black and looked a little like Nick in some ways. This had to be Xavier.

"Xavier, this is Cathy and Cathy, this is my husband Xavier." Emily introduced us. Xavier nodded my way.

"Hey." I smiled as I took in the people around us. I didn't know anybody else and Emily didn't introduce us. They must have been friends.

It didn't take long before Nick was beside me again. Dean was still latched on to Nick's hand.

"Hey, Dean, this is my girlfriend Cathy." Nick squatted down beside him as he looked up to me. Dean smiled my way.

"I'm Dean. Uncle Nick calls me Deano." He was so small but so confident as he looked to me. He definitely took after his uncle Nick, or maybe even Emily. Xavier didn't seem at all that charming, but he was handsome and kind nonetheless.

"Hey, Deano." I smiled down at him. I squatted down just like Nick until I was eye level his way. He looked to the tattoos on my skin which were evident on my arms.

His little arm came out until he was touching one of them.

"I want one." Dean pouted. Nick and I both laughed at him.

"Not until you're a big boy." Nick replied. Dean nodded before running away from us both to get his toys. We both stood back up and Nick wrapped an arm around my waist.

"I love that boy." Nick sighed. "I think he likes you."

"He does?" I asked.

"Well, people say he's just like me. He's even starting to take fascination in your tattoos. That boy is going to love you."

The word love made my heart stutter. It seemed as if Nick didn't really know what he said. He smiled my way but I couldn't help but look at him.

I shook my head to banish my thoughts. When the time was right, the time was right. Right now, I wanted to enjoy time with his family. It meant a lot to me to be here.

Suddenly, Emily came barrelling over and she took hold of my hand. She pulled me away from Nick, and even though Nick didn't seem too happy about it, he still let go out my body.

"Don't frown, I'll bring her back." Emily stated.

She pulled me over until we were both sitting on one of the garden benches away from the crowd of people.

"You have a lovely home." I stated. "And a lovely boy."

"Who you talking about? Dean or Xavier?" She joked. I couldn't help but laugh. "Xavier isn't much of a socialist, but he'll get comfortable soon."

"I understand." I replied. Emily moved forward.

"You don't know how happy we are that Nick has finally met somebody. He's helped our relationship out so much, I think he deserves this. He was a bit of a play boy, you know, a ladies man and what not." She waved off. "But my God, Xavier and I didn't expect to see the day."

"It's hard to believe."

"For the record, he's crazy about you. Don't doubt that. I've never seen him like this, ever, and I've known him for a few years." Emily mentioned. "He's still staring at you now."

I looked around and true to her word, his eyes were on me. I smiled his way and he smirked before turning back around.

"He's totally in to you." Emily said. "I know that look, Xavier looks at me like that. That boy is head over heels."

"We're just taking things slow at the moment." I replied. "I'm in too deep and I don't want us getting hurt."

"Hurt is their middle names, darling." She sighed. "But they only love once."

"Love?"

"It's undoubtable and totally inevitable. You both may not know it yet but I can see it."

My heart stammered in my chest.

"I could recognise that look from anywhere." She looked to me and smiled. "There's no way you're getting rid of him now."

CHAPTER 16

As soon as the food was done on the barbecue, I followed Emily over to where the rest of the group was sitting. I cuddled in to the open side Nick had given me, his arms wrapped tightly around my body as soon as I got close.

Nick continued to talk to Xavier even though his eyes flicked down to my awaiting body. He held a beer in one of his tattooed hands and he was a hard slab of muscle beneath my finger tips.

When Xavier left Nick to help Emily with the food, Nick turned to me.

"Alright, baby?" He asked, his bright eyes focused on me. I nodded.

"I love your family." I said with a smile. "They're very welcoming."

"Of course they are, I've never brought a girl back to meet the family." He smiled my way, blowing me backwards at the sight of it. It had the ability to make any woman a panty dropper for him.

When did I ever get so lucky?

"Then I must be special." I replied back, humour dripping from my voice.

"You have no fucking idea." Nick muttered. He then turned from my body as he smelt the food coming our way. Nick took two burgers off of the tray and gave one to me with a small smile. I took it off of him gratefully.

With a burger in one hand and a beer in the other, he looked so appetising it hurt. I took his form in, drinking him in like a dog on heat. I tingled.

"Stop." I heard Nick's strangled voice come out from beside me. My eyes latched on to his in surprise. "Stop looking at me like that when we're in public. You don't want to be bent over the table in front of my family, do you?"

"I wouldn't mind being bent over." I shrugged as I smirked. He shook his head with exasperation before eating the remaining part of his burger. He then laid down his bottle on the table before grabbing my burger and putting it beside the half empty bottle.

Nick proceeded to grab my wrist before pulling me indoors. We met Emily on the way.

"Where are you taking her?" Emily asked Nick. Nick didn't stop in his tracks and Emily had a large smirk on her face, as if she knew exactly what was happening.

I didn't blush, I didn't need to. If Xavier was anything like Nick, she would have understood.

"We won't be long." Nick let out as he took me through the renaming parts of the house. However, just as we got to the front door, it opened. A man I had never met before entered the house which caused Nick to stop dead in his tracks.

As soon as the two men caught sight of each other, they both bristled with tension. Nick stood before me, his body stiff and unforgiving. I looked between the two men, really not sure what was happening.

The man before me was tattooed and had a ruffled dirty blond hairstyle. He was handsome, in his very own way. He didn't top Nick, I didn't think anyone would.

His eyes suddenly flickered down to mine, he smirked. Nick moved to the side to cover my body as he continued to stare the man down. It was clear to see these two men hated each other with a passion, what for? I didn't know.

Nick took hold of my hand behind him. I squeezed him tight.

"We've got places to be." Nick stated, his voice deep and menacing.

"Where are you going?" The man asked back.

"None of your business." Nick snapped. I heard the deep chuckle resonate across all walls. Nick stiffened.

"Why don't you stay? Introduce me to your girl, Nick."

"Fuck off." Nick growled.

"I'm just trying to be friendly." He feigned innocence, it didn't sound genuine.

"I've told you to fuck off."

"Introduce me."

With a huff, Nick took a hold of my hand and stormed off in the opposite direction, back out in to the back yard. He mumbled childishly under his breath as I struggled to keep up with him.

As soon as we got outside, Nick let go of my hand and stormed up to Xavier who was holding Emily tightly in his arms.

"Why didn't you tell me Michael was going to be here?" Nick hissed their way. Xavier patted him softly on the back as guilt was evident in his eyes.

Catching sight of me, Emily left Xavier's arms and made her way over to me. I was grateful somebody was going to save me, or maybe to tell me what the hell was going on.

"I'll just let them boys talk." She said sheepishly. I looked to her, one brow arching.

"Who's Michael?"

"An old pal, I suppose." She shrugged. "Nick and Michael don't get along, at all." Emily laughed nervously.

What is it she wasn't telling me?

"Why not?"

"They're similar people, personality clash and all that."

"Are you lying?" I asked. Emily looked to me, a piece of hair in between her finger and her thumb. She couldn't look at me, she wouldn't.

"No." She huffed. "Yes." She turned to me and whined. "Don't tell Nick I told you, please, you've got to promise me." Her hands came across to squeeze my shoulders as she pleaded.

"I won't." I replied. "I promise."

"Right." Emily took hold of my hand until we were seated in the living room, away from prying ears. She sat down beside me. "Michael is a bit of a man slag, just like Nick."

I looked to her, she spluttered.

"Not anymore!" She shrieked. She calmed herself down before continuing. "What I mean is-"

"I know what you mean." I replied, to urge her to continue with the original story.

"Anyway, they've always been in competition with each other, especially when it comes to the women they sleep with. They've had each others sloppy seconds, so on so forth-"

"Gross." I scrunched my nose up in disgust. The jealousy moving inside my body was painful, it twisted around my heart and pulled. I didn't want to think about Nick and his activities with other women. I tried to forget about it, so it wouldn't effect me. But truthfully, it hurt more than anything.

"Yeah." Emily sighed. "That's all there really is to it."

"Is that it?" I asked. There had to be more to it than that, their hatred for each other rolled off of them in waves.

"That's it."

"Then why wasn't I allowed to know?"

"Nick is very clear that Xavier and I are not to tell you personal matters. I kind of agree with him, he's always been so reserved and I suppose he would rather tell you himself." Emily stated. "It's not nice hearing things from others when it should be fromhim."

"You're going on like they're all bad things."

"Most of them are, I'm sure he's told you something, right?" She looked to me, her eyes on mine with intensity. I wanted the ground to swallow me up. No, Nick hadn't told me anything about his past or who he was before I met him.

Was that a good thing or a bad thing? Shouldn't he have told me something by now? What was he keeping from me?

Shit, I had all these questions running around my head but no answers. The only person to give me the answer was the man outside, going rampant because his frenemy had entered the building.

"By the look on your face, he hasn't told you anything has he?" I shook my head in reply. "That's okay, it takes time, it's a hard thing telling someone else about your past."

It was hard, I knew that first hand. I had laid myself open to Nick and he hadn't even bothered to meet me halfway.

Irritation started swimming around in my veins.

"It is hard." I repeated. It was fucking awful, the worst thing I ever had to do was to tell Nick about my scarring past.

With that, I got up from the sofa with a quick smile to Emily. We were going to get along so well.

"You're the best." I stated her way.

"Don't have to tell me twice." She smiled back. I gave her a quick hug as a thank you. A thank you for telling me something Nick should have told me and a thank you for letting realisation dawn on me.

I needed to know more about Nick. Would he be open to tell me? I didn't know, but I had to find out.

I left the living room and made my way back outside. Now, Nick was sat on the table with a sulking expression in his face. I went over to him.

"Hey." He wrapped his arm around me.

"Hey."

"Are you sulking?" I asked. He looked to me and smiled.

"I guess I am." He shrugged before taking another swig of beer.

"Aren't you driving?"

"We could always get a taxi." He shrugged again. Simple. It was always that simple with Nick.

"I need to ask you something." I stated. His brow arched as he looked to me. "Why haven't you told me anything about your past?"

Suddenly, Nick stood up straight.

"What's Emily said?" He asked, his eyes setting in to panic but his lips going straight. He didn't look happy, not one bit.

"Nothing." I let out quickly. I didn't want her getting in to trouble, not when she hadn't done anything wrong. "I was just wondering why you haven't told me anything."

"There's nothing to tell you, that's why." Nick let out. "I had a boring childhood and a boring adult hood."

"Nick-"

"Enough." He snapped. His eyes were swimming with irritation.

"Nick-"

"I said enough." His voice took on a menacing tone.

Jesus, I was just asking, he didn't have to speak to me like that.

With that, I huffed his way before turning my back to him and stalking forward.

"Cathy!" He called after me. I ignored him. "Shit." He whispered.

I continued to walk forward until the next thing I knew, I was stalking forward in to a hard chest. The wind was knocked out of my body as I crashed.

"Woah." The voice came out. "Watch out, sweetheart." I looked up and found myself face to face with Michael himself. He really was handsome, but he did nothing for me.

His tattooed arms came out to steady me. I couldn't help but flinch away.

"You should watch where you're going." He smirked my way, his eyes alight with humour. I turned my head but Nick was not in his current position. No, he had gone, disappeared just like that.

"You should watch where you're going, too." I stated. "It takes two to tango." I pushed past his body and made my way in to the kitchen. I grabbed a drink from the counter.

Michael followed me in to the kitchen until he was leaning against one counter. He watched me.

"You seem pissed off." I took hold of my drink again and took a swig. Oh, he was observant. Of course I was pissed off, I had every right to be. I didn't mean to pry, I would never do it to be nosy, I just thought he'd tell me something, lay a little bare just like I had to him. In fact, I was all too quick in telling him my dirty secrets.

When I ask about his past, he talked to me like some little child. I wasn't going to stand for that.

"I am." I stated back. I had no shame.

"What's he done this time?" He smirked.

"That's none of your business." God, I was starting to sound exactly like Nick.

"Well, if you're not happy with him-"

"I'm more than happy, thank you." More than anyone would ever know. Nick made me forget things I've always wanted to forget. He made me happy, made me feel things. I had never felt so alive. This man had a nerve.

My irritation was growing by the second.

Suddenly, Michael stalked forward. I walked back until my back hit the back door. He continued to stalk my way.

"What are you doing?" I questioned, warning in my voice.

"You're Nick's girl, but I'd happily make you my girl." He smirked. "Tell me, have you had sex yet?"

"Get the fuck away from me." I spat.

"Come to me when he dumps you on the street." He said. I couldn't swallow past the lump in my throat.

"He's not going to leave me." I said confidently. "We like each other. We're together."

"He's amped things up a bit, has he?" He mused. Michael took a piece of my hair in between his fingers. "That's not like him."

"I'll kick you in the balls." I threatened. Michael chuckled.

"I love how feisty you are." He said my way.

"You think this is a joke?" I questioned. "Nick's my boyfriend, so get the fuck away from me."

"I can give you more."

"No-"

"Yes." His stubborn voice came back out. I squeezed my eyes shut.

"Leave me alone." I punctuated every word.

"Cathy, you know he's not worth your-" before he could finish his statement, Nick had him by the throat.

I gasped loudly as I took in their figures. Michael was held against the pillar in the kitchen whilst Nick's hand was wrapped around his neck. He held on so tightly, Michaels face went red almost immediately.

"She's mine." Nick growled. I stood still, in shock at the sight of them.

Fuck, Nick would kill him, I knew he would.

"Get the fuck off me." Michael wheezed. Nick let go of his throat, but before Michael could move, Nick laid a hard punch to his face. Michael fell to the floor.

"I gave you all my sloppy seconds, you could take them, I didn't give a fuck, but this girl's mine. Touch her again and I'll kill you." Nick spat.

"I want her, too." Michael let out.

"She's fucking mine!" Nick roared. He laid a kick to his rib cage, Michael groaned out.

"Jesus, Nick." I gasped, not knowing what to do or how to stop this. Nick's knuckle was bleeding from the impact, but he didn't seem to notice the pain.

As if they could hear the noise coming from the kitchen, Xavier and Emily came running in to the room. Xavier took a hold of Nick as soon as he saw the scene. Emily stood with her hand across her chest.

"Nick, I swear to God, this kitchen is new." Emily moaned. "There's blood everywhere." She looked distraught at the mess.

It was clear to see that Emily was used to the fights that went down in her life. It was also clear to see that none of them had taken place in her kitchen.

"Lay another hand on her, mate, and I will fucking kill you." Nick growled. "She's not just another lay, she's my girlfriend and she's fucking mine. Go and find someone else to play your mind games with because this girl is taken."

"Nick, that's enough." Xavier let out.

"She's mine." Nick said again. His eyes were wild with panic and anger as he looked to the man beneath him.

"I know, Nick, I know. Come on." Xavier tried to get him to move, but he was still out of control. His chest heaved as he stood there. My heart broke just looking at him, he was so distressed.

"Nick, move away, baby." I said. I moved forward, Xavier looked to me with warning but I ignored him. Nick was my boyfriend, he needed me.

I took his face softly in to my hands and waited until his eyes finally flickered my way. As soon as he took me in, he sighed, relief evident throughout. Without another warning, Nick smashed his lips down to mine with violence and roughness.

I didn't care about the people around us, not when Nick needed me the way he did.

"Don't you miss the passion, Xavier?" Emily asked dreamily. I couldn't hear her, not when the blood was rushing around my body with need.

"I give you passion, Angel." Xavier mused. "You know I'm still waiting for baby number two."

"Before you get excited, I'm going to check on our first spawn." Emily sighed. "All this noise and my baby's probably still sleeping." Emily left the scene before her.

My arms wrapped around Nick's neck as I pulled him tighter to my body. The anger and irritation of the last hour was evident in the way he kissed me. I loved it, loved the need and passion he exerted in to it. It got me all kinds of hot.

"Come on." I heard Xavier grunt as he picked up the body on the floor. He carried him out of the kitchen and took him else where. Michael groaned as he was moved.

"Nick." I moaned against Nick's lips as soon as we were alone.

"I'm sorry." He took my face in to his large hands. I sighed at his touch. "I'm a mess, I have been since I've met you. Everything you do makes me crazy."

"You know you're not the only one."

"It's easier when you know how much you deserve."

"And you don't?" I asked. I searched his eyes for something, anything, but he was blank. All I saw was the affection shining my way.

"I see you in my dreams, kissing men who are not me." He whispered. "I see you finding what you deserve."

"Nick, I only want you, why can't you see that?"

"I wake up gutted, gutted that I know I'm not what you need. But, I'm happy, happy you could see your way past me. I'm fucking selfish, Cathy, I'll keep you because I don't want you to go, even when I know you're better off without me."

"Don't be fucking stupid." I snapped. "You're everything I needed, you're everything I have ever wanted."

I loved him, why couldn't he see that?

I admit it now, I fucking loved him.

And there was nothing I could do about it.

"You fight for me, and that means a lot to me." I mentioned, just as realisation had hit me like a ton of bricks. It scared me, but I reveled in the way it felt.

"You deserve to be fought for."

And even though I couldn't quite believe him, I took his face in to my hands and kissed him again.

"Nick, do you believe in magic?"

He replied, "No." against my lips.

"Okay." I smiled.

"That was random." He stated.

I shrugged but I didn't say another word. I looked to him, stared right in to his soul. I wish he could feel the way I felt for him, I wish he would know without me having to tell him and scare him off.

He looked right back at me, his eyes almost searching my soul in return.

I love you, Nick.

He blinked, but he didn't say a word.

CHAPTER 17

"I'm not wearing one of them." Nick looked to me with disgust evident on his face. As I held up the small bandage, Nick was visibly hating on the thing.

"Why not? Your hands look battered." They were bloodied and bruised from the impact of Nick's strength. It amazed me just how physically strong he was and how willing he was to keep me safe.

"There just a few scratches, babe." He mentioned. He sat before me, his legs spread wide and his body now one of calm and relaxation. I stood before him, dangling the bandage in front of his face.

"Stop being a baby." I muttered. I went to grab his hand but he moved it out of reach. I huffed. It did nothing to stop him from smirking my way, his chest moving slowly up and down as he watched me with darkened eyes.

"Drop the bandage and sit on my lap."

"Excuse me?" I spluttered. The small demand had my heart racing. I'd sit on his lap any day of the week. His muscles were just too strong and muscly to resist.

"Drop the bandage." He demanded slowly, his tongue forming the words so seductively.

I couldn't help but drop the bandage right to the floor. I stood before him waiting for my next command. This was a thrilling game, one he knew so well to play.

"Come here." His voice was rasping as he patted his thigh. I didn't waste another second as I scrambled in to his legs. Once I was straddling him, I laid my head against his heart. He was so tall, I fitted him like a glove.

His arms came around my body, his hands rubbing small circles in to my back. I had chance to finally let out the breath I was holding. He was the most intense man I had known to date, it didn't help that he liked to beat up everything in his way for me. I relished in the feeling, even though it was quite a scary thought. What if one day he really hurt himself? I couldn't live with myself if I knew it was because of me.

"You're a stupid man." I said in to his chest. He continued to rub circles on my back. He let out a shaky breath.

"Tell me about it."

"No, I'm serious Nick. One day you're going to get yourself seriously hurt. Couldn't you have just talked, man to man, face to face?"

"Men talk with their fists." Nick stated.

"Do they?" I questioned sardonically. "I don't think they always do."

"Well, I do." He replied. "I'm not saying sorry for protecting you and I never will. The prick deserved it and I'd rather make sure you're safe, that's the most important thing to me."

"You're a brave, stupid, stupid, man." I breathed.

"And you're my woman." Nick replied. "Fuck trying to be civil and talk like men. I'll fight for what's mine, I'll show everybody in this place exactly who is off limits."

"Nick-"

"I'm not arguing about this." Nick injected. "I'm not arguing about how I'll protect you. I'm doing it my way, I'm doing it the the only way I know how."

"Fine." I huffed. I got up to look at him, his stormy eyes caught me off guard. "You know I'm still grateful, right? For everything you've done for me in these last few months."

"You better know I'm grateful, too." Nick smiled, his pearly whites on display for everybody to see. It really did knock me for ten.

I snuggled back in to his chest. We stayed silent, basking in each others silence and company for as long as possible.

It wasn't long before Emily was bounding in to the room again with Xavier right on her heel. I smiled at the sound of her calming but bubbly voice. She reminded me of the girl I used to be, before everything had changed my life for the worst.

"I swear I was there for decades trying to rub the blood up from the kitchen floor." Emily huffed. "Yeah, that's fine Nicholas, punch the guy and then sit on your arse like a king. Your peasants will do all the hard work."

Nick chuckled beneath me.

"My hand hurts like a motherfucker." He stated. "But thanks for doing my dirty work."

"It looks sore, mate." Xavier said as he sat on the sofa beside us.

"I tried getting him to wear a bandage." I heard a loud laugh in the distance. Emily looked to me with one of hysterical humour and pity.

"You won't get any one of them boys to wear a bandage, it's like satan in their eyes."

"Just let the air get to the wounds instead of fussing." Nick rolled his eyes as he stated his words. I looked to him and copied. Nick smiled my way and I couldn't help but smile back.

"You guys make me sick." Emily said, but her face said otherwise. "You're like love sick puppies."

"As if." Nick scoffed. I half expected him to comment on the 'love' part, however, he didn't. "I'm too manly to be a puppy."

"I like puppies." I replied.

"In that case, I'll be a puppy." Laughter erupted around us. Nick chuckled, but he looked my way, his eyes crinkling with happiness.

I took him in, all of his beauty and more. He was enchanting, he really was. And yes, he had a ruggedly handsome face and an amazing body, but there was just so much more beneath him that pulled me to him. I had never felt anything like this, he brought feelings I had never experienced.

The topic of conversation changed quickly before I had chance to catch up. I could stare at Nick all day, but I'd never get anything done.

"How's that death trap of yours?" Xavier asked, his attention moving from the TV to Nick.

"I love the death trap." I jumped to its defence. It was rattly and rusty, but it worked like a dream. The way Nick drove it, too, was enough to really get my body going. He handled the van with so much power and authority, I just couldn't help but keep looking.

He made it look so easy.

"You do?" Nick questioned.

"I do." I nodded. "I think it would be fun to drive."

"You want to drive it?" Curiosity peaked in his eyes.

"I do, actually." I shrugged. "I've never driven a truck before."

"Neither have I, actually." Emily said. "It does look fun." She smiled my way. I nodded.

"It's just like driving a normal car." Nick chuckled. "You women have weird fantasies."

"And you men don't?" Emily scoffed. "Double standards."

"Nick, I wouldn't wind her up tonight, you know she shouts at me." Xavier said, his voice full of humour but still serious, too.

"It's fine, Cathy and I are a team." Emily stated. "We've finally balanced the ratio of men to women."

"You know damn well that Cathy is on my team." Nick replied.

"Like hell."

The arguments and banter went back and forth as the night progressed. It was a few minutes passed midnight when Nick decided it was time to head home.

"I hope you both come up to see us extra soon, it's been so fun having you along." Emily took me in to her arms. "I've left my number on a piece of paper. Just ring me if you ever need to." She smiled as she handed me the piece of paper. I took it gratefully.

"You'll be hearing from me."

She turned to Nick as I hugged Xavier goodbye.

"Hate you." Emily said to Nick. He moved out of the threshold of the front door.

"Hate you more." He stated as he walked to the van on his drive. Emily laughed as she watched us.

We both clambered in to the van and Nick got the van in to motion. We waved out the window and made our way out of the drive way. It only took a few more seconds before we were heading home.

Nick turned the radio up as we sped down the country lanes. He looked relaxed as he took us home. I looked out of the window and hummed quietly to the songs I knew.

I loved Emily and Xavier. It was easy to see that Nick was close with both of them and that they all adored each other dearly. It was amazing to see Nick so relaxed and calm in the presence of others. I loved seeing Nick so happy and content.

Just as I thought we had to go straight to go back home, Nick turned right, until we were driving up narrower country lanes. My head snapped his way.

"I think you went the wrong way." I stated. Nick smiled.

"No, I didn't."

"Then what are you doing?" I asked.

"Making your little dreams come true."

"What is that supposed to mean?" I asked again. He looked amused as he stopped the calm in the middle of a dirt road track.

"You said you wanted to drive the truck." He shrugged.

"What? Here?" I questioned, worry setting in. Only because he was a cop, didn't mean I thought we were safe from getting in trouble. "I don't want to ruin your truck."

"I wouldn't let you ruin it." He said with a smile. With a smile of my own, I didn't even have to think anymore as excitement bubbled through my veins.

"Are you sure now?" I asked again. I didn't want him to be gutted if I actually did ruin his beloved truck.

Without another word, Nick picked me up until I was in the drivers seat and he was in the passengers seat. Nick buckled me up tightly.

"I haven't driven a normal stick for years." I said as I fondled the steering wheel.

"Well, biker girl, lets see how well you do."

With that, I started the engine, put the stick in to gear and revved. I smiled devilishly his way. I opened our windows all the way to let the cold night air in, and released the handbrake gently.

To get used to the truck, I started off slow and steady. After a few minutes, I was ready. With a small smile, I put the accelerator to the floor and watched as the speed of the truck grew fast.

" 'atta girl." Nick smiled my way.

My hair whipped across my face as I sped through the dirt road track and got to a field so big I couldn't see anything else around us. I sped on the grass, the mud flicking upwards behind us.

I screamed with joy as the truck sped faster and faster by the second. The wind was refreshing against my skin. I was loving every second of this.

Adrenaline sped through my veins but peace over came my every feeling.

This was being adventurous, this was being the old me.

I welcomed back the old me with a new perspective. Nobody could bring me down again, not when I had Nick by my side.

NICK

I couldn't take my eyes off of her.

It didn't matter what she did, she did everything so sexily. I had never seen anyone drive a truck so amazingly in all of my life.

My heart felt like a fucking rocket.

Her hair whipped across the truck but what really got me was the smile on her face. Not the flirty smile, or the shy smile I had gotten used to seeing, no, this smile was made of pure happiness and joy.

I would walk across hot coal to see that smile again. If I could see that smile every day of my life, I'd be a very, very happy man. It made me feel so intensely, but joy and pleasure was not something I was used to feeling.

Now, I welcomed it with every fibre in my body.

"Fuck." I said as the truck sped across the field beyond.

"Cathy." I tried to grab her attention. She couldn't hear me, she was in her own world as she handled the vehicle we sat in.

Feelings over took me so strongly I couldn't think straight.

Would it always be like this?

I only had to look at her and I was a done man. I would do anything she asked me to, just to see her happy. I would put my own life on the line because that was how much I wanted to see her happy and smiling.

I was fucking whipped, but I couldn't give a shit.

I had never wanted to say the L word. I hadn't since I was a few years old to my parents.

But this, this was all too much. Her scent drove me wild, and my throat was having a hard time keeping the words in.

I wanted to shout it. I wanted the whole world to know it.

I wanted to know if it was killing her like it was killing me.

"Cathy." I tried to get her attention again, my heart beating fifty miles a second in my chest.

She shouted in joy as she spun the car around.

"Fucking hell." I whispered as she laughed.

There was no doubt in this world that this woman was for me. My heart would tear out of my chest if she left me now.

"This is so fun." She giggled like a little school girl. Everything went hard. My world stopped.

"Keep going, baby." I said, even though I was sure she couldn't hear me anymore.

"Nick!" She screamed my name as she turned on the grass again. We skidded a little, and she laughed.

I groaned at the pain I felt. All these feelings, all too soon. So intense, too much for me to handle. I didn't know how she felt about me, but I knew exactly how I felt about her. It didn't take a genius to know it when you felt it.

My fucking God did I feel it.

"For fuck sake." I groaned. "I love you."

The words escaped my lips so fast I couldn't stop them.

She didn't hear me, but she looked to me once I said them.

Her eyes were bright as the car kept moving.
I had fallen in love.
And she smiled as if she knew it, too.

CHAPTER 18

Nick carried me out of the truck as I laughed in his arms. His face was almost as happy as mine, his eyes twinkling as he looked to me.

"You're fucking beautiful." He breathed. I couldn't help but let my smile grow. Everything was going so well and I was so happy. I wanted to cling on to these memories forever and to never let them go.

Nick buckled me in to the passenger seat before placing himself back in to his seat and holding on to the wheel. Exhaustion took over my body fiercely and I yawned.

"You look tired, baby." Nick stated.

"I am." I couldn't help it. All this excitement and fighting today was enough to make anyone exhausted. I couldn't wait to get to bed.

"Fall asleep, Cathy. I'll take you to bed once we're home." My eye lids fell and they went heavy with tiredness. I couldn't help but let sleep evade me as the gentle rumble and noise of the truck lulled me in.

The engine had stopped only ten minutes later and I was back in Nick's arms. He carried me gently in to his apartment and in to bed where he stripped me out of my clothes with so much care and affection, my heart leapt in my chest.

I woke up to look at him.

"Hi." I croaked his way. His eyes flew to mine and he smiled.

"Hi."

He gently pushed me down in to bed once my clothes were off. Once I was in, he stripped and laid in to bed next to me. I couldn't take my eyes off of his body, no matter how tired I was.

Nick pulled me in to his arms and I sighed with content.

"Thank you." I muttered, indoctrinated by my own happiness and joy.

"For what?" Nick asked, his voice deep and his breath tickling my ear. I wiggled against him and he hissed through his teeth.

"For everything." I replied.

"You never need to thank me." His voice was now gruff and as I wiggled against him more, he laid his hands roughly on my hips and thrust forward. "You need to stop."

"Why?" I smiled mischievously.

"Because you're tired and I won't be able to stop myself."

"Then don't stop." I replied.

With a small growl coming from Nick, he pushed me on to my back and got on top of me awaiting body.

This was the life.

Nick and I had hardly gotten any sleep. It was now 5 in the morning and we were still up. Now, we were talking about things and just generally getting to know each other. He was my boyfriend, but I didn't mean I knew he more than anything just yet.

Hopefully, that would change.

"So your mum never found out?" Nick asked, his eyes full of worry and anger.

"Never." I replied. "I kind of hoped she never did, I was mortified at myself and at him." I shrugged. It was hard when I didn't want anything more than to tell her. I couldn't, he made sure I never did. But also, I was embarrassed, what if she didn't believe me? I loved my mother and in Australia, she was all I had.

"It makes sense." He sighed. With a small silence beginning to fold, I sat up a little straighter.

"What about your mum?"

"What about her?" He was already getting defensive as he moved on to his back. I followed him.

"Come on, Nick, give me something."

Nick sighed loudly.

"She's dead." He stated, matter of factly. I gasped.

"I'm so sorry." I couldn't help but sympathise.

"Please, I don't want your pity, just forget I told you."

"Nick." I took hold of his hand. "They're your family, I know it's hard talking about things it's just, you can't keep it in and let it over take you."

"I don't want to talk about it." Nick replied like I little boy. I sighed in defeat.

"Okay, fair enough." I laid back down on my back and began to close my eyes.

"Don't be mad at me." I heard his voice come from beside me.

"I'm not." And I wouldn't be. I understood that people told information in their own time. It was the hardest thing to ever do and even though I felt extremely vulnerable as my darkest secrets were out there, I still understood.

Everybody was different and you couldn't ever expect anybody to do the things you did. I didn't have to tell him and he doesn't have to tell me.

"Do you promise?" He questioned. I always see other sides of him since being with him. He had a soft and insecure side, his most vulnerable side, and he let it show.

"I promise." I replied. I turned over to lay on his chest and he sighed. He wrapped me up tightly. He didn't have to say anything but I knew he was thankful.

At precisely half 8, I woke up to get ready to go to work. Today, I promised my dad I would help him at Tattoo Rouge. I regretted it as soon as my exhausted head decide to pound.

Great.

I was already moody, groggy and sleep deprived. This wasn't going to be good. I was also hungry, which added fuel to fire. I hope my father could forgive me for my bad mood today.

Nick was also tired and groggy today as he drove me in to work. He hadn't said much since waking up and even though it didn't scare me, it still made me worried. I wondered what was eating him- if anything. He could just be tired.

"Are you working today, too?" I asked. Nick turned down the radio a notch before replying.

"Yeah, until four." He stated.

"I finish at half three I think." I replied. "I'll start dinner before you're home."

"Sounds good."

"That's if you want me there?" I questioned. It wasn't that I felt rude staying at Nick's place, it was just that the way Nick was acting this morning, I thought maybe he would want time on his own.

"No, come. I want you with me."

"Are you sure?"

"Of course I am." He flickered his eyes my way. "You know I sleep better if you're beside me."

With that, Nick pulled up in front of Tattoo Rouge. I leaned over to lay a small kiss on his cheek.

"Is that all I get?" He asked with a small smirk. I smiled. With that, I pulled his face down to mine and laid my lips against his.

Once I pulled away, Nick smiled.

"That's better."

I left the truck with a bigger smile on my face than I entered the truck with. Maybe my groggy mornings wouldn't be so bad after all if I had Nick beside me.

I entered the parlour ten minutes before my shift started. I was extremely lucky to have gotten this job as soon as I moved back home with my father. He knew I was artistic but I didn't really have the experience he did. We were both lucky that everything turned out fine in the end.

"Hello, stranger." My father was at the front desk as soon as I walked in. The quiet buzz of music played in the background and also the quiet buzz of the tattoo needles working their magic. It was soothing.

"Dad." I beamed his way. I walked around the counter to sit on a stool and began drawing some rough sketches as I waited for some more customers.

"The bastards hogging you." Dad grunted as he continued to work beside me, his glasses perched on the top of his nose.

"Don't be grumpy." I laughed.

"Well, I've only just got you back and now he's just whipped you off your feet. Fucking boy." He shook his head but a small smile played on his lips. "Him, out of all the people you could have gone for."

"He really isn't that bad." I stated. "He's treated me better than anyone has ever before. He's amazing, dad." I couldn't help but feel like a melted puddle every time I talked about him.

Suddenly, Glenn whipped around on his stool to face me. A knowing smile played on his lips but worry was still evident. I looked to him and he sighed.

"I know that look." He pointed out. I looked to him in confusion. "That look of love and admiration."

"Dad-"

"Just be careful, okay? He's my bestfriend and I know him more than anyone. I trust him but I'm not exactly feeling comfortable at the moment. I know what he's like, Cathy, trust me."

"I'll be careful, dad, I promise." I replied. "Trust me, I really like him." Glenn came over to wrap his arms around me.

"I know you do, but I'm your father and all I'll ever do is worry."

"You know I love you."

"You too, Birdie, always."

After the heart to heart with my father, customers started to file in and the shop got busy. My father and I set to work for the day and I was able to finally breathe and take my mind off of things that I didn't need to worry about.

Nick hadn't texted or rung all day so I assumed he was busy working, as was I. I missed him terribly but the time away was also refreshing even if it was only for a few hours. I think I would always miss him now, no matter how long we were without each other.

At four o'clock, I said goodbye to my father and left the parlour. As Nick was working, I decided to walk and take the bus back to his apartment.

The walk was refreshing and slow, I had enough time to put my headphones in and listen to music as I let myself think of everything I needed to think of. It was nice to relax a little, especially when everything was so intense with Nick.

I had fallen for him, hard and fast, there was no doubt about it. I wondered if he felt the same but I didn't want to dwell on that too much. People feel things at different times, I had to realise that, even though knowing he felt the same way about me as I did him would be extremely nice and would stop me from worrying.

Nick was a man I had never had the pleasure of being with before. He was everything and more at the moment, and I couldn't wait to spend more time with him.

I got on to an awaiting bus and after five minutes I was outside of Nick's apartment. At the small corner shop I picked up some fresh ingredients to make Nick a nice meal with. After that, I entered the apartment building and made my way to his floor, juggling the bags as I went.

With one of the spare keys under the mat outside of his door, I opened the apartment and made my way inside.

I dropped my bags and almost screamed at the figure in front of me.

"What the fuck!" I shouted. The figure turned around and in front of me was an older looking woman in a long flowered dress. She had striking eyes and greying hair. "Who the hell are you?" I asked, not meaning to be so harsh but I was a little bit creeped out to see somebody else in Nick's apartment.

"Who the hell are you?" She replied back, her voice husky as if she had cigarettes on the daily. She held herself with grace and poise, even though something was totally off.

"I'm his girlfriend." I stated back, keeping the door open so I could run if needed be. I had my phone in my hand ready to call Nick. "Now tell me who you are and what you're doing in his apartment." I let out firmly.

I was going to be so pissed off if this woman was one of Nick's one night stands. I didn't think he liked older women.

"I'm Nick's mother." I forced a laugh.

"He said his mother was dead." I said. "Nice try." I narrowed my eyes at her, she held her chin up strong.

"Well, that's not surprising." She muttered. "He's obviously lying to you, darling, because I'm standing right here."

I took a second to step back and look at her. Her eyes were almost as striking as Nick's but I wouldn't say the resemblance between the two was all that uncanny.

"He looks like his father." She interjected. I looked to her, really unsure who this woman was. Has Nick been lying to me?

"Where is he then?" I asked. He had said his mother was dead and now she was here, he could be lying about everything else he had told me.

"He's dead." She replied. "He died when Nick was about seventeen years old." She sighed. "He doesn't tell you much, does he?"

"Yeah, well, at least he doesn't tell people that I'm dead." I replied back defensively. She was obviously judging me and everything I stood for. She was judging our relationship and I would never stand for that.

Even though I was pissed off with him.

"I don't know why he did that."

"There must be a reason."

Just as she was about to reply, I felt Nick's presence behind me. Just him being here now really did irritate me. He was a liar and I was never going to stand for that, especially off him. I had a bad past too, but I never even dared to lie to him.

How fucking dare he?

I turned around with such speed my head went dizzy. I took him in, his body lined in his uniform. I wish he wasn't so hot.

"You fucking liar." I said his way, harshness and sadness dripping from every word. He opened and closed his mouth like a fish, his eyes wide and in shock. He didn't know what to say and how to do it.

With that, I pushed past him.

"Cathy." His voice was full of emotion but I didn't bother turning around and running back in to his arms.

"Leave me alone." I demanded. "How dare you fucking lie to me, especially when I told you everything about me." I pointed his way. He stepped back in shock at how pissed off I was at him and at how serious he knew this was.

"Please-"

"Leave me the fuck alone." I hissed before stalking off down the stairs. I didn't bother with the lift, I just ran and ran until I was finally outside. I was able to take in a well needed breath as my eyes started to well up.

I took my phone out of my pocket and decided to ring Danni. I didn't want to go home where Nick would know where I was. Also, I didn't want my father seeing me upset.

She answered after the third ring.

"Bitch." She greeted. I sniffled. "Oh no, what's wrong?"

"Can I stay with you for tonight?"

"Sure!" She gushed. "What's he done, now?"

"I'll tell you when I get there."

"Okay, hurry. I'll get some ice cream and wine."

"You're the best." I said as I was able to smile.

"I know." She replied.

I hung up the phone and started walking to the bus stop. Luckily Danni's apartment wasn't that far away from Nick's, but hopefully he wouldn't find me there, not tonight anyway. I didn't want him knocking down doors and ringing me all night, making things worse.

With that, my phone rang, it was Nick. I turned it off and put it in to my hand bag.

Just as I got on to the bus, I saw Nick running out of the building, searching the streets with a look of panic on his face. He didn't see me but I saw him and it was enough to depress me even more.

Yeah, he looked petrified and upset but he had no right lying to me in the first place.

This could have been avoided if he would just tell me the truth.

I was never going to judge.

CHAPTER 19

"What's he done?" Danni asked as soon as I barrelled in to her apartment with tears streaming down my cheeks.

"It's complicated." I sniffed. Danni sat me down on her small leather couch and sat beside me, waiting to listen.

"I'm the master of complicated." She stated. "So, tell me."

"He said his mother was dead." I looked to her. Danni looked to me with confusion on her face. "She isn't, she was just in his apartment once I got back from work."

"Well, fuck me sideways." She let out breath. "There is obviously a rational reason for this."

"I know, I know there probably is." I laid a hand to my head. "It's just the fact he lied to me, Danni. I told him about my past and he doesnt trust me with his."

That's what hurt the most. If I hadn't had told Nick my ugly past, maybe then I would be able to understand, not wanting to be a hypocrite in the slightest. I, for one, knew how hard it was to tell people about those demons, to confront people and make it all a reality but lying about it was never going to be the best outcome. It hurt to know that Nick had lied to me, he had gone against that trust we were slowly building for each other. That hurt.

"Well, I'm not the best with relationship advice but I will always be on your side no matter what. I want to make this better but I'm not really sure how I can do that." Danni grabbed hold of my hand. "So I'm just going to say what I know."

"Which is?"

"He's a twat." She stated bluntly. Even through the tears, a small smile formed on to my face. That was just typical Danni, always being blunt about what she thinks but also cheering you up in the process.

"You can say that again." I giggled. "But it's difficult, isn't it? I want this to work."

"I know you do. You're in love with him." Danni said, as if she had known all along.

"Dan, I think I am." And that petrified me, especially to say it out loud to my best friend. It made it all the more real, and I was shaking in my shoes at the thought.

How could this work if Nick couldn't even tell me the truth about his past, like I did mine? He lied to me, outright. I would never have known if his mother hadn't turned up to the apartment after all. When was he going to tell me?

I was angry, very angry, but I was mostly left feeling deflated. I felt defeated.

"It doesn't take a scientist to figure that one out." Danni stated. She got up from the sofa in the middle of the room and I watched her walk in to the kitchen. Two minutes later she returned with a glass of wine in her hand and some chocolate. "Here, comfort food."

"Thanks, Dan." I smiled her way. I took the wine and chocolate with greed and enthusiasm. I was definitely a comfort food eater and I ate whenever I was feeling low.

"I would have suggested vodka but I don't want you paralytic tonight."

I laughed in reply.

Danni put on a film so we could both watch it. She hoped it would take my mind off Nick even only for a little while. I turned my phone off on the way to Danni's, so I didn't know whether he had tried ringing me in the last hour I was here.

I was missing him already, though.

The film didn't really help to take my mind off of Nick. Somehow, he was always on my mind. I understood where he was coming from in terms of not telling me about his past, I knew how hard it was to do so. His lying, however, was just something I couldn't understand.

Once Danni was asleep on the sofa, snoring softly beside me, I grabbed my phone and turned it back on. I didn't want Nick to worry but I still wasn't ready to talk to him just yet.

Nick had been calling non stop, so many missed calls flooded the screen of my phone and I let out a breath.

I jumped as soon as the phone rang again. Nick appeared on to my screen and I wanted so badly to not answer. I couldn't speak to him, I knew I would cave. However, I didn't want him to worry, so I picked up the phone to tell him where I was.

"Cathy." He snapped as soon as I answered the phone. His angry tone shocked me as soon as I heard it. "Where the fuck are you?" His breathing was ragged as if he could barely breath.

"At Danni's." I said, my voice cracking. I hadn't expected him to be so angry with me, not when it was me being angry with him.

"Are you out of your fucking mind?" He roared down the phone. "I've been trying to find you for hours."

"Nick, what's your problem?" I snapped back. His tone of voice was starting to piss me off more than necessary.

"You need to get home." He demanded. I let out a fake laugh.

"Do I now? Nick I am not-"

"This isn't a fucking joke, Cathy. You need to get home." He sighed, as if he was trying to calm himself down as much as possible. "Something's come up and you're not going to like it, hell, Cathy, I'm going out of my fucking mind."

"What's happened?" I asked, my anger dissipating and worry starting to enter my being. Was it my dad? Was he okay?

"I can't tell you over the phone." He replied. "I'm coming to get you."

"Nick-"

"I'm coming to get you." He snapped.

"Don't bother." I snapped. I didn't bother saying more, with worry seeping through my bones and anger taking over my body, I hung up the phone.

With that, I rang my dad. It was late in the evening but I was petrified something was the matter with my father. Asides from Danni and Nick, Glenn was the only person I had here. If anything was to happen to him, I wouldn't know what to do with myself.

"You're my daughter and I love you but it's night time." His voice flooded my ears and I sighed in relief. He sounded fine to me.

"Dad." I let out.

"What's the matter?" He asked, worry starting to be evident in his voice.

"You're okay?" I questioned. "For sure?"

"Are you drunk?" Glenn asked back. "Do you want me to come and get you?"

"No." I couldn't help but laugh. "It doesn't matter, I just wanted to know if you were okay."

"Of course I'm okay." He chuckled deeply down the phone. I couldn't help but smile. My father's presence was enough to cheer me up.

After saying goodbye, we both hung up the phone and I let him go back to bed. Now I knew my father was okay, I didn't really understand what Nick was on about. Was it just a ploy to him to get me back home with him? Would he really end up lying to me again?

With that, I woke up Danni. I wasn't going to wait for Nick to get here because quite frankly, I didn't want him around me, not yet. I was still boiling mad and stupidly upset.

"What do you want?" She asked, groaning as her eyes squinted at the lights I had turned on.

"I'm going to get a taxi home, okay?" I said. "I think Nick is coming to get me but I'm not going home with him, tell him I've left."

"Will do." Danni replied as she hadn't really woken up fully yet. With that, I said goodbye as soon as I called for a taxi and left through the front door.

The taxi was outside of the apartment building by the time I got outside. I jumped inside just as I saw Nick's van come flying down the street. I told the taxi to move and to move quickly, and soon we were driving out of the street and on the way to my house.

Looking back, Nick wasn't behind me. Not yet anyway.

I relaxed in to the leather and closed my eyes tightly. I just wanted this night to be over already. Why did things have to be so difficult with Nick? We took one step forward and two step back, always. I wanted so badly for things to work out between us but I would never tolerate his lying, ever. I deserved more than that.

I paid the taxi driver once I was dropped off home and proceeded to grab my key. The lights were on in the living room and the hall way, which meant my father was now up. I felt bad for waking him up and not letting him sleep.

"Dad!" I called and shut the door behind me. I locked it before kicking my shoes off and walking in to the living room.

My heart stopped as soon as I caught eyes on the two figures in front of me. My father was sat one the edge of the arm chair with apprehension on his face but happiness all the same.

I, for one, did not feel happy. No, I was petrified as the man in front of me smiled. What the fuck was he doing here? My heart was beating against my chest with force, I was starting to panic but I didn't want to show my father or my mother who was also smiling largely my way.

"Mum." I said, my voice cracking. I couldn't look at the man stood next to her. I couldn't or I would have caved.

"Darling." She gushed. She walked over to me, fussing over my standing body and tutting at the tattoos on my skin. I recoiled away from her but tried to look happy to see her.

I was happy to see her, I really was. However, I wasn't happy to see him, the man who was giving me the eye behind my mother's back. I felt sick to my stomach.

"What are you doing here?" I questioned, my voice breaking.

"I wanted to surprise you." She smiled. "It had been so long and we missed you terribly."

"We did." His voice came out and goosebumps evaded my skin. His voice gave me shivers and in the worst way possible. It made me think of all the times he had talked to me, told me to be quiet and to be a good girl for him. It made me sick then but now it made me even worse. I didn't want to see him, I didn't want him here.

"That's great." I faked a large smile to my mother, hoping it looked real. "I've just got to use the toilet." I stated before rushing off in the opposite direction. I needed to get out of that room.

As soon as I made it into the bathroom, I shut the door harshly against its hinges. I was on the verge of breaking point. I was still pissed off with Nick but now, that didn't matter. What mattered was the man downstairs and what he did to me as a child.

After a few more minutes of trying to compose myself, I left the bathroom. I had to try and be strong otherwise I would crack. It was hard faving your demons head on, literally, but this was the case and I was going to have to get on with it. I was an adult now and I had Nick, nothing would happen to me now.

As soon as I left the bathroom, my heart rate sped up as the figure before me took in my presence. He was upstairs now, his eyes on me and his body leaning against the rail of the stairs. I couldn't breath as fear took over my every being.

"What are you doing?" I asked, trying to be strong. I wouldn't show him I'm afraid because I knew that's what he liked; what he wanted.

"I've missed you, you know." He smirked my way. His slightly greying hair looked exactly the same as it did before I left. It hadn't been that long but it felt much longer to me.

"I'm leaving." I said as I began to walk downstairs. I couldn't take this. However, he grabbed me by my arm and pulled me back until I was stood before him.

"You look older, more mature." He stated as he took me in.

"I bet you don't like that." I snapped back. He was a vile, dirty pig and I hated him with everything I had.

"Hey now." He let out, his voice deepening as irritation was evident in his blazing eyes. "I did what I had to do."

"You're vile." I spat. He smirked my way and anger boiled in my veins even stronger.

"You never complained."

"Fuck you." I hissed. Just as I was about to move again, he grabbed me. "Get the fuck off me."

"Catherine-"

"She said get the fuck off of her." Nick's voice boomed as he walked up the stairs. I hadn't even heard him coming closer until he spoke. His body was rigid and his face was full of anger. I had never seen him this angry before.

"Who's this Pansy?"

"You're lucky I haven't fucking killed you yet you dirty fucking prick." Nick said his way. His voice was not to be messed with and even I was scared to be in his presence.

He grabbed my body and pushed me behind of him. I now couldn't see but I was still able to hear. Nick was physically shaking in front of me with anger but I was able to feel stronger now Nick was here to protect me.

"What the fuck are you going on about?" He questioned back, I could tell by the tone of his voice that he was getting defensive.

"As if you don't know." Nick scoffed. "Let's get one thing straight." He walked forward until they were nose to nose. "Don't you touch her ever again or I will seriously break your fucking neck."

With that, before he could reply, Nick took me by the hand and pulled me away from the man in question. He pulled me down the stairs and opened the front door. I didn't bother to put up a fight, I was just ecstatic that he was here to keep me safe.

I followed him until we were inside his van. He didn't speak for a few minutes as he stewed. I let him. He was still shaking with anger, anger I had never seen before.

"Nick."

"Don't." He let out. He turned his head away from me to look out of the window.

"What's your problem?" I questioned.

"My fucking problem is you." He snapped. His eyes were ablaze as he now took me in. He wasn't calming down, not one bit. "You didn't tell me where you fucking were, you wouldn't pick up the phone when I called and then I see you and that rapist together talking!" He roared.

"I didn't know he was going to be here!" I shouted back.

"I was trying to fucking tell you, Cathy, but you left before I could."

"I was pissed off with you." I replied truthfully. It's hard to think straight when you're so pissed off. Also, I would never have known they were going to come back, it was a massive shock to me.

"Fuck sake!" Nick hit the wheel in front of him and I jumped at the loud bang it made. "I want you safe and it's difficult when you don't listen to a word I say."

"I didn't know he was going to be here, do you know how difficult that is for me? Today's been shit, Nick. You've lied to me and now my childhood demon is coming back to haunt me." Tears welled up in my eyes all of a sudden. I was exhausted and this day had been shit. "Stop being selfish, Nick, I know you worry about me but what you've done to me today has hurt me beyond words and now this? This has killed me."

"Cathy." He tried to take hold of my hand but I pulled away.

"I'm glad you're here to protect me from him, Nick, I really am, but who's here to protect me from you?"

"What do you mean? I would never fucking hurt you, Cathy."

"No?" I fake laughed. "Lying to me is enough to hurt me just as much."

"Don't be like this." Nick groaned.

"You lied to me, Nick, who's to say you haven't lied about everything else?" I sighed. "It's becoming hard to trust you."

"No." His voice was strong. "Don't say that."

"It is though." I shrugged. "I've told you everything about me because I wanted us to work and I wanted you to know. Never have I ever thought about lying to you, I wouldn't, because I wanted us to have that foundation of trust."

"I never wanted to lie to you, either." He laid a hand to his head.

"Well, what's done is done now." I stated. I opened the door and got out before Nick could stop me.

"Cathy-"

"I can't think straight." I shook my head.

"You can't go back in there, not with him."

"Nick, I can't stay in here with you, I need to go."

"Cathy don't you fucking dare." He warned.

"I can't." I shook my head again, my mind so exhausted and jumbled I couldn't think. I was a mess and my brain felt like it, too.

I shut the door before Nick could say another word. I heard him shouting for me before getting out. I ran inside and shut the door in front of him.

I ran upstairs and in to my bedroom, not caring that I was being rude considering my mother had come to see me. With that, I shut the bedroom tightly and laid on top of the covers. I couldn't move, so I slept in my clothes.

I heard the front door open beneath my room and heard Nick talking to Glenn. Soon, it all went quiet.

With that, I fell asleep with tear strained cheeks.

What was I going to do?

CHAPTER 20

I woke up the next morning feeling like absolute crap. Now I had slept on my feelings and on the mess that had folded last night, I had chance to clear my mind and to think of my next step.

Firstly, I was being dramatic. Nick had lied to me but there must have been a valid reason for doing so. He had his reasons and I had mine for doing the things I did. I needed to hear him out.

Also, was I out of my fucking mind? My childhood rapist was down stairs and I had no intention of running for the hills yesterday. Today, I had to get out of here. I had to leave and fast, too.

Once my eyes had opened up fully, I rubbed away the sleep from my eyes and looked around the room.

My heart sank when I saw Nick sitting infront of the door of my bedroom. A small 5 o'clock shadow was forming around the bottom of his face, showing that he hadn't shaved for some time now. Also, his back was hunched and his head rested above his risen knees. He was sleeping in front of the door to make sure I was safe.

I got up from bed where I was in Nick's t shirt and not my own clothes. He must have changed me last night and I was grateful.

I went over to Nick's body and sat down beside him. Shit, how could I have been so stupid yesterday? This man did everything to protect me and keep me safe and I was just an over dramatic fool with a tendency to kick off over everything I thought was wrong.

There was nothing wrong with showing my feelings and showing them quite strongly, however, I felt guilty now watching the man I loved keep me safe when all I had tried to do was push him away.

I slowly leaned my head against Nick's shoulder, hoping not to wake him up. I felt much safer when Nick was here and I had no intention of leaving this room until Nick was right there beside me. If it wasn't for him, I'd be having a mental breakdown right this minute.

I couldn't thank him enough.

As soon as my head touched his shoulder, he sighed.

"What are you doing?" His voice sounded sleepy and gruff all at the same time. My heart seized in my chest.

"I don't know." I replied. I didn't know what I was doing or why. This man had every ability to fuck me up and make me a mess. I cared so deeply and that was the root of the problem.

"You're an idiot." Nick muttered. He sighed again. "You're so fucking stupid."

"I know." I whispered his way.

"How could you be so stupid?" He moved his head until he was looking at me. His eyes were a stormy blue, full of irritation and anger.

"I don't know." I didn't really know what to say.

"The guy who hurt you all your childhood is downstairs and living under the same roof as you. You couldn't even come back to my place just to be safe." He stated. "I know I lied to you, Cathy, but I hadn't raped you for years and neither did I mentally abuse you." Nick was livid now the more he spoke. I didn't what to say because after all, he was right.

I was fucking stupid.

"I was a mess." I stated. "Seeing him shocked me and I didn't know what to do or how to act. I didn't think I could cope." I shrugged my shoulders as I moved to look at him properly. "Being faced with the man who abused me as a teenager was fucking hard going."

"I know but it still makes me fucking mad that you won't help yourself." He fumed. "I just want you safe, Cathy, is that too hard to understand?"

"I know you're angry but have you ever had your childhood demon looking at you right in the eyes?" I questioned. "It didn't help that I was trying to make sense of you."

"Of me?" He asked back. He was still in the same clothes as he was last night.

"You and your lies. It's your family and I would never force you to tell me something if you didn't want to tell me but just saying I don't want to tell you will be enough for me. You don't have to lie." I took his face in to my hands. "Why did you lie to me?"

I had to ask Nick for the answers to my questions. I couldn't live like this with him. I needed honesty and truth to be a part of this and I needed him to co operate. I had never felt this way before and I knew we had something special.

"It's an old habit to lie to the women I am with. I know you're different but lying to you was my safest bet. I regret it completely, I really do." I looked in to his eyes and they looked sincere and genuine. I believed him, of course I did. We do things we're not proud of but that was all part of the learning. Nick wasn't used to being in a relationship and neither was I, we did things differently and that was that.

"Promise you won't lie again?" I questioned. "I need you to just tell me the truth or not to say anything at all."

"Of course." He kissed my firmly on the lips. "And don't ever be so fucking stupid again, got it?"

"You care that much?" I asked.

"Yes." He said. "I lo-" just as he was about to say his sentence, somebody knocked at the door. Just as I jumped out of my skin, Nick got up and picked me up with him.

The door knocked again and Nick opened it as he pushed me aside.

"We're all going out for lunch, do you want to come?" I let out a breath as I heard Glenn's voice at the other end of the door. Nick opened the door up fully and I moved to see him.

"We've got plans, sorry." Nick said before I could speak. I couldn't think of anything worse than to go out for lunch with my mother and her husband. I missed my mother extremely but there was no chance in hell I was going to sit there whilst he was there. Also, there was no chance in hell Nick was going to let me.

"Are you sure?" Glenn asked. His eyes swivelled to me. "Cathy?"

"Maybe you, me and mum can go out tomorrow?" I asked. "Nick and I have plans today but I'd love to catch up with mum sometime soon." I plastered on a smile.

"I'm not a big fan of him either." Glenn whispered between us. His knowing smile made my fake one turn in to a real one and I also let out a small giggle.

Even after all these years, my father still knew exactly what I was thinking. Maybe my feelings were all over my face but I still imagined that my father knew exactly what I was trying to say.

My father loved my mother strongly. It was a shame it didn't work out for the both of them because I knew just how inlove they were. I wasn't too sure on why they divorced but there are parts of me that still think my father is inlove with my mother even after the years apart. Falling in love was the easy part, I supposed.

"I hate him." Nick said, the shame in his voice not evident at all. It was easy to see that Nick hated him with every part of him, however, it was dangerous to show his hatred for him when my father didn't know what had happened in Australia.

"You do?" Glenn asked as he looked over at Nick. A small amount of shock was painted on to his face but he seemed quite smug that his best friend also hated the man married to his ex wife.

"He seems like a twat." Nick pushed past Glenn and I had every right to follow. "Your ex wife is out of her mind."

"Nick." I hissed quietly his way. "Be quiet." Nick turned to glare at me. Nick wasn't coping well under this roof, not at all. I couldn't wait to leave.

"Are you saying I'm better?" My father asked with a small smile on the edge of his lips.

"Yes, you silly fucker." Nick shook his head before grabbing my hand and pulling me down the stairs. "It's time to go."

"You're going so soon?" My father asked as we all descended the stairs. Just as we got to the bottom, my mother came in to the hall way with her husband on her heels.

"You're going, darling?" My mother's inky black hair was an exact replica of mine. Her eyes were piercing and she was in every way stunning. I loved my mother but I just couldn't look her in to the eyes when my nightmare was standing behind her.

"I am." I smiled her way, even though it was fake and extremely hard to pull off. "I'm sorry." I tried to act apologetic but I just couldn't wait to get out of this God damned house. Even being in the same room as him made me completely on edge.

"That's okay, I'm sure we can do something tomorrow."

"Sure." I said through teeth. I looked in to the eyes of my demon and regretted making that decision. I tried to be strong, a lot stronger than I was. My skin crawled and my heart beat accelerated as he took me in.

"See you tomorrow, Catherine." His voice made the oxygen in my lungs leave. I couldn't talk as my throat dried up. Just as I felt I was going to scream, Nick grabbed my arm and pulled me out of the house. He slammed the door behind us and almost threw me in to his truck.

He quickly got in to the drivers seat and started the car, just as he slammed his wheel with his fist.

"I am so close to fucking killing him." Nick spat. "I will slit his fucking throat." His body was physically shaking at the wheel.

It was easy to see that this man was affecting Nick aswell as myself. I was scared of him but Nick was having a hard time trying to reign in his temper. It was hard when I didn't want my mother or father knowing what he had done to me whilst they weren't around.

Nick respected the fact that I didn't want to tell them, so I understood how hard it was for him to keep his emotions in check, especially now when the man who stole my innocence was looking at him in the eyes.

"I'm sorry." I said. I didn't really know what to say. I guess this was all my fault, I was damaged and I had baggage and I hadn't really thought of that when pursuing something with Nick. A part of me thinks I am being selfish but the other part is telling me that I shouldn't ever regret doing something just because of my past.

I want Nick, I have since I met him, that isn't ever going to change. In fact, I had fallen in love with him. I couldn't stop that because of something I couldn't control.

"Stop with the bullshit sorries." Nick blurted, he liked to me with them stormy eyes and I couldn't hold in the tears. "It's not your fault, it's his. I can't have you apologising for something that is out of your control."

As the tears streamed, Nick pulled over on to the side of the road before unbuckling my seat belt and pulling me on to his lap. He kissed me all over my face until there weren't any tears left to see. I'm sure Nick was the only person who could mend me when I felt like I was breaking.

Nick took my face in to his hands and he looked me in the eyes. His were full of a deepened anger, sadness but also full of something special, I couldn't quite peg it.

However, in that moment I realised I couldn't have fallen any harder for him.

"Better?" Nick asked, his voice gentle. I nodded my head and Nick kissed my forehead before placing me back in to my seat. "We need to get a move on, my mother is still at my apartment."

"She is?" I asked. We hadn't gotten off on the best foot and I internally cringed at the first impression I just have gave off.

"She is." Nick stated with a small nod. "I guess it's time to be honest."

"You don't have to." I said as I looked to him, my full attention on him.

"You deserve it, you've given me everything and I've given you nothing."

"That's not-"

"Listen." He demanded. "Just listen." He let in a big breath before continuing. "My mother was admitted to a psychiatric unit a few years after my father died. She went bat shit crazy and I was without a father and without a mother as she was not fit enough to look after me. I mean, I was almost twenty at that time but it was fucking hard. She was all I had left and we were inseparable."

"Shit." I mused.

"I loved my mother, I still do but she still isn't right in the head. She misses my father even to this day." He sighed. "She talks about him as if he's still alive."

"So is she allowed out of the psychiatric unit or did she escape?" I couldn't help but ask.

"She didn't escape." He chuckled. "She's allowed out, it's not a prison. Usually if you're that crazy then somebody like a carer will be there with you. My mother had gotten better over the last few years and is allowed out on her own most of the time now aswell."

"And you didn't visit her?" I questioned.

"I did." He stated. "Just not a lot. You could call me a coward, I suppose." He shrugged. "I couldn't bare it. I lied because it was easier than going through the whole story."

"I understand." And I did. Telling people your life story was not always easy and it took time. There was also a possibility that somebody wouldn't understand. Luckily, I did, I had been through a lot too but that's what made our connection so special.

"If she does something weird then just ignore it." Nick said. "She's my mother so you're not allowed to be mean." His voice was full of humour and playfulness, I knew he was only kidding but also I knew that he loved his mother a lot. It was clear he did.

"You know I wouldn't be mean." I said truthfully.

"I know." With that, Nick laid his hand on to my knee and squeezed gently. Having this contact really did brighten my mood and talking to Nick made me forget everything else around us.

We got home a few minutes later and I was finally able to breath properly now we were away from my father's house. My only safe place was now one of danger.

Once we got in to the apartment, we dumped our things in to the bedroom and found Nick's mother in the kitchen.

She was making dinner and setting the table. I kind of worried if she was allowed to use the stove but Nick didn't seem to mind so I guessed everything was okay with her using the cooker.

Nick sat down on one side of the table and I sat beside him.

"I told her you were coming for dinner." He whispered. "She's quite old fashioned and she said she wanted to meet you."

"I met her yesterday." I stated. "Remember?" I questioned, wondering if I was the one going crazy instead.

"She doesn't remember." Nick replied. With that, Nick's mother came up behind me and tapped me on the shoulder. I turned around and got up from my seat to greet her. Just as I was about to open my mouth, she pulled me in harshly for a hug.

"You must be Nicholas' girlfriend." She squeezed tightly and I hugged her back with equal enthusiasm.

"I am. Nice to meet you." I said.

"It's so lovely to meet you too, lovely." She kissed me gently on the cheek before letting me go and wondering off to the kitchen. I sat down in my seat again and Nick chuckled at my shocked expression.

She seemed a lovely lady now that we weren't squabbling over the invasion of privacy. She was tiny and frail in my arms and smelt like flowers.

"She's lovely." I said truthfully.

"She is." He smiled my way with pride evident on his face.

Nick's mother started to dish out the food around the table a few minutes later. I was shocked when I saw her making four plates of food instead of three. I looked to Nick and he smiled.

"Is dad having some?" Nick asked. He flickered his eyes to me. "She always makes dad a plate." He whispered my way.

I smiled once I watched her. If Nick's father was alive now, I knew his wife would have taken very good care of him. It was sweet to see her caring for him even though he wasn't here.

"He is." She said before putting the plate beside her place at the table.

We ate in silence for a few minutes before Nick's mother looked to the two of us. She got up from her seat at the table, leaving her family of unfinished.

She went over to the stereo station at the corner of the room and went through the rack of CD's Nick had before placing one in to the stereo.

Nick watched her do so, his lips pulled up in to a small smile.

Once the song started playing, Nick's small smile turned in to a big one.

"Do you remember this, Nicholas?" His mother turned to beam his way. Nick nodded.

"I sang to you almost everyday." Nick stated. "You always chose this." He said as the song What A Wonderful World played throughout the apartment.

I looked to Nick and I swear I couldn't have fallen in love any harder.

"Sing it now, Nicky." She said as she looked to her son with pride and love.

"Aw, ma', I can't." I almost laughed at the small blush that creeped up his neck and to his cheeks. "My girlfriend's here."

"Sing to us both, Nicky." She pleaded. "Please."

"Go on, Nicky." Nick looked to me, his eyes trained on mine. After a while, he sighed but a smile made its way on to his face.

"Fine." He breathed as he rolled his eyes. "But you owe me." He pointed my way before leaving the seat and making his way over to his mum.

"Are we dancing aswell?" She asked. Nick chuckled.

"I can't dance aswell as sing, ma'."

"You can." She went over to her son and snaked her arms around his waist. Nick laughed before gently swaying with her fragile body in his arms.

I watched as a huge smile took over my face. When Nick started singing, my breath left my body in a rush and I'm sure I melted onto the floor. The man was talented and all mine.

Well I see trees of green and red roses too,

Nick flickered his eyes to mine as he continued.

I'll watch them bloom for me and you

He winked as he sang my way.

My heart was soaring in my chest as I watched him. There was no doubt in my mind that I loved this man.

No doubt at all.

Nick's eyes didn't sway from mine as he continued to sing. His eyes bored in to mine and my chest heaved. The smile was now gone from his face and that serious look was painted on to his features.

And then he sang the lyrics

"They're really singing, "I, I love you.""

chapter 21

My heart hammered in my chest as he sang me the words. Did he mean it or was it just part of the song? What was he really, truly thinking?

I flickered my eyes down to the table and watched my fidgeting thumbs. I broke eye contact which I really did need to do. I couldn't look at him as he danced with his mother and sang the words I wanted him to tell me.

What if he didn't love me? He was with me, but Nick wasn't used to love and what this whole relationship entailed. Neither was I, but I was sure on my feelings, I wasn't on his.

Once the song had finished, Nick's mother flung herself on to the sofa as she giggled like a school girl. Nick laughed with her and I had never seen him look so happy before. It also seemed as if his mother had never seen him look so happy before either.

"You seem different, Nicky." She said, her voice a little breathless. Nick looked to her and even though he smiled her way, his face was still one of confusion.

"How?"

"You seem happier."

Nick didn't say a word as he went to the dining room table and started to clean the plates and cutlery away. His mother had barely touched her food but Nick didn't seem to have minded, I guessed she barely ate at all.

I helped Nick tidy up and we worked in synchronisation and harmony. It was nice to work along side him, exactly like an old couple. It made me think that this was what I wanted and that I could have gotten used to it, easily.

Once everything was tidied, Nick and I sat down on the sofa next to Nick's mother. Nick switched the TV on and wrapped an arm around my body. Nick pulled me close and laid a kiss to my head.

We all watched a film together but half way through the film, Nick's mother had fallen asleep. Nick picked her frail body up with care and gentleness and laid her in to his bed.

Once he was back, he sat on the sofa next to my body and sighed. I looked to him but he seemed nervous as he sat there.

"Nick?" I said his name to grab his attention. He seemed zoned out and distracted with his thoughts. I wondered what was eating him. "What's the matter?" I asked, starting to worry at the look on his face.

"Nothing." He sighed again. I narrowed my eyes his way.

"Why do you look nervous?"

"I'm not nervous." He shook his head.

"Nick." I warned. "Tell me." I demanded.

"Nothing's the matter." He snapped. Taken a back, I looked to him.

"Jesus, Nick. I don't want you angry with me I just wanted to-"

"I want you to move in with me." He snapped again. "I'm fucking shitting myself because I know this is getting serious and I want you to move in with me because I don't want you over there especially when they make surprise visits." He laid his hands to his head. "I've never asked a girl to move in before."

"Do you really want this or are you asking because you're worried about him being near me?" I asked. I didn't want to move in with him if he didn't deep down want this. I wanted him to want it so badly, I wanted him to want me here because he couldn't live without me. I didn't want it to be because he was scared. I understood but it wasn't going to work otherwise.

"Of course I want you here." He moved until he had my hands enclasped in to his own. "I can't live without you. I want you to move in, babe, believe me."

"Do you?" I asked again, unsure.

"I want to protect you, Cathy, you know that but I also want you here because I think we've reached that kind of level. It pushes me to want you here more because of him but that's not the main reason." He shook his head, his eyes genuine. "I'm just nervous because I've never been this serious with another girl before and this is a big fucking step for me."

"It is for me too." I breathed. "I want to move in with you, Nick but isn't this going too fast?" Nick lowered his head until he was looking at his legs.

"Maybe." He sighed. "But I really fucking want this."

"I don't know." I mused. I was unsure. Of course I wanted to move in with him. I had fallen for Nick so hard, I could barely live a day without him, so moving in with him would be the best feeling for me. However, I was nervous to do so. I didn't want to rush things, I didn't want to go too fast with him and ruin it all.

I didn't want him to get bored of me.

"I'm worried, Nick." I stated truthfully. "I don't want this to be ruined because we're going too fast."

"I get that but I want you and you want me and that's that, Cathy. Time isn't anything when you're meant to be."

"How do you know we're meant to be?"

"Because I wouldn't feel this strongly with just anybody. No one can match you." He took my head in to his hands and pulled my face up to his until his lips were on mine. "Just trust me."

"I'll think about it." I said as I kissed him again.

"Okay." He left it aside. "What do you think about me going back to university to do an art degree?" He asked. He looked to me, the earlier topic forgotten now. His eyes were alight with curiosity.

"I think it's a brilliant idea." I said truthfully. "Is that what you want to do?"

"Yeah." He stated. "I've been drawing since I could hold a pencil. I wanted money and my talent went to waste but you make me want to be the real me and to pursue my dreams."

"I think it's an amazing idea."

"Do you?" He questioned. "I'm worried because I'm stable and I do have an income coming in at the moment. I need money so I can look after you."

"Stop it." I pointed his way. "Stop thinking of me. This is your dream." I emphasised. He couldn't stop his goals because of me, he couldn't be worried about his monthly income. He had changed his life for his mother and for the fact that he needed money. This was his change to do whatever he set out to do in the first place. I was all for it. "Besides, are you even any good?" I questioned.

I had never seen any of his drawings.

"I think so." He said. "Do you want to see?"

"Sure." Nick took my hand and pulled me up. He then pulled me along until we were outside of the room. He opened the door and inside were so many paintings and drawings. He didn't have anything else but a desk and stacks of paper. I was in wonder as I looked around the room.

I went up to a few of his drawings, not believing any of them were his. They were so dark and brooding, so creepy and spooky. He had his own style of art and they were amazing. I couldn't take my eyes off of the pictures before me.

"Are you sure these are yours?" I asked. I was blown away. A picture caught my eye near the window. This picture was half done but the colours were so much more colourful and the lines were less sharp and dark.

I went over to the picture and studied it. Even half finished, it still looked better than anything I could do. It was a picture of the bottom half of what seemed to be a woman but there was no face as of yet.

Nick walked up to me and I felt his back behind mine. He was so close to me I could feel the warmth of his body.

"Do you like it?" He asked as he looked at the photo too.

"I love it." I breathed. "It's amazing."

"I'm glad you like it." I could hear his smile as he talked. "It's you."

"What? Really?" I turned around on the spot until I was looking at him.

"I've spent my whole life drawing pictures when I've felt depressed and angry at the world. My pictures have no colour, my tattoos have no colour but you turned up in my life and made my world in colour. I drew this because I wanted to finally be able to draw my happiness on to a canvas." I melted in to a puddle on the floor as he spoke. "You're my happiness, Cathy."

"I love it." I said again, my throat dry and my mind going blank. He had that effect on me.

Nick pulled me in to his body and hugged me tight. It made me realise for sure that this was what I wanted. I wanted him forever. I was sure of it.

"Look at this one." Nick left my body and walked over to a large painting. It was dark and was a drawing of a forest. I didn't know the meaning of it but it looked so haunted.

"It looks so sad." I said.

"I was sad." He stated. "I drew this a few days after my dad's death."

"Oh, Nick." I looked to him with sympathy. The drawing was so upsetting I could see his feelings in the picture without me having to even ask how he felt. He felt haunted, empty, dark and depressed. Even thinking about how Nick felt at this time was enough to make me feel it too.

His pictures were so effective.

"I was so angry at the time. He killed himself along with my uncle. It was a shit time in my life, nothing could ever compare." He looked to the drawing which sat on the floor. "Well, unless you left me."

"Nick-"

"No, I mean it. If you left me I wouldn't know what to do with myself. You don't realise how much I need you, Cathy. I go on about how much I want you but I need you more than anything."

"I need you too." I stated truthfully.

"Then we're good, aren't we?" He smiled my way.

"I hope you never feel like that again." I pointed to the picture below us.

"Babe, I feel like that." He pointed to the colourful picture at the near end of the room. "All because of you."

It was clear to see Nick drew the way he felt. It was so raw and real, it struck me so hard. I wasn't sure whether it effected me so much because I loved Nick or whether because his paintings were that striking.

I think it was a bit of both.

It was also clear to see though that Nick's paintings belonged in a gallery. They didn't belong in a small room where nobody could see them, they belonged somewhere where the whole world could see them. I wanted him to get the recognition he deserved.

"I want to get to a point where I'm as colourful as you." Nick touched my colourful tattoos with care. He looked to them and then looked to me. His eyes bored their way in to my soul. "I want you to colour me red."

"Colour you red?" I questioned. "Colour you red how?"

"Make me feel, make me believe, make me love." He stated. "You make me feel something, just like art, you make me feel something."

"These are worth money." I looked around the room. They were just too good.

"And you're priceless." He looked to me. Seconds went past but it felt like minutes. He continued to state my way, his eyes showing me things he could quite tell me.

Soon, Nick grabbed my body and pushed me up against the wall. A wall where no paintings were. My body was tight against the white of the wall and his body. He smacked his lips to mine and soon our tongues were dancing and fighting for dominance.

Nick was unbuttoning my jeans before I knew it. He lifted my top with quiet impatience. He was moving so roughly and quickly, I loved it.

I was a puddle in his hands before he knew it.

I was writhing and pleading in to his mouth, my body shaking as he continued to touch and grope me.

"Nick, please." I moaned and groaned.

"I know." He rasped. "I know."

"Hurry."

"I need you, Cathy." He grunted. "I need you so fucking badly."

Nick unbuckled his jeans and before I knew it, he was showing me just how much he needed me.

It was a good thing I needed him too.

I was sweating and panting as I looked to the half finished drawing of me. I studied it for some time as I came down from my high. My heart was beating wildly as the love for the man beside me grew.

"When are you going to finish it?" I asked, my voice still sounding breathless as I turned to face him. He laid there, his chest heaving as he looked to the ceiling. He was content and happy, a good mixture for him.

"Soon." He said. "I'm going to make it my mission."

"I love it already, anyway." I looked to the painting again, humbled that Nick had even thought to draw me the way he had done.

"I'm glad." He smiled.

"And university is something you want to do?" I asked. "Your drawings are so good, you wouldn't need an art degree."

"I want it." He stated. "I don't know where I would go after that with it but I've always wanted an art degree. I'm going to do it."

"I'm so happy for you." I looked to him. "It's time to start thinking of yourself."

"Myself and you." His lips pulled up again as he shyly smiled my way. I couldn't help but smile back, he looked adorable.

"I can look after myself. I want you to have this, it's never been easy for you, Nick, but you don't give up." And that's why I loved him.

"I'll do it." He nodded firmly. "I'll start applying tomorrow."

"Good."

The room was silent again. We basked in each others company as light turned in to dark outside of the small bay window in the room. It casted a small glow on to our bodies which gave off a romantic aura.

It was maddening how things were changing for the both of us.

"Do you remember the other week you asked me whether I believed in magic?" He asked. I looked to him and cocked my head to the side as I remembered back. I remembered the day up Xavier's and Emily's, where I did indeed ask him whether he believed in magic.

He had said no and I wondered why he had brought it up. I also wondered how he had remembered I said it.

"I do remember." I said. "Why do you ask?"

"I've changed my mind." He stated. "I do believe in magic. I believe in fate now too."

"You do?" I asked back. Nick looked to me.

"I do." He nodded. "They brought me to you."

CHAPTER 22

I was on cloud nine the next morning, even though my body was stiff as I woke up on the floor of Nick's studio.

Nick was snoring gently beside me as he slept in peace and serenity. He looked like a young boy as he slept and he looked trouble free. I loved sleepy Nick, he was always so adorable.

The things Nick said to me last night gave me every bit of hope that Nick felt the same way about me as I did him. We spent the night in the studio together, the lowly dimmed lights adding to the romance of the whole scene before us.

I woke up the happiest I had felt in a long time.

It was petrifying just how easily and how quickly I had fallen for Nick Abel, the play boy and the police officer from this small old village. It was maddening how much he had supposedly changed from before I came back until now. Even my father had noticed the change in him, even though he was still a little wary.

My father only wanted what was best for me.

I laid on the dark wooden oak, taking in the pictures around me. Even though most of them were so dark and depressing, I still felt at peace around them. It could have been because of the fact I knew Nick had drew them. Whatever it was, I liked it.

It was clear to see my man had a talent. I was so excited for his future, whatever he had, he was going to use it to make him the man he always wanted to be. I was proud of him regardless. The last five months I've known him, I just couldn't seem to not be.

Five months didn't even seem that long with Nick. And it was clear to see I had fallen very quickly for him. I wasn't going to put a time on anything though. I had fallen for him and it was as simple as that. I just hope he felt the same because he had every power to break my heart in two.

A loud knock on the door resonated around the studio room. Nick stirred beside me and grabbed me tighter in his arms.

I got out of his hold and heard him moan and groan as I did so. Without wanting to wake him properly, I went to the door and opened it, knowing it was only going to be Nick's mother.

Once I opened the door, Nick's mother was pacing the hall way. As soon as she heard me approaching, she turned to face me.

"Where is he?" She questioned. Her face was one of panic and worry.

"He's in his studio, he's fine." I soothed. I took her frail hand and she let me enclasp it with my own. Her eyes were red with unleashed tears and right now, I was able to feel for her. Empathy came over me like a wave.

This woman had to look after her broken hearted boy after her husbands death. It was clear to see she loved him and she loved her son too. It must have been hard for the both of them when she was admitted to the physiatrics unit.

"Oh." She looked to the floor as if she was now embarrassed by her outburst. I knew she was only a little better but she had further to go. I understood that.

"It's okay." I said. I gave her an encouraging smile. I didn't want her to feel uncomfortable around me. I wanted us to get on, I wanted her to feel okay around me, not scared and uncomfortable.

I knew it was hard for her though. I was a new face and the girlfriend of her son. I doubt she had ever seen Nick with another woman before.

"Do you want to go and see him?" I asked. She looked up to me and her grateful smile was enough to melt my heart. Just the way Nick always did.

As soon as I turned around, I jumped at the sight of Nick. He was leaning against the door way of the studio, his eyes trained on me. His lips curved up in to a smile as my eyes flickered to his.

"No need, I'm here." He walked over, his chest bare and his shorts riding low on his hips. Shit, he was breathtaking.

I was never going to get used to his body. He was muscly, his body stocky but lean too. He was gorgeous and I was a lucky woman.

Before Nick got to his mother, he gave me a kiss on the cheek and leaned in my ear.

"Keep checking me out, baby." He whispered. "See where it takes you."

"Hopefully to your bed." I whispered back, my mood mischievous and playful as my happiness over took me.

Nick's eyes darkened as he looked to me, his eyes searching mine.

"Behave." He quietly growled. He stood up straight and moved to his mother. He took her in to his arms and pulled her to the kitchen of his apartment, laughing with her and improving her mood.

Nick was so good with his mother. He didn't treat her differently, he didn't bow down to her illness and treat it as anything but what it was. He didn't ignore it but he didn't pay attention to it in a way that would embarrass his mother. He just aimed to improve her mood and to make her forget all about the outbursts and actions she takes.

I could watch him all day.

As Nick took his mother to the kitchen, I heard my phone ring in my bag on the sofa. I picked it up and fished out my phone quickly, wondering who was ringing me.

"Hello?" I questioned, not bothering to look at the caller ID.

"Birdie." Glenn greeted me. "Do you want lunch?" He asked. Nick looked to me and I smiled his way, showing him that everything was okay.

"Sure, what time?"

"One should do." He said. "Bring Nick."

"Of course I will." I laughed a little. Glenn let out a small chuckle.

"I don't even know why I said that." He chuckled some more. "I used to think Nick and I were joint to the hip. Now, he's replaced me."

"Are you jealous?" I asked playfully.

"No." He let out. "I'm glad you've taken the fucker off me. He can pester you now."

"You love him really." I said, Nick looked to me just as if he knew we were talking about him. His brow arched as he made coffee for the three of us, his eyes never leaving mine.

"I do." He sighed. "Sadly."

"You're so mean." I giggled. Nick's smile grew.

"So is he. Ask him if he loves me." I laughed. "Go on." He encouraged.

"Nick, do you love Glenn?" I shouted to him.

"No." He said back. "He's a twat."

"Did you head that?" I asked, moving to sit down on the sofa.

"Loud and clear, love." He chuckled again. "So I'll see you at one?"

"Yeah." I said just as I remembered my mother and my demon was also here to stay. "Uh, is it just us three?"

"Sadly not." His voice lowered as if he didn't want to be heard. "But your mother wanted us all to be together and who am I to tell her no?" He sighed.

In that moment, I wondered if my father still loved my mother. He never spoke about it and he never said he did, but by the way he spoke about her husband, it wasn't because of anything but the fact he knew she could have done better. My father was good at judging people and I had no doubts that he knew he was a bad man.

He was the worst man.

My heart wrenched anyway. I would have done anything to see my father happy with my mother. My mother and I had stopped being so close once she remarried and I wished everything was different between the three of us and all I wanted was for the two to be happy.

My mother loved her husband and was incredibly happy. It was a shame I hated him with everything I had.

"Great." I tried to plaster on a fake smile which would hopefully aid me in the fake happiness of him being there.

Glenn didn't question me, he knew I didn't like him either. If only he knew half of it. I shuddered at the thought of him knowing what happened back in Australia. He couldn't know, ever. And neither could my mother.

Once my father and I had hung up the phone, I placed it back in to my bag and sighed as I leaned further in to the sofa.

My heart kept in fright at the thought of sitting around the table with my childhood demon. However, this time I wasn't on the verge of a breakdown. Nick was going to be there and I knew he would do anything to protect me.

I knew I was going to be safe.

Nick sauntered his way over to me and placed a cup of coffee infront of me. I took it and looked to him, my now bad mood evident.

Nick caught on to my mood straight away, his face dropping as he took me in.

"What's the matter?" He questioned.

"We're going to lunch." I stated. Nick looked to me in confusion.

"Cathy, forgive me if I'm wrong but since when have you been in a bad mood because you're having food? You love food."

Nick sat beside me and placed a gentle arm over my shoulders. I already felt better under his arm, his warmth seeping in to my skin.

"My mother's going." I stated. I watched as his face dropped even further. His eyes filled up with irritation.

"Why?"

"Dad said mom wanted us all to be together." I shrugged.

"Well, why didn't you say no?" He snapped. I knew the mention of him was enough to get Nick angry and irritated. He hated him almost as much as me.

"Because I couldn't. I want my mother to be happy, Nick." I said. Nick's face softened up as I said so. He understood that, I know he did. He looked to his own mother before looking back to me.

"Okay but I don't want you leaving my side."

"Nick-"

"I mean it." He clipped. "You're not leaving my side." His face said don't push me but his eyes pleaded in the lost vulnerable of ways.

I sighed.

"Fine." I finalised. "I won't."

Nick kissed my forehead before getting up, gulping down his coffee and walking over to his bedroom door.

I got up and followed after him, wanting to get ready. I had to shower and change as it was already eleven. We had two hours to spare.

This was going to be fun.

Nick and I got to the small cafe with ten minutes still left to spare. Nick was quiet on the way to lunch and didn't speak a word.

I understood his nerves and the anger that coursed through his veins. It wasn't nice to be around somebody who would do such a thing to me. For me, it wasn't nice to see my nightmare and to look him in the eyes.

I was petrified.

We picked a table for five and sat down before the others came. Nick made sure I was in the corner so he could keep an eye on me there. I felt a little safer knowing he was beside me and was there watching over me.

I was so grateful for him.

My father was the first to walk in to the cafe, his face one of joy to see me but annoyance at the man behind him.

He was definitely jealous of his ex wife and her newest husband. I could tell.

"Cathy." He kissed my cheek over the table and slapped Nick's cheek lightly as he started to talk about the football scores. As he was doing so, my mother's husband quickly rounded the table until he was sitting opposite me.

As Glenn spoke, Nick's eyes flickered his way and his hands bunched up in to fists and his body became stiff. He was ready to explode.

My mother's husband looked to me and kept his eyes trained on mine. My heart started beating loudly in my chest as he continued to look at me. I leaned in closer to Nick, his eyes following my movements.

As soon as my mother's hand touched his shoulder, his eyes left mine and I was finally able to breath. Still, Nick seemed ready to kill him as he physically shook beside me.

I stood up from the table as my skin felt slick and sweaty with panic. My heart kept beating and my head went light.

I couldn't do this.

Nick stood up abruptly from the table as soon as he saw me moving to the toilets. He didn't bother apologising and neither did I, even though we could both hear my father's voice calling for the both of us.

I opened the bathroom door for the women's toilets and Nick entered with me.

"I just need some time, Nick." I stated, my voice cracking as I did so. Nick watched me intensely, his chest heaving up and down.

"Cathy-"

"I just need some time!" I snapped loudly. I knew I was taking my fear and anger out on Nick but I just couldn't help myself. I just needed some time and some time alone to gather and collect my thoughts.

Nick didn't bother answering back as he opened the door with force and slammed it shut. I knew he was going to stand out there watching over me. I knew him too well but I was grateful.

I splashed some cold water over my face and took in a few deep breaths. I tried to calm my beating heart before it got worse. It would only be a matter of seconds, I knew.

Just as my heart was calming, another door opened in the toilet. I didn't even know the door was there until it moved. My heart lurched again but it went in to full throttle as soon as I saw his body sauntering in to the toilets.

He clocked me before I could move.

Just as I was about to scream, he held a hand over my mouth after running towards my shaking and trembling body.

I tried to scream but he clamped my mouth shut.

"Shut up you bitch." He spat. "You think you can get away with leaving me?" He laughed so evilly the panic came back to hit me.

I couldn't breath.

No. No. Please. Nick.

Help me.

"And now you've got a new man too?" His face came closer until his breath hit my face with force. His chest heaved as he breathed heavily. Those eyes of my nightmares were exactly what haunted me.

They were dark, promising, determined. I knew what they meant and I wished I didn't.

Nick. I need you.

"You know don't you." His eyes glinted. "You know you need to be punished for this, Catherine."

I tried to struggle free as soon as he said the words but as I did so, he grabbed me harder. His nails dug in to my skin, probably drawing blood in its path.

I tried to bite down on his hand, the adrenaline speeding through my veins.

He leaned back and looked to me with a new wave of anger. In a quick flash, I was on the floor as he hit me. I was too scared to make a noise, the adrenaline pushing every thought of pain away from me.

I needed to run. I needed Nick to help me.

I tried to crawl away but he came over and picked me up. I tried to scream again but his hand came to my neck.

I struggled to breath.

"You've missed this haven't you, petal?" He asked, his eyes a light with something I had never seen before. He wanted to hurt me, badly. He got a kick out of it. "Don't worry, you'll have me soon. Right now actually."

No. No. Not again.

"I can't wait any longer." With his hand still on my neck, he undid his jeans with his other hand, the sound of his zipper making a tear fall down my cheek.

I couldn't breath and I was slowly moving in to darkness. It wouldn't be long before I passed out, I knew.

Just as he was about to move forward, the door burst open. As I started to black out, my eyes moved over to the door.

Please, Nick, help me.

However, Nick wasn't there.

In front of the door was a man who was shaking in anger. His eyes were full of shock, his face crumbling in my view.

And behind him was a murdering looking Nick. He ran forward with a shout and as soon as I was let go, I collapsed forward. Someone grabbed a hold of me, sobbing was heard but I couldn't move.

I couldn't breath.

"Fuck!" I heard the scream before I blackened out and I knew the voice before me.

Dad.

CHAPTER 23

I walked through a darkened tunnel, my vision leaving me in an instant. I didn't know where I was going or why I kept walking, I was willing my feet to stop, they never did.

The tunnel was cold as I trudged in wet mud, my heart raced in my chest, seizing me and coiling me tightly.

I heard his voice before I could block him out. I heard his whisper, his growl, his haunting roar. He was everywhere in the darkness.

"You're mine now, Petal." I heard him almost as if he was beside me. "You've always been mine."

His words made the panic really set in. I quickened up my pace until I was sprinting, sprinting away from all of the sounds I could hear of him. I wanted him gone, I needed him gone.

Who was going to help me?

I ran and ran until I couldn't breathe.

Soon, I came to a stop. My eyes adjusted to the darkness and I took in another figure before me. It was a woman, a woman who looked like me.

"Mum?" I said her name, my voice coming out as merely a whisper.

She didn't answer me as she turned. Her eyes darkened with anger and her fists clenched so tightly it hurt to look at.

"You're a liar." She whispered. "You're a liar!"

I woke up and tried to regain the oxygen in to my lungs. I spluttered and gasped as I panicked in my wake. I was disorientated, confused and utterly petrified.

Where was I?

My eyes adjusted to the dark and I realised I was on my own. I was in Nick's bed, my heart slowed down as I took in the safety net of his scent.

However, I was still scared and I tried to scream. I couldn't, the noise wouldn't leave my throat.

With that, I got up from my lying position, my legs shaking as I rounded the bed and made my way outside.

Please, Nick.

I heard their voices before I could see their presence. I walked until my eyes set on the two of them. I mentally relaxed as soon as I did so, he was no where in sight.

Nick paced up and down the living area as Glenn sat solemnly on the sofa. They looked haunted but anger was deep in their veins. My father was physically shaking, his eyes glazed over with something more bone chilling.

Before I could walk any further, Nick lost his temper and hit one of the vases off his coffee table, his knuckles now visibly bleeding and his face looking ready to kill.

Glenn shot up from his seat, murmured something I couldn't hear in to his ear and sat him back down.

"Nick." My voice was weak as I called out his name. As soon as I did so, his face snapped my way and his anger left him in a hurry.

He got off the sofa and made his way over to me. Once he got to me, he took me in to his arms with gentleness and ease. I couldn't help but cry.

"Baby." He breathed. He soothed me down until I was able to talk again. He made me feel safe in his arms, the worry gone even only for a little while.

Nick took my hand once he pulled away. He took it and pulled me along until we were both infront of my father. He looked to us for a few seconds.

"Dad." I said. I didn't know what to say. He knew everything now, or most things, and I was at lost for words. I was embarrassed of what had happened to me, angry with myself that I hadn't told him before he found out.

I just couldn't do it.

Suddenly, Glenn flew up from his seat on the sofa. His eyes were wild and his body physically shaking in anger. I had never seen him like this, I had never seen him so full of anger and hatred.

"Why didn't you tell me?" He roared. I stepped back in fright at the look on his face.

"I-I-"

"I've been stuck here thinking everything was fine and it wasn't!" He shouted. "You were miles away, Cathy, you were half way across the world!"

"I know and I'm sorry but-"

"Does your mother know about this?" He snapped. I wasn't used to seeing my father shout at me like a little girl.

"No." I whispered. Tears welled up in my vision and I felt so helpless and vulnerable. I understood why my father was so angry.

"This is a pisstake, Cathy!" He shouted again. "Why didn't you tell me?" I looked to him, his chest heaving as he breathed. I tried to speak but the words just wouldn't form. I didn't tell him because

I was embarrassed, I didn't want him to worry. I didn't know the right words to say. "Answer me!" He roared.

"That's enough now, Glenn." Nick snapped. "You're taking it too far. Cathy's been through a lot, you should be supporting her."

I stood there in silence as Glenn's stare flickered on to Nick. His nose flared as he took him in.

"You knew about this." He said. "You knew all along. I am her father and I knew nothing." His voice was threatening as he took in Nick.

I couldn't stand this anymore. I couldn't stand the arguing, the fighting, the anger. I wanted this to stop and I wanted everything to be fine again, just like before. I didn't want my dad to be angry, especially not with Nick. I didn't want any of this.

"I know you're angry, Glenn-"

"Angry?" He let out. A tear slipped down his cheek as he looked to Nick as if he didn't have a clue. "Angry isn't the right word for this."

"Dad, I'm sorry I didn't tell you, it was just too hard. I could never find the right words. I never wanted to make you upset or angry, I just wanted you to be happy." I pleaded. He wouldn't understand it from my point of view.

"How could I ever be happy knowing this happened whilst you were away?" He snapped. "I gave your mother one job, one fucking job to look after you and she can't even do that." He shook his head. "I can't right now, Cathy. I can't."

He moved away from our two bodies and moved over to the front door.

"Dad, stay-" my words died down as he slammed the door shut behind him. I fell to the floor and cried as soon as I heard the door shut.

Nick stood still, but I could feel his eyes looking at me. Soon, he bent down.

"I've got to go." He said, his voice strained. "I'm so sorry."

"Don't you dare." I looked to him, anger flooding my every vein. "Don't you dare leave me, Nick." I warned.

"I have to." He said.

"You don't have to!" I shouted. "You can't leave me." I pleaded. Nick laid a kiss to my forehead and stood up again. I scrambled up after him. I held on to his arm tightly. "Don't go."

"I'll be ten minutes." He said, but the look in his eyes told me he'd be much longer. As anger hit me full force again, I released his arm as if it burnt me.

"Go then." I said. I turned my back on him, hoping he'd leave me to it. If he was going to go, I wanted him to. What was he even planning on doing? Why would he want to leave me now?

"Cathy-"

"Get out!" I screamed. Even though this was his home, he had to go. I was so angry I couldn't bare to look at him. After what happened this afternoon, I needed him, I needed him to stay but instead he was off else where.

Why would he want to leave me?

With a small sigh, Nick dropped his hands to his thighs loudly. He left the room a few seconds later and closed the door softly behind him.

I fell to the sofa and cried some more.

Now, I felt lonelier than before.

I walked in to Nick's art studio, the small box roomthat held all of Nick's thoughts and feelings. I went up to the photo he had started to paint of me, the progress no where near finished yet.

I fingered the picture gently and sighed. I couldn't go home because I needed to give my father time to get over this. I hope he wouldn't stay angry for too long. I needed him and I knew he was upset, I would be too.

I sat down on the small plastic chair before a small table. I grabbed a piece of paper spare and laid it before me. I then decided to grab a pencil.

I had been tattooing way before I came back here. I was experienced enough to understand the concepts of everything to do with tattooing, my drawing having to be good.

I was no where as near as good as Nick, but I was good enough.

I started to sketch a cartoon drawing of Nick and I together. It was silly and it was cheesy but it made me feel a little better. I had to trust Nick in everything that he did, I loved him and I needed to let him do what he had to do.

I was angry he left me when I needed him so much but I trusted him enough to let him do his thing.

Still, I missed him.

He had been longer than ten minutes, almost being gone for two hours now.

A door bell suddenly rang out around the house. I jumped at the sound and laid my pencil down on my drawing.

I walked through the apartment and made my way to the front door. I peeped through the small hole in the door and confusion swept through me as I saw the girl Nick worked with. Alice I think her name was. She was the girl I was sure fancied the pants off my boyfriend.

What was she doing here?

I opened the door up straight away and she didn't look surprised at me being on the end of it. She smiled sweetly my way and decided to come in to the apartment without my saying.

"Uh..." I trailed off, not knowing what the hell she was doing.

She sat down on the sofa and made herself at home as if she lived here.

"What are you doing?" I asked. I had already had enough of this week and I wasn't in the mood for being nice and sugar coating things. What the hell was she doing here and why was she acting as if she lived here too?

"I've come to 'baby sit' you." She used her fingers to indicate the words. I looked to her, confusion still evident on my face and now obvious irritation.

"What for?" I asked. Alice shrugged.

"Nick phoned and I'm here." She smiled all smugly and I just wanted to slap it off her face. Why had Nick phoned her out of all people? And I didn't need babysitting!

Nick was going to have an earful off me.

"Do you know where he is?" I questioned. I stood standing as it gave me a feeling of power over tiny Alice.

"I don't know." She shrugged again. "But I heard someone in the background so I assume he was with somebody."

"What did the person sound like?" I asked. I knew I was asking too many questions but I just wanted to know where he has gone. He was in an obvious rush and I was stuck here, not knowing a thing.

"High pitched, annoying-"

"A girl?" My heart started beating. I trusted him, I had to. But Nick was Mr Playboy before me and he was used to obvious girl attention. He was in so much rush and I knew I was big baggage. What if he did have somebody else?

No, no, he couldn't have. He was just on his own and Alice was stirring things. I trusted him.

"Yes." She bluntly replied. God, I wanted to kick her out of here.

"I don't need you Alice." I was being honest. "I want you to leave." I was firm and I hoped she'd listen.

"Nick said-"

"Nick isn't here and Nick's my boyfriend." I snapped. "If I tell you to leave, you leave." I pointed to the door and stared her down. I was being petty but I had been through so much, I didn't need her here making it worse.

"But-"

"Leave!" I shouted. She looked to me before stomping out of the apartment.

Once the door slammed against its hinges, I flopped on to the sofa.

Was this day going to get any worse?

And who the hell is with Nick?

CHAPTER 24

I opened the door to my father's house and braced myself walking inside. I didn't have a clue whether he was here or not or where my mother and father were.

Quite frankly, I didn't care.

Nick hadn't come to the apartment and it had been over five hours now. I was tired of being angry and I was just overall tired. I couldn't be bothered to wait around for him when he was meant to be protecting me, not making me feel more shitty about the whole thing.

I didn't even have it in me to worry about who he was with. I had to trust him, I just had to.

Like hell I was going to listen to Alice anyway. It was obvious she was obsessed with my boyfriend and maybe she just wanted to cause trouble.

I was still angry about the fact Nick had called her over to look after me. As if I was a baby who needed looking after. I was a rape victim and a survivor, not a piece of shit who needed to be watched like a hawk.

I've always protected myself, I didn't need anyone else doing it for me.

Just as I opened the door to the house, my phone rang in my pocket. I didn't answer it until I dropped my bag to the floor and had taken my jacket off.

I answered it quickly as soon as I knew it was Nick.

"Why the hell can't you just do as I say?" He snapped as soon as I had answered the call. I was too tired to act shocked and bothered about him snapping at me at the other end of the phone.

I sighed.

"What do you want, Nick?" I sounded bored, just like I had given up on everything. Maybe I had, I didn't know. Everything was just getting too much for me lately and all I wanted to do was sleep it away.

"You told Alice to leave when I needed her to look after you." He said. "I want you fucking safe, Cathy!"

"Props to her for wanting to do your job." I jabbed. "But the girl fancies you and she was stirring shit up between us."

"Like what?" He replied back irritated.

"Making me believe you were with another girl." I said. He didn't reply but I heard his heavy breathing down the other end of the phone.

"Where are you to?" He completely ignored my statement with another question. "Are you still at the apartment?"

"Nick-"

"Answer me." He snapped.

"No, I'm at my dads." I snapped. "Were you with somebody else?" I asked.

"Why the fuck are you up there?" He boomed. "He could be at home, you're being so fucking stupid right now!" He fumed.

"Get fucking lost." I snapped. I could feel my anger coming back to me at full force. "You should have been looking after me, making sure I was okay! You were meant to be there for me but you'd obviously rather be with somebody else. I fucking need you and you're never bloody there!" I shouted.

"Cathy-"

"Leave me alone, Nick, seriously." I snapped. "Don't ring me, don't come and see me, don't even try anything." I said. "I want to be left alone."

"You can't tell me to do that, you can't tell me I can't see you!" He shouted, his voice becoming one of panic and one of irritation.

"I'll do whatever the hell I please." I said. "Have a good night."

"Cathy, no." He demanded. "That man's made your life a living hell, but you don't need to take it out on me."

"Don't you dare start this. You knew I was damaged goods as soon as I told you the story! If this is too much for you, please say now."

"Don't be fucking ridiculous!" He snapped down the phone. "Don't do this."

"Leave. Me. Alone." I punctuated the sentence carefully. "Before I tell you to never come back at all." My anger was overcoming me so much, it was hard to keep my harsh words at bay. I wanted to hurt him, I didn't know why. I never wanted to see him upset but my anger was just too much.

"You wouldn't do that." He threatened as the oanic really started to set in to his voice.

"Bye, Nick." I said.

"Cathy, please-" I hung up the phone before he could say anything else. As soon as I did so, I flung the phone on to the arm chair.

I walked around the house, my body being dragged as if I were a zombie. I couldn't feel a thing. It felt as if my body was completely numb, mentally and physically. This whole ordeal was mentally draining and I was just too past gone to even feel anything.

It was hard to cope when the person you needed didn't want to help you. It was hard to cope when you were barely coping in the first place.

I felt more alone now than I ever had before.

Walking around the house, I realised that I was alone here.

My father was no where to be seen so I rang my mother to see where her and her husband were. If they were going to come back home, I needed to find somewhere else to go. Maybe I could ring up Danni to sleep there for a few days?

My mother answered the phone after a few rings.

"Hey, darling."

"Mom, where are you to?" I asked. I couldn't bring myself to ask about her husband.

"We're both at a hotel." She said. I started to panic as I realised Glenn could have told her about what happened. "John thought it was only best as we didn't want to over stay our welcome." Oh, so it seemed John had the right idea.

I didn't know what had happened to him after, did Nick and my father beat him up? Did mom suspect something? I had so many questions now running through my mind, even though it seemed everything was okay.

"So you're not coming back?" I asked, hoping they wouldn't.

"No, darling." She said. "Unless you want to see me?"

"No." I let out a little forcefully. I had to catch myself. "No thank you, mom. I'm going to have an early night."

"Okay, love." She said. "I'll see you tomorrow."

"Yeah." I hoped I didn't have to see him. "See you." I hung up the phone and fell to the floor. It seemed I was becoming a right mess, inside and out.

I came here to get away from all of this. I moved so I could get away from him, start a new life and get happy again. Just as everything was starting to look up, my world started to move again beneath my feet.

Just as I had started to stop my quick beating heart, the door opened and my father came in to view. I looked up at him, my eyes starting to tear up at the sight of him. He looked worn down, his usual smile now a frown and his face one of depression.

I wish this could have all gone away.

"Birdy." His voice cracked as he took in my tear strained face. "I'm so sorry." He got to the floor beside me and took me in to his arms. "I never meant to have a go at you. None of this is your fault. I'm just so angry about the whole thing, my one dying wish was to make sure you're always okay. I was so mad to find out the worst whilst you were away. It was never meant to be like this."

"I couldn't stop it." I sobbed. "I tried and I just couldn't stop any of it."

"Cathy, don't." He whispered. "None of this is your fault. None of it." He sounded firm.

"I tried to leave but mom wouldn't let me come and see you until I was an adult. After that, I wasn't allowed because he kept black mailing me until I was strong enough to do it." I stated as I started to hiccup. "I needed you but you were so far away."

"If only I had known." He said. "If I had known, this would have never happened, I promise."

"I wish I never left you, dad." I looked to him.

"I wish you never left me either." He replied. He took my face in his hands as he continued to look my way. "He won't ever hurt you again, Cathy, do you understand?" He looked serious, his eyes one of determination to look after me. I believed him when he said it.

"I understand." I breathed.

"He will never, ever, touch you again, I promise you this with my life." His voice was strong. "You have to believe me."

"Of course I believe you." I said. "You're my father and I love you."

"And you're my daughter and I let you down."

"No you didn't." I snapped. "How were you meant to know?"

"I don't know." He shrugged. "A father should just know when their little girl is in trouble."

"You weren't meant to know, I made sure you didn't." I said. "None of this is your fault either."

"I'm just broken inside, Cathy. You're the only thing I have left. Knowing what had happened to you..." he laid his hands to his head. "God."

"Stop this." I pulled his hands away from his head. "We can move on from this now. We can. Hopefully mom and him will go back to Australia soon and we can move on with our lives." I sounded hopeful.

"Yeah." Glenn didn't seem too convinced. He got up from the floor. "Where's Nick?" He asked.

"He's out and about." I looked down to the floor, hoping he wouldn't catch on to the fact we had argued.

"What's the matter?" Glenn asked. He knew straight away something wasn't right.

"Nothing, we've just argued that's all." I shrugged as if it were no big deal.

"I'm sure you'll be okay." He said. "The man worships the ground you walk on." He stated. "He's lucky he does or I'd break his neck too."

"Maybe." I wasn't entirely convinced anymore. Not after tonight.

"There's no maybe about it. And it's obvious you love him too."

"I do but..." I shrugged, not really wanting to talk about it. My father caught on quickly and sighed instead of replying.

My father came over and gave me a helping hand to get up off from the floor. I took it and was standing up in no time.

"Look at me." He said. I looked to my dad.

"I promise you everything's going to be okay."

"I believe you." It had to be okay, it just had to be. I couldn't continue living like this, not knowing what was going to come creeping up on me. I didn't want to be scared to turn my neck and see him there. I didn't want to be scared anymore.

"I'll do what I needed to do before this all started."

"What's that?" I asked.

"Protect you."

I walked through a darkened tunnel. The sounds came back to haunt me, again and again and again. They never went.

I could hear him again echoing in my ear. He told me he wanted me, he told me that I was his and his only.

I tried to run again and my legs worked faster as the minutes went on. I was running at full speed, my lungs exhaling and inhaling oxygen quickly.

I needed to get away.

Suddenly, I got to the end of the tunnel. The noises stopped and I saw a figure before me. This figure was one of a male's, not a female's, and I recognised it instantly.

"Nick?" I called his name. He turned to look at me, his eyes shining brightly as he saw me, but his mouth was turned in to a frown.

"You did this to us." He said. "You've ruined everything."

"What do you mean?" I stammered. "What have I done?"

"Your baggage has damaged me." He scowled my way. "Now I'm locked up and trapped here."

"Nick-"

"We're never getting out."

I woke up with a frightened start. My head was saturated with sweat but my body was freezing cold. I had to stop my beating heart from rattling against my rib cage.

Just as I was about to pick up the phone to ring Nick, I heard the front door shut downstairs. Was somebody coming in?

I was about to pick up the bat beneath my bed, my half sleepy state making me think that he was coming back for me, to hurt me again, before I heard the sound of my father's car drive off in the distance.

I called my beating heart and flopped back in to bed. My father used to always drive off in the middle of the night whenever he was feeling low. He was probably going for a drive to clear that head of his after the last twenty four hours.

I didn't blame him.

Anyway, I picked up my phone and texted Nick quickly.

Where are you?

He still hadn't come back to see me but hopefully he was back at his apartment by now.

In under a minute, my phone pinged with an incoming text. I picked my phone up quickly.

Go to sleep. Everything will be okay.

I text him back.

Are you at your apartment?

Hopefully he was.

Yes. Nothing to worry about. Go to sleep.

Okay, so he was back at his apartment. I started to relax again and was able to leave my phone and try and get back to sleep.

It was a restless night and I tossed and turned for the majority of it. I just couldn't sleep, no matter how hard I tried. Sometimes, I got in to a small slumber but was easily jumpy and I jumped out of it most of the time.

I was even awake for when my father got home not long after he left.

But finally, I was able to sleep at around four in the morning. However, after what seemed like half an hour of a light sleep, my phone rang beneath my pillow.

Who the hell needed to ring me at this time?

My mother's name flashed upon my screen.

"Mom?" I was confused as to why she rang me. Soon, I heard her sobbing on the other end of the phone.

"Cathy." She sobbed. "He's dead." My heart started leaping.

"Who's dead?" Was my father okay? He had left only a few hours ago and I knew he was home now. Nick had texted me a few hours ago too, so they both should have been fine.

"John." She cried. "John's dead."

CHAPTER 25

I never considered death a good thing, in fact, it was something I feared during many sleepless and thoughtful nights as a child. When I started to grow up, I wondered whether death would be the most peaceful thing, a happier place to be.

Death to me wasn't always a thing to celebrate, but tonight, even though it wasn't always acceptable, things were different. A part of me was so relieved I wanted to celebrate.

I mean, have you ever laid awake praying that something would all stop? I prayed so hard, I cried in to my pillow as I wished upon every star to get me out of there.

It was a little too late now but something had worked. He was gone and some kind of weight was lifted off my shoulders.

I was free.

And freedom never felt so good.

I laid a wake the rest of the night, my eyelids not closing once. I didn't lay there in fear anymore, I didn't have to be afraid that he would walk in any moment. I could lay here in peace, and if felt so good.

Still, my heart turned in my chest when I thought about my mother. How did she not find out about what he had done to me? When was the right time to tell her?

There were still so many questions running around my mind. Also, how the hell did John die? My mother didn't tell me much on the other end of the phone, she had to hang up as soon as she told me, she seemed a mess and in no need to talk to me.

I felt bad for her, even though this was what I wanted.

Of course I wanted my demon dead. Anybody who lived in a walking, day time night mare wanted the monsters dead.

Hopefully, somebody was looking down on me and decided to make his death a peaceful one. Peace wasn't something I wanted for him, but I had gotten what I wanted and the least it could have been was peaceful.

He was gone, I didn't need to hold a grudge any longer. I could now move on with my life, my life with Nick.

When the sun came up and birds started to chirp, I knew there was just no way I could fall asleep now. I rolled out of bed like a sleep deprived zombie and made my way to the kitchen.

Once I got there, I wasn't surprised to see my father also awake with a coffee in his hands.

"Can't sleep?" He questioned my way before I was in his line of sight. I sighed and moved to the coffee machine.

"Not a wink." I stated. "Has mom rang you?" I asked. She rang me so early on the morning I hadn't asked anyone whether they knew. Did Nick know? Should I text him?

"Yeah." He sighed. "He's dead." He said the words but his words weren't full of remorse. He seemed almost as relieved as me.

"How do you feel?"

"Hell's the best place for him." He mumbled. I looked to him, agreeing, but the words would have never left his mouth before.

My father was never a horrible man, he was always so full of humour and light and now? My father was a man full of hatred and hollowness. "Don't look at me like that."

I held my hands up in mock surrender. He was obviously hurting just like I was.

"I'm not going to feel sorry for him, I'm not going to pretend I feel sad he's dead." He replied. "I'm happy he's dead, I hope he died in torture for what he did to you."

"I'm only shocked because you've never spoken about a person like that before." I replied truthfully.

"Well, I'm hurting, Cathy." He looked to me, his eyes one of sadness and anger. There were evident bags beneath his eyes. "I'm allowed to feel this way."

"Of course you are." I said, my face softening. "I don't blame you one bit."

Once my coffee was made, I cradled the cup to my chest and stared off in to space. I really needed Nick right now, it was maddening how much I missed him once he was gone. I hadn't heard back from him since the texts last night and even then it sounded like he didn't want to talk to me.

Was it too much for him to look at me? What was going on with him?

I loved that man, well and truly. I had fallen in love with him and even though I was trying to act strong, I felt like breaking. This was already too much to handle and Nick not being here just made me crack that little bit more.

I needed him, that was all.

My father and I continued to sip our coffee's in silence. My father hadn't been to the shop in quite a while and I hadn't worked there. The rest was nice but I think the distraction of tattooing would be good right now. I needed something to take my mind off of the drama that has unfolded.

"Are you opening up the shop today?" I asked as I moved to sit down on a barstool next to my father.

"Nah." He said. "I can't work today, I have some things to take care of." He sighed. "I probably also need to see your mother."

"You're not going to tell her are you?" I started to panic. I knew I really needed to tell her what had happened and what had gone down whilst she was away on night shifts, it's just the thought made me physically sick. I didn't have to tell my father, he found out and my mother was a whole different story. She loved the man.

"No, but you really do need to tell her someday." He stated. "And soon. She needs to know, as a parent, hiding something like this does more damage than good."

"I know." I sighed again as I laid a hand to my head. "I promise I will tell her soon."

"Don't leave to too late." Glenn got up from the barstool and put his cup of coffee in to the sink. He came over to give me a small kiss on the top of my forehead before going to leave.

"Where are you going?" I asked.

"I'm going to get changed and then go and see your mother." He said. "God knows what she's going to be like."

"I'm sure you'll cheer her up." My father could cheer anybody up and easily too.

"I'm not sure anymore, Birdy." He looked to me. "I can barely cheer myself up."

I walked over to the tattoo shop that my father owned. He hadn't opened up today and left the place closed as he went to see my mother, however, that didn't stop me from going to the place anyway and having a look around.

I needed a distraction and this was the quickest one I could think of. I had my phone clutched in my right hand and the key in my other. I unlocked the shop and closed it behind me.

Firstly, I wanted to give Nick another ring. I was angry last night, the fear really got to me and it seemed my past had caught up with me. I didn't want him to leave me alone, I didn't want to be alone full stop.

I hoped Nick wasn't too busy now to come and see me. I was missing him and it felt like I needed him now more than ever.

I called him but he didn't pick up.

That was weird. Nick always picked up the phone, especially if he knew I was calling. Was he purposely ignoring me or was he just not near his phone? Even when he was working, he'd usually pick up.

Did I piss him off that much?

I laid down my phone with a huge sigh. I then moved over to the tattoo bench and used my fingers to gently probe at the utensils beside it.

I just felt so lonely. My father wasn't his usual self, he was upset, hurt and pulled back. It was usual and I didn't blame him but I felt as if everything was my fault. I felt as if Nick didn't want to see me, he didn't even pick up my phone call. I really needed to see him. As for my mother, we used to be close and then we drifted a part once she re married. I missed having her as a mother and right now, I needed my mother to speak to. She just didn't know any of this.

My life was one big utter mess and I was feeling the backlash.

Behind me suddenly, I heard the door open of the shop. Thinking it was my father, I turned around.

Before me was Nick. He wore his police uniform and he looked so utterly handsome. His face made me want to cry, he was here, as if answering my prayers.

"Nick." I smiled his way, relief flooding my every being. However, Nick didn't smile back. He looked to me, his face drained and his eye bags evident, just like my father's. He looked a mess, just as bad as me. Something was troubling him tremendously, I could tell. "Are you okay?" I asked, my smile leaving my face and now a look of worry evident there.

Nick didn't reply. Instead, he walked forward with hesitancy, almost as if he didn't know whether to or not, as if he didn't know what to say.

"Nick?" I called his name again. His eyes looked glazed over, like his head wasn't at all here, like he wasn't at all here.

Nick moved forward and sat on the tattoo bench before me. He looked down at his spread knees, not at me. It looked like he was physically shaking before me but he didn't say a word.

"You're scaring me." I breathed. "What's wrong?" My heart was beating fast. What was wrong with him? He was acting so weird lately.

"I've had an offer back from university." He said. I waited but he didn't say anything more.

"That's amazing." I stated truthfully. Why was he looking so ashen? This was amazing for him! Something he's always wanted! And he got an offer back so quickly too. "Why aren't you happy?"

"It's not a University around here." He stated.

"Okay, so where is it?" A few towns over? Maybe in another state? That was okay, I would follow him wherever his dreams took him. I wanted to get out of here anyway.

"Italy." Italy? Jesus Christ, that was ages away.

"Well, that's cool!" I stated. "We could save money and go there together, buy a cheap flat over there and-"

"You don't get it!" Nick snapped. "I'm going without you." He struggled past his words and his face looked up to look at me.

"What do you mean without me?" I questioned. I shot up from the place I was sat on and looked down at him, panick setting in and anger washing over me. He was going to leave me right now? After everything that had happened? I fucking needed him! "You're going to Italy without me?"

"Yes." He swallowed strongly. "I've got to."

"You're a fucking joke!" I shouted. "You've found somebody else haven't you? Somebody who hasn't got baggage and someone who can fuck you any day you like." My words were harsh as the tears poured down my cheeks. "So now you're leaving me?"

"No!" He shouted. As he looked to me, his face fell again. "Yes." He breathed.

"Get out." I gritted my teeth together as I pointed to the door. "Get the fuck out of here!"

"Cathy, please-"

"I fucking loved you." I sobbed. I still did and my heart was breaking. "I had fallen in love with you. I'm so fucking stupid." I cried. "So stupid!" I knocked a hand to my head.

"No." He breathed, his eyes becoming teary themselves. "No!" He shouted. He went to move towards me but I took many steps back.

"Don't you dare." I hissed. "Don't you fucking dare touch me or I will scream this bloody place down."

"You love me?" He questioned. He looked to me, his face full of guilt and heartbreak itself. Well, I wasn't going to be on the other end of his pity.

"I used to love you." I pointed in to his chest. "But now I hate you." My words were still so harsh and it looked like they hit him forcefully with every word. He took a step back from me as if I had burned him.

"Don't say things you don't fucking mean!" He growled loudly. "You don't hate me, you can't hate me." He seemed panicked.

"You're leaving me when I need you the most you selfish prick." I snapped. "You don't love me, you never have!"

"Don't say shit!" He roared. "Don't say fucking shit!"

"Get out!" I screamed as I pointed to the door. "Get out and don't ever come back!"

"Cathy!"

"Have a good time in Italy, Nick. I hope you find somebody out there who has more patience than I ever did with you." I glared at him, my eyes looking right in to his soul. "I hope you fall in love someday instead of messing with everybody else's feelings."

"I never-"

"Get out." I stood my ground. Knowing I wasn't going to budge, Nick looked to me before sighing. With teary eyes and a few more seconds, Nick turned his back.

I thought I heard him say I love you, but I knew it was just something I wanted to hear.

I had wanted to hear it since the day I realised I had fallen in love with him.

But sometimes, people fall in love with somebody who doesn't love them back.

I was one of them.

CHAPTER 26

As soon as the door slammed against its hindges, my body kicked into over drive. No, he couldn't leave. I loved him too much to watch his back turn and to watch him leave me like this. I loved him too much to not work this out.

I ran out of the shop after him, my body running on adrenaline and what seemed to be the energy from my breaking heart. And it really was breaking. I needed him, I couldn't watch him leave me.

"Nick!" I shouted. His body turned on the pavement and he watched me run after him. He didn't move but his intense eyes on my body gave me the confidence I needed. They always did. "Please, you can't go." I pleaded. I stopped before him, my breath coming out in short pants.

"I-"

"We can talk this out, I can make this better." I was desperate now, so desperate. I needed him to see sense, I needed him to want me. "Just don't go, don't leave me, please Nick, please." I was almost sobbing as I now clutched on to the sleeve of his sweatshirt.

"I have to." He breathed. "I have to."

"You don't have to." I looked at him, his eyes showing me that he was also breaking. If this was too much for him, why was he doing it? We could be happy together, we were anyway.

Nick sighed before laying two hands to my face. I let him touch me, his touch already making me feel calmer, safer.

"I have to." He repeated. "This was never going to be easy and I wanted to leave you angry, not like this." He looked to me. "I wanted you to hate me so leaving would be easier."

"Don't leave at all!" I cried. "Nick, please, I love you." A tear fell from my eyes and Nick wiped it away. As soon as he did, he squeezed his eyes shut tightly. He shook his head as if he didn't want to hear the words at all.

"Don't." A strangled cry left his lips. "Don't make this harder than it is."

"I love you, Nick." I repeated forcefully. "I'll do anything, I promise."

"Cathy, stop." Nick snapped but his eyes started to tear up. I looked to him, wondering why he was feeling this way. Why did he want to leave me? Didn't I make him happy? Was I too much baggage? I had so many questions and no willpower to ask them. I needed him to stay first, because watching his back turn was just too much. He was hurting me, couldn't he see?

"I'll do anything for you, Nick. I'm sorry if I've never showed it, I'm sorry if I haven't made you happy but you walking out on me is going to kill me, Nick, I fucking need you, I need you more than anything." I didn't want to lay all the cards on the table this way. Should I have told him I loved him sooner? Didn't I make it obvious? I was a closed off person but I tried to show him I loved him. Because I did, and something like that was hard to cut off.

But he didn't realise how much I needed him.

"Cathy, you're guttering me." He breathed, a small tear left his eye as he said the words. He didn't bother wiping it away, I think he wanted me to see it, to see how much I was effecting him.

"I just want you to come home with me, Nick." I whispered, my throat closing so tightly I couldn't breath. I hadn't realised Nick leaving would make me hurt this much. Or maybe I had, I just hadn't thought about it. The thought was too much, and this was damn right unbearable.

"These last few months have showed me exactly where my home lies and it's with you, but I need to leave and you need to trust me." He looked to me, his eyes pleading. "You need to trust me and just give me some time, okay?"

"How much time do you need?" I asked. Could I give him time? "What do you want from me?"

"I've got to go, Cathy." He looked to me. "I need to leave." He flickered his eyes around us.

"Nick, tell me you're not leaving me." I pleaded. He left my body feeling bereft as he started to move backwards. "Nick!" I cried.

"I'm sorry, Cathy, for everything." His eyes started to tear up again, his face serious and so genuine. He was breaking, I could tell, I was feeling it too.

"Nick, no." I sobbed. "No." I could barely breath.

"I love you." He sobbed before he turned his back towards me and left. I watched his back leave, his words hanging in the air.

I collapsed to the floor, his body now gone with my heart leaving with him. He had torn me up inside and I felt like nothing.

If he loved me, why did he walk away?

Was this the way love was supposed to feel? I didn't feel loved, I felt bereft and hollow inside. My heart felt stomped on.

I couldn't breath as I gasped for breath on the side walk. I could barely sit straight as my body and mind wrecked havoc.

God, it hurt so much.

This was not how love was supposed to feel.

It was starting to become dark and I was still on the pavement. My tears had dried up and now I felt nothing. No sadness, no anger, no nothing, I felt like a body where all my organs had left me.

It was easy to say I was heart broken and it seemed the world had slowed down minute by minute. My world was turning on its axis and I just wished I didn't feel this way.

Walking home was a lot harder when it was difficult to move, difficult to stand up straight without wobbling and difficult to breath when the air felt so thick around me.

I was struggling, it was clear. I was lacking support and love from the people I needed it most from. I needed more than this, I needed something because the nothingness I felt during my time in Australia was fast approaching I would do anything to not go back to where I was before.

I needed my dad right now.

Once I got to my house, the lights were on throughout. The feeling of relief washed across my body. I couldn't be alone right now, no, isolation was the worst thing I could do.

I walked in to the house but heard talking almost straight away. In the living room sat my father, my mother and a police officer. The sight of his uniform was enough to make my heart crack that little bit more. Nick wore that outfit and he always looked so good in it.

I shook the thoughts away and appeared before my parents. They both looked to me, my father's arm around my mother and her eyes all tear strained and blotchy.

I hadn't seen my parents so close since their divorce many years ago.

"You okay, Cathy?" My father asked, his face looking concerned at my probably blotchy face. I couldn't speak, the lump in my throat growing bigger. Instead, I nodded and sat down on the arm chair which was vacant. The police officer standing in the middle of the room looked to me. I paid him no attention.

The officer started to tell my parents what he came here for.

"We're still researching and we've got a very good team working with us at the moment. They're checking to see whether John's death was a suicide or a killing." My mum made a noise at his words.

"Who would want to kill him?" She wailed. I looked to my father and he looked down as soon as I looked over. My eyes narrowed his way.

A killing? Could he have been murdered? By who?

"What are you suspecting so far?" Glenn asked. I watched him as he looked up to the police officer. It was evident to see he didn't give a shit about John. I was becoming suspicious.

"I can't tell you, I'm afraid. We haven't had much information back yet." The grey haired man replied. My father nodded.

After a few more minutes, the police officer left. My mother continued to sit on the sofa as she sobbed. And even though I wasn't upset about the news, I knew exactly how she was feeling. Her heart was breaking, she loved her husband, I gave her that, and now he was gone, she was obviously hurting.

Nick wasn't dead but I felt just as hollow without him as my mother felt without her husband.

I didn't know whether I could tell her yet what he did to me. How would she take it? This was already too much for her and I didn't want her to continue feeling like this. Not if she felt the same way I did. At the end of the day, she was my mother and I loved her dearly.

My father left my mother with a few soft words as he announced he was going to make coffee. Still feeling suspicious, I followed after him and closed the kitchen door behind me.

"Why are you closing the door?" He asked. I looked to him, my tear strained cheeks must have been evident. "What's wrong?" His concerned father look was straight back on his face.

The lump got bigger again and before I knew it, I was sobbing in my father's chest, forgetting the reason I came in here.

"What the hell's the matter?" He asked, his voice beginning to panic. "Has something happened?"

"He's left me." I sobbed as the tears kept coming. "He's gone."

"Who?" He asked. As if it finally clicked, he said "oh."

"Oh?" I cried. Oh was all he was going to give me?

"The fucking bastard." Glenn shot out. "I'm sorry, Birdie." He soothed. "Did he say why?"

"He said he's going to Italy for University as he had an offer, but without me." I said. "So he left me."

"He doesn't know what he's missing." My father replied. "It's his loss."

"You don't get it, dad." I snapped. "I love him."

"And he loves you, I know he does." My father stated. "He loves you more than anything."

"So why has he gone?"

My father couldn't answer, didn't answer. The room was filled with a silence and I was struggling to be silent right now. I wanted answers but it was clear to see I wasn't going to get any.

"Dad?" After a few moments of silence, I gathered his attention. "Did you kill him?" I was just going to be blunt. I wanted to know.

My father moved away in an instant. He looked to me with shock.

"Of course not!" He shot out. "I wanted him dead but I don't have a killing bone in my body." He looked appalled. "I thought about it but I would never have gone through with it, it was just a fantasy of mine."

"You just looked suspicious, that's all." I studied him but his face looked genuine. I couldn't see my father killing anyone either. It just wasn't in him.

"I'm just as shocked as you are at his death." He replied. He quickly turned his back to me and started to make the coffee.

"Dad-"

"I didn't kill him, Cathy, I swear."

"I believe you." I said, and I did. But John's death was the least of my worries.

"And you don't have to worry about Nick." He stated. "If you both love each other that much, you'll find a way back."

"But that's the thing, I don't know if he loves me. He said he did, but he's leaving me, what am I meant to think?" I asked.

"All you can do is believe him, Cathy." He said. "He's never been with a girl more than a week, let alone tell anyone he loves them. I don't know what's going on with him but what I do know is that that boy loves the socks off you. He'll make his way back to you, he will because that's how love works."

"And you're so sure?" I liked his hopeful thinking, I wish I could keep on to it and hold it close. But I was feeling negative about everything, I wasn't so sure he was ever going to come back to me.

I wanted him to.

"You don't move on quickly, I mean, look at me, I'm still in love with your mother even after all these years."

"You are?" I asked shocked.

"Of course I am, can't you tell?" I hadn't really looked at it closely, my mind had been else where since she came here.

I was still shocked to silence. My father still loved my mother? I guess it was easy to see. He had a lack of female companions, he never really talked about my mother but when he did it was always out of love and niceness, never bitterness. And when John came here, he hated him from the start without having any reason to at the beginning.

It had been years and he let her love someone else.

I couldn't let Nick love someone else. I couldn't watch him do that.

"And I need you to promise me something, Cathy." He said. He looked to me and I looked to him, listening. "You need to tell your mother what John did to you. You need to tell her everything."

I knew I had to some day, but the words still made my heart pound in my chest.

"She deserves to know and you deserve to tell her." He said. "This is your chance to move on, she's the only way you can."

CHAPTER 27

Two days had gone by and I hadn't gotten better, in fact, it seemed as if I was just getting worse. I didn't have high hopes for Nick texting me or even ringing me, but I had tried and I felt a little less hopeful everytime he ignored it.

I had had my fair share of boys in the past but no one quite like Nick. I hadn't ever felt like this before. The things I felt for Nick were so strong, so real, now he's gone all those feelings felt just as strong. I wanted him back with me, I needed him and he knew it.

I still didn't know why he left. He said he loved me, he said he didn't want to leave but he had to. Why? Why did he have to go? For university? I knew it was his dream but I'd have gone along to support him in anything he did. Maybe he just didn't love me anymore, I guess that was okay.

My heart didn't feel okay, though.

Someone needed to come and pick up the pieces.

I hadn't eaten much these last few days. I'm sure I was losing weight and it took so much effort trying to get out of bed every morning. Dad still had the shop shut and I was grateful, I couldn't work feeling the way I did. I could barely walk without shaking on the pads of my feet.

Love really took a toll on you and a part of me regretted ever falling in love with him. I should have known this was never going to work. He was a playboy, a ladies man and I guess a leapord never changed it's spots.

I shook my head. I couldn't think like this. I loved the man so much, I knew I couldn't continue like this. He obviously wasn't going to come back to me so I needed to move on.

But even the thought of doing so took the breath out of my lungs. I didn't want to move on, I didn't want to be without him full stop.

"Cathy?" My dad's voice came out from behind my bedroom door. I laid in bed and as I stared at the ceiling, I willed my tears to stop. I was going to run out of them.

"Yeah?" I croaked back. I heard him sigh.

"Can I come in?"

"Sure." My voice was small but he heard me nonetheless. The door creaked open moments later and he hesitantly walked in to the room, a look of apprehension on his face. His comical stare was laughable, I just didn't have it in me to laugh.

My father sat at the end of my bed and looked to me, his face one of guilt and one that seemed out of its depths. He didn't know what to do with a broken hearted girl and I was right there with him. What could you do when your heart felt in two?

"You haven't eaten for days." He stated. "And you've barely gotten out of bed." I nodded my head but I knew my stare was vacant.

Glenn sighed again.

"I will literally call the doctors if you don't start improving. This isn't healthy, love, not one bit."

"I know." I breathed. "I can't help it." I wanted to go back to my normal self and I knew one day I would. I had gotten out of this state before and I knew I could do it again, but this time it felt a whole lot different. It was easier to get rid of someone hurtful than to bring back someone who doesn't love you anymore.

He said he did but the more he goes, the less I believe him.

"You can't give up on him yet, Cathy, you know that don't you?"

"What more is there to do?" I looked to him, I knew he could see the pain in my eyes.

"You're my daughter, we don't give up the fight." He stated.

"You did. Mum married another man and you were left lonely, dont you get that?" I asked. "The woman who left you didn't love you anymore, just like Nick doesn't love me. You can't force something if it's not there."

"You really believe there isn't something there between you and Nick?" He spluttered. "How many times do I have to point it out? Nick wouldn't have ever acted the way he did over just anybody. He didn't act like he did for anything but the fact he adores you. There's something up with him at the moment and you have the power to get it out of him, you know, you're the only woman with the power."

"I don't know." I just didn't know. It hurt to think and thinking made it all the worse. I didn't want to lose all hope but I didn't want to gain any either, just incase. I wanted to fight for us but how much did I have to fight? I didn't see Nick trying to save us, he only ever wanted to leave lately.

"You need to go and talk to him properly." He stated.

"I've tried."

"Then keep trying." He pressed further. "I gave up too soon with your mum, Cathy, way too soon. You can't make the same mistakes as me, you can't let him brush you off like this. Settle this before you go insane."

I felt already passed it.

Just as I was about to open my mouth and reply to my father, my phone rang on the side table beside my bed. My heart sky rocketed, could it be Nick on the other end of the phone? What would I say if it were him?

I knew I couldn't let myself feel hopeful like this but I just couldn't help it. My father looked to the phone and urged me to answer it. I almost jumped to it.

Once I saw the caller ID, my heart fell. It wasn't him but it was Emily. Emily never rang me, we texted a lot but she never really rang. If she wanted me she would usually ring Nick first.

I picked the phone up without hesitation.

"Hey?" My greeting was almost a question. Was everything okay?

"Cathy, what the hell is happening?" She gushed down the phone. Her voice was full of shock and irritation.

My father left the room quietly, he gave me one last look before shutting the door behind him.

"What do you mean?" I questioned.

"I swear to Jesus if this is true I'm going to flip a shit."

"What are you talking about?" I'm sure Emily always talked in riddles. I never quite understood what she was trying to get at but that made her more the endearing.

"Xavier's just announced the news that Nick had left you!" She was getting louder on the phone as the seconds went by. As soon as she said the sentence, I couldn't help but burst in to tears. "Oh, no, Cathy. I'm so sorry, honey." Her voice was now a lot softer and I couldn't help but cry all the more.

"I miss him already." I stated. "I just want him back."

"I know." She soothed. "I don't know what the fuck he's playing at."

"I love him, Em, I really do." I couldn't help but state what I was feeling. I knew Emily knew my feelings for Nick the first ever time she saw me. She could read me like an open book, I knew it. I felt so vulnerable but it was so comforting to know that she new exactly how I felt.

"I know, babe." She sighed. "I know exactly how you're feeling. Xavier and I never had an easy relationship, you know. We broke up at one point and it was the hardest thing I ever had to go through. It's hard to watch the man you love go, no matter who calls the shots."

"I don't know what to do. I'm so lost and it's killing me."

"When you're lost you either die or you make your way home." She stated. "And you're going home, Cathy, Nick saved my relationship once, it's time for me to do the same back."

"But what if he doesn't want me back? What if he doesn't love me?-"

"Don't be so absurd!" She shouted. I jumped and the phone nearly fell out of the grasps of my hand. "Meet me at Nick's apartment this afternoon."

"Why?" I asked. Was I ready for that today? I had barely left my bed since he left. Could I really put myself through any more trauma?

Emily and Xavier knew nothing about my step dad and what he did to me. That was also a big part of this.

"We're going to sort this and we're going to sort it together." She said. "So get ready and make a clear head."

"I don't know if I can do it-"

"You're doing it." Emily stated. "And try not to be so hard on yourself. It's destructive."

I caught the bus to Nick's apartment. It was different to the feel over his rusty old van but I'd take it over this bus any day.

My heart was beating fifty miles a minute and it seemed the further we got to his apartment, the worse it became.

I wanted this to go well. Would Nick welcome me with open arms or push me away? I wanted him to want me and I wanted him to love me the way I loved him. If this didn't work this afternoon, then I didn't know what would. Maybe then, I'd have to give up on us. I can't be the one making all this effort to get us back.

If he didn't want me, I wanted chance to move on.

Once I got to the apartment, I saw Emily and Xavier standing outside. I exited the bus and made my way over to them.

"Hey, babe." Emily hugged me tightly and I willed the tears to stay in my eye sockets. Xavier gave me a quick hug which was so like Xavier before moving away.

"Are you sure he's in?" I asked. He could easily be working or out with his friends. When did he even leave for Italy? He barely told me anything about it.

"Xavier text him this morning. He's in all day." She said. "But I think he's in a bad way." She looked to Xavier and he nodded solemnly. "He only replied to Xavier by text, he wouldn't answer the phone when we rang him." She shrugged.

"Luckily I've got a spare key or otherwise we wouldn't be seeing him at all today." Xavier stated. God, was he really that bad?

Xavier led the way and Emily and I followed after him. I was almost shaking as we made our way to his apartment. The elevator ride felt like it took forever but it realistically only took a few seconds.

I remembered the memories we had in this elevator, the first time he took me to his apartment was my most fondest. Something he never, ever did with a girl.

I was the first and now probably not the last.

Once we got to Nick's apartment door, the loud music coming from behind the wooden door was easily heard. Once Xavier unlocked and opened the door, the music was now ten times louder and it shook the whole apartment.

Emily looked to me with furrowed brows but it did nothing to comfort me. Once all three of us were inside of the apartment, Xavier turned to us both.

"I think it's best if I talk to him alone!" I had never heard Xavier shout even when it was just to be heard over the music.

I looked around the floor and there were beer bottles and vodka bottles thrown all across the floor. Some were smashed to smithereens and some were whole bottles.

I gasped at the mess of the apartment.

"No." I shot out. "I need to see him." Now I was here, I wasn't going to leave without him. This wasn't the way he usually lived and there was no way I was going to let him live like this, with or without me.

The apartment was a pig sty and there was no doubt Nick was the same.

Without further instruction, I started to walk around his apartment to find him. My movements were rushed and the longer it took to find him, the more worried I became. This behaviour just wasn't Nick and something was off.

I almost ran to his studio. The small room that held all of his feelings and thoughts. As soon as I opened the door, I knew he was in there.

Nick was leaning against the wall opposite me, the painting of me beside him. All of his pictures across the wall were now ruined and damaged, they looked as if they had been shredded with scissors or punched by bare hands.

The only photo in tact was the photo of me.

"Nick!" I shouted over the music. His eyes were closed and his head lulled against his chest as he heaved. He started to grow a beard and his eyes were puffy and extremely baggy.

He didn't hear me.

I rushed over to him and crouched beside him. I wished the music would just shut up!

"Nick!" I shouted again. He heard me this time and his eyes shot to mine. They were blood shot and very red. Even though he was looking at me, his eyes were glazed and were not focusing.

He was drunk.

Extremely drunk.

"Shit." I breathed. I went to touch him but his body flinched away from it. I looked to him with ears pooling my eyes.

Where was my Nick? What had he done to himself?

"Cathy." He slurred. "What are you doing here?" His mouth was almost turned to a sneer.

The music suddenly turned off and a few moments later I could feel both Xavier and Emily stood behind me.

"I came to talk to you." I said. "I came to make things right."

"What's there to make right?" He laughed but there was no humour involved. "Nothing's right."

"Nick-"

"Leave me alone." He sneered. "And don't touch me. His words made me jolt back as if he had shocked me. I felt as if his words hand burnt me beyond repair.

Xavier stepped forward just as soon as I flew back from him.

"That's enough now, Nick." Nick pushed Xavier away forcefully. Xavier didn't seem effected by it but there was a bit of irritation there in the depths of his eyes.

"Don't be a fucking twat, Nick." He growled.

Emily laid a hand to Xavier's shoulder, knowing what Xavier was capable of.

"Get yourselves out of here." Xavier stated to the both of us, but looking in to Emily's eyes. We didn't move. "Now." He snapped.

Just as he said those words, Nick took a hold of the painting of me that was still unfinished. He looked at it for a few seconds before throwing it across the room. It fell to the floor beside me with a loud bang.

I stared at the painting for what seemed like an eternity.

"All of you get the fuck out of here." Nick slurred. "You need to get her away from me." Nick pointed to me and I felt the force of it.

Emily grabbed a hold of my hand and dragged me out of the room. I didn't struggle against her grasp but I continued to stare at the thrown painting of myself on the floor.

I was almost in shock.

This wasn't Nick.

He painted me with love and affection, he painted me and he kept me there beside him. Now, I was thrown to the floor without a second look.

As soon as I was out of the room, Emily took me in to her arms and I broke down.

I could still hear loud noises coming from the studio room. I so desperately wished everything would be right again.

I was lost and this time, I wasn't going to make my way home.

How could you move on when you're heart wasn't home?

CHAPTER 28

"D o you want to go home?" Emily soothed my arm as she looked to me with a huge amount of pity. "He will come round, Xavier will make sure of it."

I shook my head. No, I didn't want to go home. I wanted to stay, I needed to speak to him. I couldn't speak to him drunk so I would have to wait until he was sober enough to talk.

Emily sighed but she didn't push me further. She took hold of my hand gently and moved me away from the now silent room and dragged me to the living room. I let her.

As soon as she had me sat down on the sofa, she went to the kitchen to flick to kettle on.

"It's not always the easiest thing, Cathy, and I know exactly how you're feeling and what you're thinking." She said from the kitchen. I looked to the wall across me but I didn't have the energy to answer her. I knew she knew but I wished she could help these feelings.

Anger started to seep through my bones as I thought back to what had happened only a few minutes before. I was in shock, Nick had never treated me like that and he had absolutely no right to!

Okay, this was good. I wanted to feel angry at him, I wanted to be pissed off. He treated himself as the victim but this was all his fault, he was the one who left me so he gave him the right to treat me the way he did?

I stood up from the sofa with force which caught Emily's attention almost immediately. She looked to me from her stance at the counter.

"Cathy-"

"I'm pissed off." I snapped out. I hadn't meant to snap at her but the emotions running through my body were just too over whelming.

All I wanted was a relationship with Nick. Instead, he was the one playing games with my head. He said he loved me but then he left me. I wanted to talk this out with him but all he wanted to do was treat me as if everything was my fault.

Did I deserve this? Absolutely not. I wanted him to be there for me after a stressful two weeks, instead, he was doing the opposite.

When did he become so selfish?

My thoughts were only adding fuel to the fire but I was glad. I wanted to be angry, I wanted to be red hot bloody angry at him before my tears washed me away.

"I've had enough." I stated as I looked to her. "I have honestly had it up to here." I used my hand for good indication and all she could do was look at me. "I've tried everything with that man, Em, everything. He's not helping and he obviously doesn't want this. I don't want to keep running to him when all he's doing is running away. This isn't fair, this isn't fair on me."

"Maybe you should just-"

"No, Em, you're not getting it." I walked towards her in the kitchen. "I've spent my whole life trying to get it together. The one time I'm finally happy, everything has to ruin it and I'm back to where I was before. I'm too weak and way too naive to keep thinking this is a good thing. He doesn't want me and I'm not going to keep begging him to." I shrugged. "I'm over this, I'm over everything."

"What are you going to do?" The sadness in her eyes was evident. She had started to become like family to me, her, Nick and Xavier.

"I don't know yet." I stated. Maybe earn some money to leave the village. Maybe my father and I could go travelling together. We both needed a brain refresh.

"You've been hurt before haven't you?" Emily asked as her head cocked to the side. "Somebody hurt you."

"Maybe not in the way you're thinking." I quietly replied. Her eyes were just too knowing.

"I know it by the way you speak, the way you move. Xavier used to be exactly the same." She touched my arm gently. "I know when a person is hurting."

"I'm hurting." I nodded. "And not just because of Nick."

"You don't have to tell me anything but from experience, time heals everything. Xavier and Nick are both troubled men, they've both been through so much and you did all you could for him." She sighed. "He just doesn't help himself."

"Will you wish him the best for me?" I asked Emily. I had to keep the tears at bay even though I knew this had to be the end.

"Of course I will." As soon as a year escaped down her cheek, mine did too. "I don't even know why I'm crying." She chuckled a little and I did the same. "I guess all I wanted was for you both to feel the love I feel. Everyone deserves it."

"Maybe one day, hey." I smiled her way even though it was a little forced. I didn't want to fall in love with some one else, if I ever could. I wanted Nick and I wanted my love to be shared with him.

Emily and I shared a tight hug.

"Please keep in touch." Emily stated. "Or I'll have to come to your house."

"I will." I said.

Before we let go, a cough resonated throughout the kitchen. Xavier stood behind me, leaning against the counter and looking at the two of us.

"Angel, let go of her, Nick wants to talk."

"With who?" Emily asked.

"Who do you think?" Xavier shook his head before making his way over to Emily. He slid an arm around her.

"Tell him I don't want to speak to him." I said to Xavier. Xavier's eyes flickered from mine to behind me. I knew Nick was behind me now and my heart was beating a mile a minute. I didn't want to speak to him anymore, he made his feelings clear and now it was my time to be strong and to move on with my life. I wasn't going to end up the way I did before. Not this time.

"Cath-"

"We're done." I said to Xavier. "There's no point stretching this out any longer."

Nick moved forward until he was closer to my back. As he did so, Xavier dragged Emily out of the room and she left with a small sheepish smile.

I stayed with my back turned to Nick.

"So, we're done?" He repeated my words with deflation. I whipped around as anger started to bubble to the surface again.

"What do you mean we're done?" I snapped. Nick's eyes were red as if he had been crying. He looked just as broken as I felt. "You've made it pretty obvious what you want, Nick, don't play the God damn victim all the time!" My voice got louder. He tried to move forward but I made a huge step back.

"I'm a mess."

"I'm past caring." I sighed. "You've brought this all upon yourself." I looked to him with a sneer. "All I ever wanted to do was love you and be loved by you. If you don't want me, leave me alone so I can move on, these head games you're playing are fucking with my head." I laid a finger to my temple.

"I never meant to hurt you, I never wanted this." He said. "I don't even know what I'm doing." He laid two hands to his head.

"Well, I know what I'm doing." I said. "I'm giving up, I'm giving up because I've had enough of being desperate for you." I shook my head. "All men have been my whole life is upset and heartbreak and this time I'm not letting it make me feel like there's a ton of sand bags on my back. I want to be free from this feeling, I want to be happy."

"I want you to be happy." Nick pushed. "I want you to be fucking happy, Cathy. God, it's killing me seeing you like this."

"It's killing me, too." I said truthfully. All of this was killing me.

"No woman had ever made me feel the way you did, the way you do. All I had to do was feel your skin against mine and it felt as if my heart started beating again. I'm being a soppy bastard and I know it but you don't even know how much I need you, how I can't stand life without you."

"I do understand because I felt exactly the same way." I said. "But I'm so confused as to what you're trying to do here. Is my past too much for you to handle? Can't you stand touching me in places I had been touched before?"

"That's not fucking it!" Nick roared. "I don't care where he's touched you because I'd do anything in my power to fucking wash it away. I'm so obsessed with you, so possessed by you I want your whole body to be drowning in me and just me alone."

"Then what are you trying to do?" His words were everything I wanted to hear but I was just too confused to make them mean something. Was he telling the truth now? Why did he want to leave if he felt like this? Was it something I did?

"Cathy, I wanted him dead from the moment you told me what had happened. I wanted him to burn in hell and for you to feel safe in my arms."

"What are you trying to say?" I asked, my voice now cracking. My heart was beating against my chest.

"You gave me life, Angel, and I took one away."

"Nick." I felt sick. Nick, he murdered John for me? Fuck. How hadn't I put two and two together? Why hadn't I thought about this?

My previous Nick, he shouldn't have ruined his life for me.

"You killed him?" My voice was barely a whisper.

"I wish." He chuckled darkly. I had never seen him look so deadly and in that minute I knew he'd do anything to keep me safe.

After all this time, he didn't want me gone, he wanted me safe.

"Then what?" I was shaking.

"His blood is cold but they're not on my hands."

"Then who's hands are they on?" My brows furrowed with fear. What had he done?

"It doesn't matter."

"Of course it-"

"Cathy, stop it." He came forward. "Do you feel safe now?"

"I don't know." I shrugged. "I felt safe knowing he was dead but I-I-"

"You're scared of me?" He breathed. It seemed as if he had been punched in the stomach.

"It's a big deal, Nick." I breathed back. "You got him killed, I wanted him dead but I just can't seem to wrap my head around everything. What's going to happen to you? What if the police know this is all your fault?"

God, I was going to be sick, I could feel it.

Suddenly, as if a light bulb had popped up above my head, a thought came to me.

"That's why you were running away to Italy wasn't it? You wanted to run from the police?"

"They're not going to find out, Cathy, believe me. I was just trying to make sure."

"God, Nick, you've put yourself in to so much danger." I looked to him with fearful eyes. "All it takes is one knock at the door and you're going to be ripped away from me. I would rather him alive than this, I would rather live in fear of him but know you're here than be without you."

"Your love for me is the only thing that could ever keep me going in this world. You power me, I'm a better man when you're here. I wasn't going to let him make you feel the way you did, I wasn't going to stand for him touching you before I ever had the chance to stop it."

"But you killed him!" I shot out.

"And I don't regret it, not one tiny little bit." He snapped. "He raped you, he took your childhood away from you and he ripped it with his two bare hands. He was sort of lucky in a way, at least he had a life before that. But you? You're here scarred from your past because of him, scared to move forward and scared to look back."

"Nick-"

"I tried to leave you because it was easier for the police to banish me as a suspect if I wasn't with you anymore." He moved forward but I still moved back. "I just wish someone would have explained to me how losing you was going to make me feel, like someone shot a whole in me and left me out for the wolves to eat."

I knew how he felt.

"They're treating it as suicide." I willed my heart to calm down. "Do you think they will leave it as that?"

"I'm hoping so."

"I didn't think you wanted me anymore." I stated.

"I want you more than you could ever imagine." He whispered. "I'm not a bad man, Cathy, I didn't do this because I have a desire to kill. I did this because the woman who saved me needed saving herself."

"I know." I sighed. It was a lot to wrap my head around but my heart felt fulfilled in a way. Nobody had ever cared for me enough to do such a thing to save me, to make me feel safe.

And I did feel safe. For the first time in my life, I didn't have to keep watching the space behind me. He wasn't here to hurt me, he wasn't here to abuse me.

"I love you, Angel." His voice rang out and I immediately relaxed at the words. It was a relief to hear them.

I thought he was leaving me for good.

But all along, he was only saving me when I thought he was killing me.

<h1 style="text-align:center">CHAPTER 29</h1>

"I need you." Nick breathed. I looked to him with wide eyes. My heart was beating, finally, with happiness. I had Nick back and it seemed as if everything was fine again. I willed my excitement to calm down, but it was just no use.

"Nick." I said his name with relief and victory before scrambling forward and rocketing in to his arms. He caught me, he always did. His arm was like a blanket, it was safety and everything I needed.

"Steady on." He warned, but his arms grasped my body tightly as if he was scared I was going to vanish any second now. He sighed as he laid his nose in my hair. My face was squeezed against his body and literally, I didn't want to be anywhere else.

We stayed in that embrace for what felt like hours but in reality it was only a few minutes. I wanted to stay in his arms forever and never let him go. Him leaving only showed me that I loved this man more than anything and I was never prepared to let him leave me again.

And I meant it.

Forgetting Xavier and Emily were still in the apartment, reality came flooding back to me once I heard a small giggle coming from

Emily's mouth. I opened my closed eyes and saw her and Xavier standing before us, smiles on their faces.

"This is the best day ever." Emily gushed.

"Have you forgotten about our wedding day?" Xavier grumbled in reply, but his eyes were a light with humour. Emily only giggled but the loving look she gave her husband told us everything we needed to know. Their day was magical because she was marrying the love of her life.

Would Nick and I ever marry? It was still too soon to be thinking of that but one day I kind of wish we would.

I couldn't really ever imagine my life with somebody else. Not after Nick, not after what he has given me.

The four of us moved from the kitchen and made our way in to the living room. Over coffee, we all talked as if nothing had happened previously. It felt surreal but the hurt was still there, deep inside my bones. I wanted to get over it now I knew what had happened and why Nick did what he did but I just couldn't make sense of it all.

Did he really get someone to kill the man who raped me? I didn't even know he had that streak in him. Was it something I could even live with?

I tried to shake away all of my thoughts. I had Nick back and I didn't ever want to let him go. Ever.

My head was a mess and a lot had happened in the last few days. I felt as if my world was spiralling out of control whilst it was trying to piece itself back together again. I was now in some sort of bitter sweet bliss and I didn't know what to make of it all.

When did life start to become easier?

"Nick, you were so stupid to let her go in the first place." Emily's voice pierced through the air like a knife and we all turned to look at her. She sat there, her face a mixture of happiness but also annoyance at Nick.

Nick didn't say a word. He couldn't. He didn't want to tell his family about what he had done and also about my own back story. We were both hiding things and it didn't necessarily feel good.

"Come on, Cathy, I'll take you home." Nick got up from the sofa he was perched on, his body a mass of lean muscle and sexiness.

"But-"

As I was speaking, Nick gave me a glare to tell me that he wanted me to follow him. Emily stared his way but Nick didn't pay any attention to it. I followed him out of his apartment and I followed him down to his truck on the driveway.

"What's up?" I asked him. He looked to me as he sauntered forward.

"I didn't want to be the bad guy." He stated quietly as his eyes searched mine. "I know I broke you when I promised myself I wouldn't." He sighed. "I didn't think I could."

"You did what you had to do to protect me and besides, you're back now, aren't you?"

"Emily's looking at me as if I killed her dog."

"She cares for you, Nick. They both do." I exclaimed. They did care for him and I'm glad he had family that did.

"And they care for you too, especially Emily."

"They want to see you happy."

Nick sighed again before leaning against his truck. It was like he was all out of energy, all out of run. I watched him lean his head against his truck. Even like this, he was hot.

His facial hair was out growing and his messy hair looked un-kept.

"Do you want to go somewhere else?" He lifted his head to look at me as he asked the words.

"What about Xavier and Emily?" I asked.

"They have a key to my apartment. They can let themselves out."

"Are you-"

"I'm sure Cathy. I just want to be alone with you." He answer was blunt but it fired a light inside of me. "And you can get that look off your face this instance."

"What look?"

"The look you always give me when you want me. I want you, too, Cathy, so fucking much but I want to wait for now. We have all the time in the world, don't we?"

I was hoping he was right.

And yes, I did want him. It had felt so long being without him and I wanted nothing more than to have him, to know he really was mine again. The connection had been lost and I needed it back.

"Yeah, we do."

Nick and I decided to go back to my dads house. Well, mostly I decided. Nick was a little hesitant on the idea once he found out I had told my dad everything.

Nick and Glenn were bestfriends, I hoped they would sort themselves out and not start something out of nothing. I knew my dad was protective over me and he couldn't help that.

"He's going to hate me, you know?" Nick mentioned. I looked to him as he parked the truck in the driveway.

"He won't hate you, he's-" just as I was about to continue, I heard the front door open from my opened window and once I looked, I saw my father storm out of the house in a hurry.

He rounded his way up to the truck and looked at Nick with glaring eyes through my opened window.

"What have you got to say for yourself?" He snapped. Nick looked at him, his face not giving away anything. You wouldn't have known how he was feeling.

"It's all in control, Glenn." He tried to brush the whole thing off. I internally laughed, as if that was going to make my father okay again.

"It's not in control, Nicholas. You've broken my daughter's heart and yet here you are. I will literally kick your ass."

"Glenn, don't push it." I could tell Nick was becoming agitated but Glenn was right. Nick had broken my heart and he did deserve a verbal thrashing from my father.

But then again, Nick had told me everything now. I understood exactly why he did what he did and I had no right telling him it was the wrong thing to do. All he did was try to protect me.

"Dad, everything's okay again." I said to him, trying to give him my sweetest smile. I wanted him to feel as if I was protected again. From the bags under his eyes to the tiredness slouch he now possessed, my father was evidently tired and worn out. Because of me.

The thought was sobering.

"I'm okay, Nick's okay. I'm safe." I grabbed my father's hand and squeezed gently. He squeezed it back before sighing and closing his eyes tightly.

"Glenn, I am so sorry for what I did to your daughter. I didn't mean to leave her when she needed me the most, the truth is, I fucking love her and I'd do anything to protect her. You have to believe me." Nick's outward affection was shocking.

Nick had never been in to public affection really. We kissed in public and had held hands before but when it came to words, they were reserved for the two of us.

To hear him say the words to my father was a shock. I wanted him to tell the world just who he loved so the more he said it, the more I believed him.

"Of course I believe it." He looked to Nick intently. "I know a man in love when I see one."

"So I'm forgiven?" Nick asked. I looked to my father and his lips twitched in to a small smile.

"You are forgiven." He stated. "But you're on your last warning."

"I got it, boss." He tipped his head but the smile was evident on his face. I knew it was a relief for Nick to know he had my father on side again. It meant a lot to me too.

Just as my father was about to move away from the truck, Nick caught his attention.

"Glenn, can I talk to you for a minute?" He asked. Glenn nodded and Nick got out of the car.

"Can I know the secret?" I asked out of the open window. Glenn smiled but Nick shook his head.

"Sorry, babe. It's boy stuff." He waved me off and I huffed in annoyance. "Don't look cute, it's not going to work." He chuckled slowly and my toes curled in my trainers.

God, Nick.

I watched Nick as he walked with my father. Their lips were moving but the more I strained my ears to hear them, the less I could. I huffed again. It was useless and I was just being too curious.

I saw my father smile and then Nick smiled in relief afterwards. With that, they shook hands, clasped each others back and Nick sauntered his way back to the truck.

"Everything okay?" I asked. He looked to me and smiled.

"It is now." He clasped my knee and turned the ignition on again.

"We're not staying?" I asked.

"I thought we could go back to mine. Emily and Xavier should be at their own house by now and I have other things on my mind." He looked to me with a wicked look.

"Oh yeah? Like what?" I gave him a small smirk but the fire was already lit inside of me and I was just fit to burst.

It had been so long and I needed him. It was evident.

"You're just going to have to wait and see." He winked before turning back to the road and getting the vehicle in motion.

Feeling playful and extremely happy, for a change, I grabbed his knee. His eyes flickered my way for a second but I didn't look at him.

Once his eyes were back on the road, my hand slowly moved further up along his leg. He stiffened beneath me and a growl left his lips.

"What are you doing?" He asked. I didn't say a word, I just moved my hand along his leg until I was close enough for him to stiffen even more. "Don't." He let out a strangled moan. "I'm driving."

"I bet you wish you wasn't." My voice was husky as I spoke. Oh, I was so ready for him.

"I will literally stop this car." He warned. "Please don't push me, you don't realise how much I fucking need you."

"I think I do." I exclaimed. "I love you, don't I?"

"Baby." He groaned. "You're pushing me over the edge."

"Good." I looked triumphant and I hoped he saw it. The shit he put me through lately, he was supposed to feel over the edge. He was supposed to feel at least half the way I did.

Maybe he did? I mean, if what he was saying was true then it must have been a shit time for him too.

Finally, however, we were nearly back at Nick's apartment. I was so excited I could barely contain myself for the night ahead. I couldn't wait to get Nick all alone.

But as soon as Nick's truck rounded the parking lot outside of his apartment, we both knew something was wrong almost straight away.

A police car was evident outside of the apartment complex in all of its fearful glory. I took it in, my heart beating a mile a minute at the sight of it and this time not from the excitement.

Why was it here?

Once the figures saw us approach, they got out of the vehicle and made their way up to the truck. Nick didn't say a word, his body looking relaxed and not in the worst bit frightened. Me, however, I was a nervous wreck.

"Nick." I whispered his name but he gave me a reassuring look. He took hold of my hand and squeezed before letting it go gently.

"Don't panic." His words did nothing but make me panic more.

The police officers went to Nick's side of the truck and Nick rounded down his window.

"Sir, can we ask you to leave the vehicle please?" A deep voice came out of a very tall man.

"Derek, what is this all about?" Nick obviously knew the man before us.

"We need to ask you again to leave the vehicle." He was adamant.

Nick sighed before opening the door. I looked to him with wide eyes and I opened my truck door quickly to be beside him.

What the hell was going on? I was shaking.

"I'm sorry to say this, Nick, but we are arresting you on suspicion of murder." The other man's voice came out and I collapsed to the floor at the words. I didn't hear him say anything else.

Nick stood there, his posture calm but his eyes fixed directly on me. He was shouting my name as they handcuffed his hands behind his back but I couldn't hear him.

This was going to break us if he was found guilty of this charge. He was going to spend years in prison. How did they find out he was involved in this?

Just as soon as I had him back.

"Cathy!" Nick shouted again. This time, I heard him and I looked up to him. I was in shock, I had to have been. "It's going to be okay, I promise you."

"Nick." I said his name. They started pulling his body to the police car and I stood up and ran with him. "Nick, please!" I was scared. I was so scared.

"I'll be out before you know it, Angel." He said, his voice so calm. How could he be so calm?! "I love you. I love you so fucking much."

"Nick, no." I sobbed. "Don't go."

"Say it back, Cathy. Tell me how much you love me." He demanded gently as he was pulled. They opened the door and they pushed him inside.

"I love you!" I shouted as they slammed the door shut behind him.

His face in the window was one that would haunt me forever.

I was sure of it.

Chapter 30

Crushed. That's how I felt. Not because I was in handcuffs, not because I was being pulled to the police station. No, it was because I wanted Cathy and I wanted her happy in my arms.

I had fucked up so much already and this was the last thing I wanted and needed. This was the last thing Cathy needed.

Everything had changed the moment I met her. I knew deep down my life would never be the same again and I was okay with that now. Infact, it was everything I wanted.

I wanted a life with Cathy, I wanted everything with her. I didn't want to own her but I wanted to have her mind, body and soul.

I needed it.

I laid my head in my hands and squeezed my eyes shut. Even now, I couldn't get her off my mind.

Every action I took I did it for her. Now, I just needed to get out of here and back to her.

Once I was chucked in to an interrogation room, it seemed as if I was more determined to get out of her. I didn't want to say shit to these people.

"Mr Abel-"

"What am I here for?" I asked. I gave the officer a glare but he didn't seem to shrink beneath it. That irked me more than I would have liked.

The police officers both sat down at the table before me. One was bald and the other had a goatee. I hated them both, hated how they had me here, hated them because I was away from Cathy.

"We know you knew Johnathan." I hated him.

"Not personally." I shrugged. "What's this about?"

"Our detectives have been investigating his death scene. A few things don't add up, that's all." They were being reserved and I was becoming pissed off.

"I want you to cut the shit." I growled. I leaned forward in my chair, my arms resting on the table before me. I knew I was digging a deeper hole but I just didn't care. I was a police officer myself, I had been in an interrogation room myself and I knew how everything worked here.

"Mr-"

"Just tell me what you're accusing me of." I demanded. The bald officer sighed before me.

"Obviously, you're a suspect of Johnathan's death."

"And why?"

"Because a few details have come to light recently. Johnathan's wife during her statement had stated that you didn't get on very well with John." Oh, so Cathy's mum really wasn't as in the dark as we originally thought. I hated John but I'm sure I didn't make it that obvious.

Maybe I was wrong.

"So?" I questioned further. "I didn't like him much but I didn't hate him enough to kill him." It was all lies, of course I hated him enough to kill him. I didn't regret it one bit, not one tiny bit. I'd kill him again in a heartbeat.

Anything for Cathy.

"Can you tell us why you didn't like him?"

"He just wasn't my cup of tea. I dislike many people, Officer." And that was vaguely the truth. I wasn't the most loving person in the world and I liked it that way.

"Disliked him enough to kill him?" The man with the goatee was now piping up. God, I wanted to smash both their heads in so badly.

"I have already answered that." I sighed. "This is pointless. I disliked him but definitely not enough to kill him. Besides, you have arrested me based on absolutely no evidence what so ever. What you have here is a shit show, it's not professional and my girlfriend is back at home, scared because she doesn't have a clue what's going on." I tried to stay calm under their watchful stares.

The two men looked at each other quickly before the bald man laid his hands on the table and stood up with authority.

"We will be back in two minutes." He stated before the two men walked out of the room.

"Fucking great." I muttered under my breath.

The minutes ticked by and I knew the men were gone longer than they said they would be. I laid my hands in to my pocket and sat back.

My finger fiddled with the metal in my jeans pocket, reminding me where my feet were planted.

I just had to get out of here.

The longer I was in here, the more I was itching to get out. There was something I needed to do, something I needed for my sanity.

I couldn't take this any longer.

Soon, the men came back in to the room. The bald head looked to me but with a resigned look, he told me to leave.

"You May be back for questioning and a later date but for now, you're free."

"About time." I said as my glare was aimed at the two men. If they saw the look, they didn't retaliate.

I got up from my seat and almost ran out of the police station. I had no way of getting home. I grabbed my phone and opened it, I was going to get a lift off Glenn but before I could ring him, someone was barrelling forward and in to my arms as I stood just outside of the police station.

I smelt Cathy's fresh scent and as I realised it was her in my arms, I gathered her up and pulled her even closer. I laid my nose in to her hair, not wanting to ever let her go again.

"So much has happened." She sobbed against my chest. My heart broke every time I saw her cry. She was so strong and she didn't deserve anything that life gave her. I wanted to change it, I wanted to make her forget and for her to finally be happy.

I was going to make it my life's mission.

"I know, baby." I was going to make you happy, Cathy. "I've got you." I soothed as I smoothed her hair beneath my fingers.

"I've been so scared." She breathed. "I just want everything the way it was before."

"And it will be." I promised. "Just stop crying, Cathy. I can't seem to think when you're crying, you're just breaking me in two."

"I'm sorry." She moved her head to look at me. I wiped her tears with the pad of my thumb and she leaned in to my touch.

"I wish you knew how much I love you." I said. "I wish you could feel just how badly I need you."

"Nick-"

"Marry me." I demanded. She took a step back as she gasped.
"What?"

"Marry me." I put my hand in to my pocket and grabbed the metal ring. I kept it on me, not wanting to let go of it until I had the chance to lay it on her finger for life. "Please." I dropped to the floor on one bended knee.

"Oh my god." Cathy looked down with a fresh strain of tears on their way. "Are you sure?"

"I have never been more sure."

"And what about your playboy ways?" I hoped she was joking.

"All in the past." And I meant it. "You're the only woman who could have ever made my heart beat again."

"You're such a soppy sod." Cathy giggled and I'm sure the world turned on it's axis.

"I'll spend my whole life making you happy. I'll do whatever I can to protect you. Just please, say yes and make me the happiest man in the world?"

"Of course it's a yes!" She almost shrieked. It was so unlike Cathy but just too right in this moment.

I got up from my position on the floor and forgetting the ring in my hand, I laid two hands to her head and pulled her lips to mine.

She pulled back after a minute, a glint in her eyes and the relief plasted on her face.

"And the ring?" She looked giddy with excitement.

I took her hand and placed the engagement ring on her finger.

"He's fucking done it!" I heard a shout and instantly familiarised myself with Emily's voice. What the hell was she doing here?

Emily came barrelling my way and soon she had her arms wrapped around my neck like a vice.

"I didn't realise I had an audience." I grumbled as I took in Xavier taking a leisurely pace up to us.

"We were Cathy's lift here. We didn't know you were going to pop the question." Xavier stated. He wasn't as excited as Emily but by the small smile on his face, I knew he was happy.

When Emily left my body to see Cathy's ring, Xavier took me in to a hug. I hugged him back with all the love I could muster.

"Congratulations, bro." He mumbled quietly.

"Thanks, man." I clapped his back.

"Jesus, this is the best day of my life!" Emily clapped.

"Are you forgetting our engagement? Our wedding? The birth of our son?" Xavier muttered the questions and Emily pouted his way.

"Okay, the fourth best day of my life." She rolled her eyes his way.

Xavier and Emily started walking back to the car as they bickered lightly.

I took Cathy's hand and pulled her along too. Cathy looked to me with a small smile.

"What?"

"I wonder what my dad is going to say." She smirked.

"He already knows." I stated. "I have already asked him."

"You asked him for my hand in marriage?" She looked to me with shock.

"It's tradition." I said.

"And you know all about that do you?" She said playfully.

"I love you enough to want to do this right."

"God, I love you, too." She bursted.

And this time I believed her when she said it. Those words alone could bring me to my knees.

She was my angel and everything in between.

And she saved me from a lot.

Chapter 31

"You can't cook the chicken in the microwave, Nicholas!" I shouted his way as he plated the chicken legs and walked over to his microwave which laid on the counter.

He wore a pair of cooking gloves that I had brought over from my house. I didn't have a clue why, the plate wasn't even hot.

"Why not?" Nick huffed. "I used to cook everything in the microwave."

"That's because you don't know how to use the oven." I replied back. I was going to house train him, whether he liked it or not. If he was going to be become my husband, he needed to know what to do.

At the thought of Nick being my husband, I crumbled in to two. I couldn't wait to marry the man of my dreams. The police came to our house every now and then but there was no evidence that Nick had even touched John.

Nick wasn't even worried.

"The oven's on, just open the door and put the chicken in." I rolled my eyes his way and he caught me.

"Why are you rolling your eyes at me?" He asked defensively. "I'm trying, aren't I?"

"You're doing amazing, sweet cheeks." I pinched his bum hardly and he shot forward.

"Careful." Nick warned. "The chicken could splatter across the floor." As if a light bulb went off above his head, he smirked. "If it did, I wouldn't have to cook and then we could just get takeout instead."

"Haha, nice one-"

Before I could continue with my sentence, Nick started to wobble his arms around and the chicken legs moved across the tray.

"Nick, don't!" I hissed his way, I tried to grab the tray but he was just too tall. "Nick." I warned.

Nick continued to laugh but I stood before him with my hands on my hips.

"Fine, no sex for you tonight." I turned around and waited. I heard him lay the chicken in the oven before coming up behind me. H wrapped his arms around my waist and laid his gloved hands against my stomach.

"Aw, come on." He pouted against my cheek. "That's mean."

"If you make this meal nice enough, I'll let you have me in anyway you want me."

"Do you mean that?" I could feel the excitement roll off of him like a wave.

Typical man.

I nodded my head and Nick turned me around quickly. He laid a kiss to my lips.

"I love you, Angel." He kissed me again and I melted in his arms.

"I love you, too." I breathed. Before he could say anything else, I smacked his bum. "Now, no more stalling, I'm starving."

"This is manual labour." He huffed again. He went over to the oven and looked through the glass of it to see his raw chicken cooking.

"Babe, the chicken ain't going to cook faster just because you're looking at it." I wanted to laugh at the dumb founded look on his face. I couldn't believe he had never cooked chicken legs in his life. He only knew how to barbecue and microwave.

Nick looked to me with narrowed eyes and flipped me the bird. All I could do was laugh.

I left the kitchen and went to sit down on the sofa. I grabbed the TV remote and put on a light hearted programme to watch.

I had a few days off work and so did Nick. I was glad we both had a few days to get back to normal with eachother after all that had happened over the last few days. It was really difficult for the both of us but I was glad we were back together and stronger than ever.

And engaged.

I looked at my ring as it glinted under the light. God, I loved it, I loved him. He had done so much for me all because he loved me. He had been involved in the killing of my step father, he had made me crazy but kept me sane all at the same time. He was incredible and I was incredibly lucky.

My father still felt guilty about the whole ordeal and found it difficult to get over everything. My mother was my mother and just as confused and emotional as the rest of us.

Currently, my mother was sleeping in my bed at my fathers and I was at Nick's. My mother needed company and I knew Glenn would always be there for her, he loved her and never stopped.

My heart clenched for him.

I couldn't imagine being without the love of my life.

"You can't sit and watch tele while I do all the work." Nick sulked as he came in to the living room. He still wore the oven gloves and I couldn't help but laugh at him. Why was he still wearing them?

"I can do as I please." I said his way with a smirk. "I'm your future wife."

"True." He said with a smile and a glint in his eyes. "But I'm your future husband and I'm currently dying of exhaustion."

"You've put eight chicken legs in to the oven, that's not an exhausting task." I laughed.

Nick pouted as he sauntered his way over to me. He grabbed the remote and flicked the TV over to a music channel. It landed on a song and before I could tell him how much I loved the song, he had my hand in his and he pulled me until I was flush against his chest.

"Wanna dance?" He asked like a naughty little boy before me. His eyes were twinkling, he lips pulled in to a smile. After every-thing that has happened lately, it was mad how much happier he looked.

"I'm not that good at it." I said. "I can shake my ass in a club but that's about it."

"Cathy." Nick growled out. "You won't be shaking your ass in the club anymore." And he looked read serious too.

"That's a shame." I sighed with a small smile. "I had a few fans."

"Your ass..." he clenched my arse in his hands. "Is mine."

"Yeah, yeah." I brushed him off jokingly. All Nick did was smile before pushing his hips forward. I gasped. He did again and I couldn't stop myself from pulling his lips to mine.

Nick moaned against my mouth.

"You're a filthy girl." He breathed. He pushed my body back, forgetting about the dance, until I felt the sofa hit the back of my knees. He pushed my down some more until I was lying down and his body was above mine.

I looked in to the depths of his eyes, knowing I still had so much to learn about him. I knew I had time, I had forever.

Nick pinned my arms above my head before taking his lips to my neck. I moaned at the contact.

"Nick-"

"I can't wait to feel-"

"Nick-"

"What?" His glazed eyes were looking at me, dark and inviting and so intense. He looked confused as to why I was stopping him short.

I wanted him to make love to me, I really did, but all I could smell was the chicken from the oven.

"You need to go and check that chicken." I said. I watched him as he narrowed his eyes and his eyebrows furrowed.

"That fucking chicken." He muttered. "Let it burn."

"We are not letting it burn." I replied back firmly. "Go and check on it."

"It's not a child, Cathy." He looked annoyed.

"Nick." I warned.

Nick huffed before pulling himself up on to two feet.

"I hate cooking." He mumbled as he walked over to the kitchen. He opened the oven door and chucked the chicken on to the counter top.

Once he was done, he came rushing out of the kitchen. Before I knew it, he had me in his arms and he was taking us both to his bed. Once we were there, he chucked me down with force and I almost squealed.

"That's cheating." I said a little breathless as I looked up to him. He took off his shirt with effort and my mouth watered at his body.

I then watched as he took off his jeans. He was now just in his boxers and I licked my lips at the sight. His eyes darkened.

"Fuck the chicken." He said as he climbed on top of me. "I want to make love to my Angel."

"I'll let you off this once." I pointed, just because I wanted it just as badly. I craved him like nothing else.

"You'll let me off all the time once I'm finished with you." He smirked.

"That's a promise, is it?"

"You know I've always liked a challenge."

I laid in Nick's arms as I listened to the hammering of his heart against his chest.

"Nick, you've never told me about your family." I mused.

"I have." He said. "You've met my mum."

"Yes, but what happened to your father, what about everyone else but Xavier and your mum." I said. Realisation had only now just dawned on me. It was evident that Nick loved his mum but he never spoke that much of his family.

I hadn't ever tried to push information out of him.

Nick sighed.

"My father was killed along with my uncle."

"Xavier's dad?" I asked as I sat up to look at him. He looked to me but he held a vacant stare.

"Yeah." He said. "They were both killed, twins they were, killed by Xavier's mum." He shrugged.

"She didn't get caught and Xavier and I didn't find out until we were older. She was a nasty piece of work but we've washed our hands of her."

"Shit." I said. I couldn't ever imagine growing up knowing my father was dead and that my auntie had been the one to do it. A killing, that didn't have to have happened.

"His funeral was the worst." Nick laid an arm over his eyes but I didn't even attempt to move it. "I sat there, as a seventeen year old boy thinking he had killed himself. Xavier thought the same about his father."

"Nick." I didn't know what to say. It sounded so shitty. Too much for a young boy to go through.

"I cried my heart out that day." He stated truthful. "It was the last time I ever did, until I lost you."

"Baby." I breathed. He cried when I left him? God, I cried ten rivers. "I'm here now and I'm not going anywhere."

Nick's arm tightened around my body until I was lying on his chest once again.

"I had a shit time when I was a kid, but you've made my life worth living." He stated. "I'm madly in love with you, I can't fucking begin to tell you."

"I love you so much." I said and my heart couldn't grow any bigger when I looked to him. He was everything I ever needed and I wasn't ever going to leave this man, no matter how hard things got.

He had my heart and he was going to keep it.

Suddenly, the sound of his phone brought us out of the loved up daze we seemed to have been in.

Nick reached out to grab his phone and sat up once looking at the caller ID.

"Alright?" He answered. He listened intently and I got up from the bed and left him to his phone call. I needed a shower.

I entered the shower after turning it on and started to wash my body. I stayed under the spray of the shower until Nick came in to the shower with me.

Gone was his earlier expression of relaxation and calm, now, he looked somber as his head bent under the spray.

"Everything okay?" I asked him. He looked to me with a drained face.

"I've been suspended." He said. "Which only means I'll probably be sacked in the next few weeks."

"What? Why?" I asked, shocked and surprised. Why did they suspend him? Nick was the best police officer I knew, even when I was biased.

This wasn't fair. Nick needed his job, especially when he had his sights set on univeristy and his art degree.

"Because I'm still under trial for John's murder." Was his only statement. I took Nick in to my arms.

"You'll be okay." I said. I didn't know what else to say. Nick would be okay, he was stronger than anyone I knew.

"Cathy, how can everything be okay?" He seemed defeated. "I won't have any money coming in. I can't save up for my art degree, I can't save up to treat you."

"Don't worry about me-"

"What about our wedding? I won't be able to afford to marry you. I need to fucking make you my wife!" Nick slammed his hand against the tiles of his shower. I took hold of Nick's face and pulled until he was looking straight at me.

"I'm yours whether we're married or not. I'll always be yours." I said. "You don't need that job, Nick, you will sort something and I'll be there with you every step of the way."

"Ever since falling for you, I've wanted to give you everything." He breathed. "A bigger place, all the best stuff, I want to wine and dine you and treat you the way you deserve. I don't have a job, Cathy, how can I do any of that?"

"I never asked for any of that. I just need you, Nick, that's all I've ever asked for." And I meant it. I didn't need expensive things,

I didn't need to be wined and dined. "You took me to a burger shack on our first date. I loved every second of it."

Nick smiled in memory.

"You did." His smile dropped. "But still-"

"I don't want to hear anymore." I said. "We're going to sort this, we're going to be okay because we're a team and that's what we do."

"I promise you now, once I find my feet, I'll give you everything this world has to offer." He seemed dead determined too.

I didn't need the world though, I just needed him.

CHAPTER 32

"I don't know what to do today." Nick stated as we started to wake up. The morning sunlight beamed through the blinds of the bedroom window and I was weirdly relaxed and content.

Nick was still upset and a little annoyed about his job and the situation that had brought on, but other than that he was also feeling relaxed as we held eachother tightly.

"Maybe you could paint some more canvases, you're good at those." I mused. He was good at everything but I wasn't going to tell him that.

"I usually paint better when I'm feeling something." He replied back.

"And you're not feeling happy?" I asked as I looked in to his eyes. "You've got me back, you should be ecstatic." I was half joking but I knew I meant it too.

"I've never had to paint happy before, except that painting of you."

"Which you threw." I couldn't help but say it. Nick rolled his eyes but by the frown on his face, I knew he felt guilty about it.

"I've got a good idea." Nick said before sitting up in bed. I moved off of his body and watched him as he pulled on a pair of tracksuit bottoms and a t shirt. They clung to his muscled frame and I couldn't help but stare.

"Where are you off?" I asked. With the blanket up to my neck and my eyes on him, he turned to look at me. He smirked as he took me in.

"I have to go out a minute, to get some essentials."

"For?"

"I'm not telling you." He smirked some more. "It's a secret." I narrowed my eyes at him but I didn't say another word. I just watched him as he moved, until he was ready and kissing me on the cheek. "I won't be long."

And he was gone, like a little boy in a candy store.

Well, what can I do now?

I got up and pulled on my own clothes that I had packed in to one of Nick's drawers during my stay. Maybe I could go and see my mum and dad? Maybe take a walk?

I had so many possibilities.

Just as I was about to do my hair and make myself look even the littlest bit respectable, the door knocked.

Weird, Nick didn't get many visitors unless it was me or my father.

I walked over to the wooden door anyway, curious as to who it may be. I opened it wide and took in the woman before me.

"Alice?" I asked, wondering why she was here at all.

"Can I come in?"

"Nick's not here at the moment." I stated. I guessed that's who she was here for. She had always had a thing for Nick and it had been blatantly obvious since day one.

"It's okay, I came to see you." Her statement shocked me. I'm sure Alice wanted me out of Nick's life, so why did she want to speak to me?

"Come in then, I suppose." I opened the door wider and she came in to the room as if she knew exactly where everything was.

Oh, please.

Alice sat down on the sofa, making herself at home without me having to say a word. I sat down on the sofa beside her and waited until she started to speak.

"Nick's still under trial for John's murder but there's absolutely no evidence at all. I'm sure he'll be let off the hook real soon, you'll be pleased to know." She said, her big brown eyes boring in to mine.

"That is a relief." I said. "He hasn't done anything wrong." At my statement, Alice smirked.

"If that's what you think." She muttered. I looked to her, my eyes narrowing her way. Of course I knew he did do something wrong, but how did Alice know anything about this ordeal?

"What's that meant to mean?" I was becoming defensive. "Do you think he killed John?"

"No, not one tiny bit." She said. "I did."

I stood up as she said those words, my eyes wide and my heart beating a mile a minute.

"What?" I felt like I couldn't breathe. How had she killed my step dad? The man who had abused me all those years? What the fuck was going on?

"I know you won't say anything because if you do, Nick's coming down with me." Her words were strong but I barely listened. The blood rushed through my ears.

"How?" I was speechless.

"He rang me up and he needed a favour."

"D-did he tell you everything?" I asked in shock horror.

"That your step daddy abused you? Yes, of course he did." She rolled her eyes as if Nick had always told her everything about himself.

Rage bubbled inside every vein that I owned inside of me. How dare she come here and pretend as if her and Nick were meant to be. And how dare Nick tell her, out of all people, what had happened to me in my past! I couldn't believe this.

"Get the fuck out." I said. I hated her, I had always hated her. Alice looked up to me with shocked eyes.

"Aren't you going to thank me for what I did for you?" She asked, her face a picture of disbelief.

How fucking dare she.

"Get out!" I screamed. Before she could move, the door flew open and Nick took in our forms. I was red and as stiff as a board looking at Alice, and Alice just looked shocked.

Nick dropped his bags to the floor, as if he knew exactly what had been said.

I didn't look at him. I couldn't. In some way, big way, I felt betrayed.

God, why couldn't he have told me? We were just starting to get back on to the straight and narrow.

When would everything just stop?

Before anyone could say anything, I stormed past Alice and went to storm past Nick, but he took hold of my arm in his hand and stopped me.

"Cathy, I can explain everything if you'd-"

"Let me go." I warned, my voice low and dark. Nick looked in to my eyes, searching. He must know how angry I am, surely.

He did because he let go of my arm as if it were on fire.

"Don't go." He said, as if they could have stopped me.

"Leave me alone." I replied back before storming past him and running down the stairs of the apartment block. I knew he didn't bother coming after me and I was grateful.

Tears pricked my eyes as I continued to run further away from him.

I really did feel hurt and betrayed. Nick had told Alice everything about my past, a past I didn't want anyone to know about, let alone her. I hated her, couldn't he have seen that?

I didn't want her to do my a favour, it pained me that all of those hours he spent away from me, he spent with her, killing someone he thought was for me.

Nick could have protected me with him still alive. A part of me would have rathered that over this.

And what hurt aswell was the fact he didn't tell me.

Once I was outside, in the morning open air, I fled down the street. I didn't have a car to go home in and by the time I called a cab I knew Nick would be out here trying to get me to come back inside.

I didn't want to go back inside with him.

I needed time to cool off and think.

I walked against the cool concrete with just my socks on. I didn't seem to care a bit, the pain and the coldness grounded me in a way I needed.

My phone buzzed in my pocket but I didn't dare pick it up. I knew who it would be and I didn't want to speak to him right now.

It continued to buzz for at least ten minutes but I continued to walk against the concrete. Cars flew past and I bet every driver wondered what the hell I was doing, especially without any shoes on.

I didn't care though.

My tears had dried up by now but I was still left livid. I didn't exactly want to be angry, I just was. But could you blame me?

He shared things, secret and horrible things with another woman, one I knew loved him just as much as I did.

This whole thing was fucked up.

Suddenly, a vehicle pulled up beside me, it drove at a slow pace beside me.

"Cathy!" Nick shouted out of the window of his truck. It rattled as he drove it but I didn't stop. "It's freezing, get in the truck."

Oh, so he wanted to be demanding now?

I didn't reply. I was being childish, I knew, but I was allowed to be.

"Get in the truck, Cathy." He demanded again. "Catherine!"

"Don't call me that!" I snapped as I turned to him. His truck stopped as did I. He stared at me as he pulled his handbrake up.

Cars beeped their horns as Nick took up half the road but they ended up having to overtake him. Nick wasn't moving, he seemed unfazed.

"Listen to me." He snapped back. "Get in the truck and let me tell you I'm sorry."

"I don't want to hear your apologies." I flung my hands up as I spoke.

"Cathy-"

"I'm hurt, okay?" I breathed. Nick frowned. "You brought up my demons to a woman who is in love with you just as much as I am."

"I don't love her back, you know that."

"It's not about that!" I shouted. "My life is my story to tell. I get to decide who knows about my past, I get to tell people what I had to go through and you had no right, no right to tell anyone!" I was breathing hard. "You know how much it fucked me up, how could you tell Alice all about it?"

"I wasn't thinking, I just wanted that fucker dead for ever hurting you."

"You don't get it do you?" I let out a laugh. "You've had to live through pain, too. You've had to pretend everything was going to get better even when you were at rock bottom. You know how it feels to grow up thinking the world was fucked up and you were the last person on this Earth who I thought could ever betray me this way."

"Don't say that." Nick breathed.

"You know how much he haunted me." I couldn't help but sob as the tears started anew. "You spent nights cuddling me to sleep when all I could do was cry, I told you in confidence and I thought you were there to protect me."

"I am!" He shouted. "I've always been there to protect you, you know that, you fucking know that."

"Do I?" I asked. "You've betrayed me, Nick, by bringing her in to my past. I never wanted her there, I couldn't even tell my parents, let alone let you tell her."

"I wasn't thinking!" Nick's eyes were full of panic. "I was so dead set on getting that fucker dead. I wanted him dead for what he did to you, that's how much I love you. She was the only person I knew who would do this, this isn't anything new to her, Cathy."

"What else have you told her?" I asked, ignoring his statement. "Have you told her what I'm like in bed? Do you laugh and giggle about how fucked up I am?"

"Of course I fucking don't." Nick growled. "I don't speak to her."

"I don't know with you anymore." I breathed.

"I know you don't mean that." Nick replied back deeply.

I walked closer to the truck and Nick's eyes started to look hopeful.

I grabbed hold of the ring on my finger and pulled. He watched me and his face dropped.

"You think you are in control." I took hold of his hand and dropped the ring in it. "But you don't know shit."

I turned my back on him and walked away.

No tears fell from my eyes as I walked. I was all out of them.

Relationships were so difficult especially when we were all just as fucked up as eachother. This was a hard pill to swallow for me. I had spent my childhood days plagued by my step dad and I told Nick in absolute confidence. I didn't ever think he would tell anyone about what had happened to me, especially her.

He had no right to tell anyone about my past.

I didn't think I could ever get over that.

It made me think, over think. Had he told his other police friends about me? Maybe they all laughed as Nick told him things about what we did in bed. How was I meant to know after this?

Who was the man I was going to marry?

I shook my head. How could I have ever been so stupid?

I could hear the truck door open and then it slammed shut. I heard footsteps running my way. I didn't do a thing.

"Cathy, you can't do this." He was pleading. He took hold of my arm and I let him. "You can't do this, not again, please." His eyes were wild with panic.

I didn't speak, I looked at him blankly.

He took hold of my shoulders and shook me. After that, I couldn't help but break down and cry. What had he done to me?

I was still so broken and just as I was trying to piece myself back together again, something comes along and rips it all apart.

"I watched you go before and I deserved it, I deserve everything I get but I can't watch you leave me again, not this time, not ever." He pulled me close to his chest, as if he was scared I'd vanish any second, and I sobbed against his chest. "Your past means a lot to you and it means a lot to me too. It was fucked up, it was vile what he did to you but it's made you who you are, the Cathy I love. You're so strong, so fucking strong and I know I've betrayed your trust but I need you to know I didn't ever want it to be this way."

"I genuinely wasn't thinking and me not thinking has hurt you." He sounded just as broken as I.

"I can't." I didn't know what to say. I was hurt but I didn't think I could ever turn my back on Nick. I couldn't, even though I did feel betrayed by him.

My god, what was I doing?

I couldn't run away every time he did these things. What he did was so wrong but I couldn't leave him, not again, not ever, just like he said. I needed him, needed him like the oxygen I breathed.

I was messed up but he was the only thing I was sure of.

"I took my ring off." I sobbed as I looked in to his eyes.

"I can assure you, you won't be doing that again." Nick's voice was low but I knew how much that had hurt him. He opened his palm again and there was my ring. "Please, put it back on."

I gave him my finger and he slid the ring back on to my finger. He kissed it once it was in place.

"My wife." He murmured. "I fuck up but I have so much love for you."

Before you have a go at me, lol, I just wanted to say that the whole point of this chapter is to show that Nick made a mistake because he was so determined to protect Cathy. It was a crappy thing for him to do but how do you expect me to end the story (which is ending soon?) by them never getting back together because of this? They had already left eachother once and I didn't want to do that again to you readers.

Cathy isn't going back to him because she's weak, she just doesn't want to run away from him anymore. She knows he's fucked up and so does he, why should she punish him anymore than she already has done?

And yes, Cathy does go running a lot. That's just the way she is. But it's character development and that's the thing she is trying to work on.

People aren't perfect, especially my characters.

Also, this isn't a gender thing. You know from my other stories that I am all about strong women and women empowerment!

CHAPTER 33

"You want me to give Nick a job?" My father asked, his eyes twinkling but the seriousness was on his face. His salt and pepper hair, which was once as dark as mine, was cut neatly on his head.

My father was heavily tattooed just like Nick. They were comforting, something that I liked on a man. Maybe it was because I had always looked up to my father and his tattooes, either way, I loved them.

"He's lost his at the police station. He wants to go to uni and do his art degree. I don't know what more to do." I sighed with defeat. I hated seeing Nick upset about his lack of employment. He worked so hard and I knew all he wanted to do was get money to make me happy.

I didn't need it but I think he thought I did.

"I'd love to give him a job here, he's artistic, creative and one hell of a good drawer." He stopped. "But that's not how Nick works. I doubt he'd want a job just because I asked, he works for the things he gets, he doesn't just take."

"I know but couldn't we at least give it a shot?" I asked, hopeful. "He doesn't exactly have a choice right now."

"Ask him and then we will talk about it." I gave my father a kiss on the cheek before looking up to my next client.

I got back to work.

Hours went by where I was able to lose the troubles in my mind of the last few weeks and just tattoo. I loved this job and I was the luckiest person alive to be doing what I had loved since I was little.

I was artistic just like Nick but we expressed it in different ways. That was the thing with art, we use it in anyway we can.

Nick liked to draw, paint, make abstracts and paintings whereas I was more in to the tattooing scene. Maybe Nick wouldn't like to work here, doing this, but I knew he'd be amazing at it for the time being.

This was the only chance he had whilst he was still on trial.

Every time I thought about Nick and his talent, I couldn't help but smile. I loved that he could draw and I loved that he was ambitious and determined enough to make a thing out of it.

I really hoped it worked out for him.

By the end of the day, I was worn out but feeling a little happier and lighter than I had in ages. My father could see the smile on my face and he smiled back at me.

I was glad I had him back, too. Seeing him so heartbroken broke me even more. I loved my father, idolised him even, and I couldn't bare to see him so torn and devastated.

I wished I felt the same about my mother. I wanted to get close to her again but every time I looked at her, I saw John, too. I didn't want to associate her with him, not one tiny bit but I did.

Hopefully that would change soon and I could also have my mother back.

John stole her from me too.

"I've been thinking." Glenn stated as we closed the doors of the parlour. I hadn't heard from Nick all day as I had been busy at work. Hopefully he was okay. He had probably been painting all day. That took up a lot of his time.

"About?"

"What you can do to help him." I looked at my father, puzzled. "I could give him the job here, that would be fine, but Nick would need training as he has never done tattooing before. He also needs certificates and training courses to be done before he's legally allowed to be a tattoo artist, just like you and I."

"Right." I nodded my head as we both got in to Glenn's vehicle.

"He wouldn't be on an amazing salary to start off with, that's for sure. I doubt he'd get enough for that university degree he wants."

"Oh." I knew I looked crestfallen. I loved Nick enough to want the world for him.

"But, I'm getting old now and I've saved up a lot of money to know I'd be happy with giving you my position at the parlour."

"What?" I looked at my father with shock. Was he going to give me the parlour?

"I earn a lot more than you do at the moment, I'm the owner of the parlour." He stated, matter of fact. "But, if you were to become owner of the parlour, you could save up for him, let him get his university degree, let him find his feet with a new job. He wouldn't have to worry and you get to do what you've always loved for extra."

"Dad..." I couldn't speak as my voice came out as a whisper. "I couldn't let you leave your job."

"I've been thinking about it for ages. I was thinking about taking your mother somewhere hot, to take her mind off everything here for a few months." He shrugged as if it were no big deal. He loved her and he'd do anything for her.

"God." I breathed. That tattoo parlour would be mine.

"I'm not the richest man in the world but it has given me every-thing and more. That parlour is my baby, my second baby." He clarified with a cheeky smirk. "I wouldn't think about giving it to anyone else, Birdie."

"I am so grateful." I said, honestly. For him to do that was huge for me, huge for Nick and I as a team.

"I know you are, you're my daughter. We work for what we have and we're grateful for what we get." He nodded firmly. "And you and Nick are going to get married soon, you work as a team like that, help eachother out when you need it and you'll realise you won't need much else."

I thought back to a few days ago where I took off my ring in rage at the man I loved. I didn't ever want to do that again, I didn't ever want to run away from him whenever something went wrong.

That's what we did, we loved then we hated, but our pasts defined us and we love the way we love. Every relationship is different and we all cope differently.

I run, like a coward, but I wasn't going to do that anymore.

Whatever life threw at us, Nick and I were going to take it and become stronger for it.

Like my dad said, we were a team.

"I love you so much." I couldn't help but say. My father looked to me, unleashed tears in his eyes, and he took a hold of my hand.

"You won't ever find a love as strong as the one you have with your children, that's for damn sure." He shook his head. "I promised to give you the world and more. I let you down and now I'm making it up to you."

My heart broke.

"You don't have to do this, any of this to make it up to me. You weren't at fault, you were never to blame. You're the only thing that got me through it. I thought about leaving and coming to see you so many times, knowing one day I would have the chance got me through everything happening over there. You've given me the world and now more."

After all, he led me to Nick.

"This helps me to move on." He looked touched. I was hoping one day the guilt would be free from his face. "And I believe in you."

I got home after our heart to heart. My father dropped me home as he wanted to pick me up this morning on my first day back, to see if I was okay.

I took a lift up the elevator and reached Nick's apartment door. I could hear gentle music as I stood outside the door and I smiled.

He was home and my heart was beating in excitement to see him. Was he painting? Having a shower?

I didn't know but I wanted to find out.

I opened the wooden door and I gasped at the sight before me. Candles were lit at almost every point of the room. I briefly wondered if he had a working fire alarm just incase it set fire to the curtains, but my thoughts evaporated as soon as I took in the petals on the floor.

What a soppy sod.

I couldn't help but smile as I followed them all the way in to the bedroom.

I saw Nick as soon as I did so, he stood before he in a pair of skinny jeans and a plain black t shirt. He looked casual but good enough to eat.

How did I ever get so lucky?

"What's all this?" I beamed his way as the music lifted up my spirits. This was so romantic. Who would have thought Nick Abel was capable of any of this?

"My apologies, my blessings and my love for you." He smiled sweetly. "I want you to remember this moment whenever I fuck up. Whatever I do, you know I'm in love with you, I have been since the day I met you and I will be until the day I die."

"Nick." I couldn't help but run in to his arms and squeeze him tightly against my body. He took me in to his arms and squeezed just as tightly back.

"I have something to show you." Nick stated. "Don't tell your dad because I know he will be mad at me for getting it done somewhere else..." he trailed off as he lifted up his shirt.

The heart I had talked about before now had my name written on it above his chest.

This day was full of so many surprises.

"Nick." I said his name again in a breathless whisper as I traced the black ink across a small part of his chest. It was still healing and Nick flinched a little bit. I looked up in to his eyes and I saw that love he had for me there straight away.

"There's no way we can be apart from eachother now." He looked devishly handsome. "We're stuck with eachother, Angel, and there's nothing you can do about it."

"Unless you get it removed." I stated playfully. He scowled.

"This will never be removed." He looked proud of what he had done. "It's my favourite tattoo." He smiled.

I couldn't help but laugh. Out of all the tattoos he had, that was his favourite? He was so sweet.

"Dad is going to be mad at you, you're right." I smiled, then I remembered what he had given me. "Actually, I'm going to be mad." I started to smile.

"What do you mean?" He looked puzzled at my suspicious smirk.

"I own it."

"Own what?" He asked.

"The parlour. It's mine once the paper work is all done." Nick opened his mouth with shock.

"Serious?" I nodded and he pulled me in to another tight hug. "That's amazing!" He gushed. He sounded so proud and happy for me, and that meant so much more than anything else.

"I know." I said back. I couldn't believe it myself.

"Does that mean I can get free tattoos from now on?" He smirked my way playfully. I gave him a light punch to the chest.

We spent the rest of the night talking and doing what we knew best.

We talked about the parlour and what I could do to make it even better than it was now. Nick was all for it and I couldn't be happier.

I didn't tell him about the saving as I didn't want him to tell me off for doing his work for him. I knew he wanted to do it all his self but I just wanted to help and I knew I'd be able to without his knowing.

Instead, I watched him as he relaxed beside me. I watched him as we both turned to realise that everything was working out for the better.

We still had a long way to go but with him by my side, life was going to get easier.

He had saved me from my past and made a future I'd never have thought possible. He came barrelling in to my life, tattoos and just as dark as I.

He says I gave him feelings again, that I coloured him red, but little did he know, he coloured me every colour there was to offer.

He didn't just give me feelings, he gave me life.

And I lived just for him.

CHAPTER 34

A year on...

"I am so mad at you right now." Nick shook his head as he looked at me. He stood before me in a worn pair of jeans and paint all across his body.

He had been working so hard with his paintings and he so desperately wanted to make a living out of what he did best. I didn't blame him, he had such a talent.

"It's just money, Nick." I stated. "And I saved it because I wanted you to be happy."

"You shouldn't have done that for me." He replied. I arched my brow his way and he sighed. "I'm grateful, I am, but I don't feel like I've earnt it."

Since the first day I owned that building, my father's tattoo parlour, I had wanted to save the money for Nick to go to university, to make a living out of his work. Hell, he could build his own gallery to display his work, I didn't care, I just wanted him happy.

Nick had pride, that's one of the many things I loved about him. We fought like cat and dog sometimes but his passion, his determination, his ambition was what I couldn't live without. That, and his love for me.

"Come on, babe, it's your wedding present from me." I said. Money was tight when we had a wedding to plan for but we both made it work. We worked like clock work and together we saved up the right amount of money for the perfect day.

Nick had started out working at the parlour, it was fun because I could boss him around and he loved it there. His real passion was art, not tattooing, and I wanted him to have the perfect career. He deserved it.

"Yes but eight thousand dollars, Cathy? Really?" He looked panic stricken.

"It's money." I said. "I make enough now." And I did make enough, just about. It had taken me a year to save it out of my monthly wages now I was the owner of the tattoo parlour.

"You're too good for me." Nick's shoulders slumped.

"I love you." I told him. I always had done. His eyes bored in to my own and a small smile started to grow on the end of his lips.

He came over to me slowly, his body, my own personal painting, one of beauty. He really was hot and I was so glad he was now all mine.

"I can't wait to make you Mrs Abel." His breath hit my cheek as he leaned down to kiss me on the lips. I smiled.

"Only two days to go now." And I was so excited. I had been waiting for this for ages and now he was finally becoming my husband.

"The longest two days of my life."

Two days really did drag.

As I looked at myself in the mirror, a long, slim dress took over my body. I liked the way I looked in it, ready to indeed become Mrs Abel.

"You look amazing." Emily gushed as he took me in. She came over to me and hugged me tightly.

Behind her stood my mother. She looked me over and a tear slid down her face.

I ended up telling my mother everything. She didn't take it badly like I thought she would have. She believed me and I was so shocked, so relieved I cried like a baby, my head on her lap. She took a hold of me that night and cried like a baby too.

She was remorseful, so sorry and guilty. I had never seen her like that. She was mad I hadn't told her, mad I didn't feel I trusted her enough to know.

I knew it was hard on her too.

"I'm glad you made it." I stated to my mother. She was tanned and glowing from her months away in the Caribbean with my father. I was so glad they were getting close again and she seemed a lot happier now than she did ever before.

"Your father and I wouldn't miss this for the world." She took me in to her arms and I hugged her tightly back.

Once I was ready, I prepared myself at the alter. My father came along, looking dashing in a navy suit. I watched him with the biggest smile on my face, my father, walking me down the aisle.

He looked at me.

"Wow." He said. His eyes started to tear up and all I could do was roll my eyes.

"Don't cry you soppy sod."

"I'm crying because I have to give you over to that dense prick." He wiped a tear that fell from his cheek and I laughed at his joke.

Of course, my father and Nick were as close as ever. Nick moaned the day he left for the Caribbean until the day he was back. He moaned that he had no one to drink a beer with. I apparently wasn't going to cut it because I talked all the way through the football.

"Are you ready?" He asked as the pianist started to play the song I had chosen to walk down the aisle to.

"Extremely." And I meant every word. Nick and I had our ups and downs, I didn't believe they would ever stop but we loved eachother too much to run away now.

My father walked me down the aisle and as soon as Nick was in sight, I looked to him. He wore a fitted suit, his hands on his pockets at the alter and I wanted to weep at the sight.

I had been waiting for this day for what seemed like an eternity.

His reaction didn't disappoint either. He looked back at me, his eyes scanning the whole of my white clad body and he looked blown away.

Once my father handed me over to Nick, he took a hold of my hand, squeezed it reassuringly and smiled big my way. I smiled back.

"You look fucking great." He murmured quietly. His words made me giggle.

"So do you." He kept a hold of my hand.

The priest started to speak but I didn't pay him any attention, neither did Nick. We looked to eachother, our eyes not straying from one another, like we couldn't turn away.

We said our vows and I was so excited to make him mine, I didn't feel nervous at all.

Nick said his vows with authority, power and the usual confidence of his. God, this man really was mine.

I got so lucky.

"You may now kiss the bride."

The priest didn't have to tell Nick twice. He pulled me to him and kissed me like there was no tomorrow. I would have been embarrassed but I wasn't, I was just too buzzed and way too happy to care.

"I love you, Angel." He said in to my ear.

We both turned to the crowd before us. They cheered. I watched my father take my mother in to his arms, I watched Xavier smile at Emily as if it were the first time he had seen her. She held Dean in her arms and he clapped his tiny little hands before him.

I couldn't stop the smile forming on my face.

For once in my life, I felt as if every puzzle was right in place.

EPILOGUE

"**Y**ou are my sunshine

    My only sunshine

You make me happy

When skies are grey

You'll never know, dear

How much I love you

Please don't take my sunshine away."

I watched Nick, his body bent over a crib, doing his nightly routine to our baby. He had a beautiful voice and our baby loved it just as much as I did.

This song held so many memories and now it held so much more.

"The other night, dearAs I lay sleeping I dreamt I held you in my armsWhen I awoke, dearI was mistaken And I hung my head and cried."

I leaned against the threshold of the door and watched intently to the scene before me. These memories were the ones that would live with me forever.

And even though it was meant to be bed time, our daughter giggled at her daddy's voice and I couldn't stand there any longer, I had to go and see them.

"She's meant to be sleeping." I said quietly, a smile prominent on my face.

"She will be asleep in a minute, won't you, Angel?" He stroked the face of our little girl and she leaned in to his touch. "She's just like you, Cathy."

"Smitten by you?" I asked. That girl was definitely a daddy's girl and I was okay with that. I loved to watch them talk- well, Nick talked and she gargled. I loved to watch Nick push her pushchair when we visited her grandparents, the way he rocked her to sleep when she cried.

He was too good to her.

We had wanted a baby, of course, but Nick was so scared that he couldn't be a good dad. He was so scared that something would happen, something that would leave her all alone in the big wide world.

As soon as we both saw her face and her big blue eyes, we were done for. The worry was still there every single day but it was totally worth it. I'd worry all my life just to see her happy and I knew Nick felt the same.

"Come on, leave her sleep." Sometimes I had to pull Nick away from her. He was just so obsessed by her and he couldn't leave her alone. It was a chore trying to get him to go in to his own bed and sleep, when all he wanted to do was keep telling her bed time stories, singing to her, talking to her as if they were the only people in the room.

Nick stood up and with one last look at our daughter, he turned the light off, leaving the night light on she loved so much.

We made our way back downstairs. I had started making dinner for Nick as it was only seven o'clock.

"Something smells nice." He murmured as he wrapped one arm around my waist. I snuggled in to his chest in the kitchen.

"How's the paintings?" I asked him. Even now, many years on, he loved to paint. Nick did go to Univeristy after all, he did three whole years in art school and came out with a degree, being one of the best in his class.

I was so proud of him.

The degree got him so far and everybody in town loved his paintings. We saved up more money and soon, we rented out a little part of the local gallery which held all of his paintings inside.

The paintings that held his happiness were the ones everybody came to see. He made painting emotions look so easy.

"It's doing well." He beamed my way. Nick kissed me excitedly on the nose before grabbing the plates and cutlery from the drawers. He set up the table and I watched his body move.

My desire for him still hadn't gone.

When dinner was done, I plated it up and we both sat down to eat, opposite one another. I loved our free time together because we could act like we did before our daughter was born.

Nick ate his food with his normal appreciation. He smiled through his bites of food as he looked to me.

"You're my perfect wife, you know that right?"

"Of course." I laughed. "Who would have thought Nick Abel was going to be a family man." I joked. Looking back to the way he was before and to the way he was now, the contrast was shocking. This man lived for me, lived for his daughter.

We lived just for him.

"Shut up." He rolled his eyes but he smiled nonetheless. "I was missing out on so much."

"Being a dad suits you." And it did.

"It's the best feeling in the world."

It truly was. This was the best feeling ever, to have a husband who I loved and a beautiful daughter who'd love me unconditionally too.

Suddenly, the door bell went. Nick shot up from the chair before I had chance to get up myself. He left the dining room and made his way to the front door.

I continued to eat my food with a content sigh.

"Where is she?" I heard my dad's voice come from the hallway.

"In here!" I shouted back. Damn, the baby was going to wake up.

"No not you." My father came in to view before me. He wore simple jeans and a white t shirt, his tattoos showing. Behind him was my mother, her new wedding band shining brightly. She looked like she was glowing. "Where's Birdie?"

"She's going to get confused, you call her Angel," I pointed at Nick. "And you call her Birdie."

Glenn shot a playful glare Nick's way.

"I'm her dad, I make the rules." Nick pointed a finger his way.

My mother laughed but she came to sit next to me on the dining room table. We hugged eachother and she kissed me on the cheek.

"How's your pelvic floor going?" She asked, with no shame involved. Did mum's ever have shame?

"Mum." I groaned. "They're going fine."

She was always making sure I was doing what I was meant to do. She knew as a new mother how difficult it could be. She wanted the best for my daughter as she feels she let me down massively. I didn't blame her, though, it was all my fault and how was she to know?

Finally, however, I had put all that to bed. At one point, I was able to visit John's grave, against Nick's advice. Yet, I felt so much lighter once I had. I had put us to bed, buried deeper than John was buried. It was all behind me and I was more than happy it was.

Glenn and Nick popped open a beer from the fridge.

"This is nice." Glenn stated. "To have a beer in your house, not mine." He clapped Nick on the back.

"Fu-" he stopped short. "I'm a dad now actually, I don't swear anymore."

We all laughed. Nick looked proud of himself.

"Where's Emily and Xavier? I haven't heard from them in almost a week." My mother mentioned.

"They're on holiday with Dean." Nick stated. I smiled when I thought about my best friends and their son. Dean was another person smitten with my husband.

"Enough of this chit chat, I want to see my granddaughter." Glenn went to lay his bottle on the island.

"We've just put her to sleep." I said.

"That's boring." Glenn frowned.

"She's a baby, dad." I laughed.

"So? I used to let you watch football with me at ungodly hours of the night."

"No wonder why I have problems." I joked. Nick laughed and I shot him a look. "Go and get her then, but if she gets grizzly in the morning, you can look after her."

"It's a done deal." Glenn said and I didn't have a chance to say another word as he was gone. I heard his foots stomping their way upstairs and his deep voice resonating even from upstairs.

Soon enough, he came barrelling downstairs with our little girl in his arms. She was surprisingly not too grizzly just haven woken up.

"Say hey to pops." Her hand held his finger and he shook it gently. "She's so cute."

My mother got up to coo over the baby too. Nick smiled as he watched the scene before us. He took a hold of my hand and squeezed.

God, I loved him.

I loved my little family.

And most importantly, I loved our daughter, our little baby girl.

Sonny Rose Abel.

www.ingramcontent.com/pod-product-compliance
Lightning Source LLC
Chambersburg PA
CBHW070753190726
48292CB00002B/528